STREET
CLEANERS

STREET CLEANERS

JOHN ANDES

STREET CLEANERS

iUniverse books may be ordered through booksellers or by contacting:

iUniverse
1663 Liberty Drive
Bloomington, IN 47403
www.iuniverse.com
1-800-Authors (1-800-288-4677)

ISBN: 978-1-4917-7326-0 (sc)
ISBN: 978-1-4917-7327-7 (e)

Print information available on the last page.

iUniverse rev. date: 07/22/2015

JOHN ANDES IS THE AUTHOR OF:

Farmer in the Tal
H.A.
Suffer the Children
Icarus
Matryoshka
Jacob's Ladder
Loose Ends
Control is Jack
Revenge
Adventures in House Sitting
Skull Stacker

Available at Amazon.com, BarnesandNoble.com, and iUniverse.com

*For centuries municipalities have employed men
to remove trash from boulevards, avenues, streets, and alleys
for the purpose of ensuring the beauty of the cities
and safety of citizens.*

For K.E.K.A.

I

At four in the afternoon, the minivan pulls through the driveway into the two-car garage and pulls to a stop next to the silver BMW Z-4, his toy. The driver looks forward to shedding her work clothes and showering off the grime of her latest tour. Then she will morph into the persona of the Mom and prepare dinner for her family. She will listen eagerly to the events of their day and read the twelve-hour-old newspaper before going to bed by ten.

She enters the house from the garage and surveys the remains of today's pizza party. There was no school due to a teachers' conference, thus reason for the party. She left for her seven to three-thirty tour assuming her children would have friends over to her house then clean up. Her assumption accuracy is one-for-two. Marveling at the diversity of soda cans, she samples a cold, dry thin slice with sausage. The taste takes her back to her college and graduate school days when dough, olive oil, oregano, basil, garlic, tomato sauce, various cheeses, and either sausage or pepperoni were the composition of her weekend food consumption.

Max, the massive German shepherd mix, the third child in the household, awakens from one of his afternoon naps and casually strolls into the kitchen. He nuzzles Liz. This is his communication for attention of some kind... food or a back scratch. Liz opts for the latter. She leans over so he can thank her with a sniff and lick. The dog has been in the family for eight years. Sandy brought the skinny puppy home from Animal Rescue. A Christmas gift for the children: a vehicle for them to learn and appreciate responsibility for another. He listens to the teens, but adores Cary. They grew up together. She feeds, walks, and bathes the dog. Liz tried to give him a bath three years ago and he growled menacingly. But he will take food from any member of the household.

She must find the day's newspaper she couldn't read before she left for work. Exiting the front door, she scours the front walk, lawn, and flowering bushes to the right and left of the front door. Bingo! Bush to the left. The kid has a strong, if unpredictable, arm. As she goes back inside she notices the headline on the front page above the fold.

Developer Cleared of All Charges

She will read the details after dinner. First, up the stairs to complete the transformation from police detective to homemaker. The department-issued Sig Sauer is placed in the lockbox. Holster, with badge and extra clip are hung over a peg in what was originally just her half of the wall-to-wall walk-in closet. A few of his clothes, her favorites, still hang in the other half. They are good reminders of him. Even after two years, his smell, though faint, lingers on the fabric and her teardrop circles mark his shirts and him as her territory. Her clothes once removed are tossed in the hamper. About half full. Or, is that half empty? This eternal question produces a smile. Naked in the bathroom, she turns on the shower. The stall once held two on special occasions when the children were asleep. Now she will wet, lather, and rinse alone. The scrubbing mitt, a gift from Cary, removes the sweat that accumulated during her long day on the job. The organic shampoo and conditioner for dry hair was a gift from Alex. Both items cost more than her ingrained frugality would let her spend on herself, but they were gifts last Christmas. As her hands gently massage the bath gel over her body, they touch places that were for him alone. Now she wonders if any man will touch her body again…before a mortician or the ME. A fleeting moment of self-pity. Towel dried, she knows a cold Rolling Rock will help her prep dinner.

"Mom, sorry for the mess in the kitchen. Mr. Wisenheimer and I will clean up."

Cary's clarion call from the top of the stairs sounds raspy and groggy. Strangely hangover-like. But, Elizabeth Kimble knows better. She raised her children with a solid set of morals and understanding of right actions. The young teens will bounce down the stairs in twenty to thirty seconds. She can predict their arrival with a silent countdown because they are attuned to the noise she makes when she comes home. It's been that way since they were munchkins. To Liz, there is comfort and security to the sound of thundering footsteps as her beloveds scramble to be the first to greet her with a kiss.

"OK, Mom, we got this. Hey, lazybones, get your scrawny butt down here and do your part."

Down lumbers the young male beastie. Alex is beginning to look like his father. He has thick blond hair and dark brown eyes. Even though he is only a freshman in high school, he is five-ten and weighs 160 pounds. Who knows what he will look like when his growing stops? Sandy was six-two and 210 when he was killed in the line of duty. Cary looks like a smaller version of Liz. Jet- black hair and green eyes. At five-six and weighing 105, she is showing the bumps and curves of an emerging woman.

Alex leans into his mother's space and kisses her on the top of her hair.

"Still using the shampoo and conditioner from Christmas. Let me know when you run low. It's never too early for me to talk to Santa."

"Well, nice to see you, lazybones."

"Shush, Cary. I'll do my part."

For the next fifteen minutes, the teens exchange typical sibling jibes about looks, clothes, friends, and schoolwork. During the yammering, Liz starts to read the newspaper's lead story. Ross Concept Living, the developer of a low-income community, Oak Villas, failed to have a safety gate installed on the swimming pool fence before the community accepted its first residents. Two very young boys toddled through the gap in the fence and drowned. The parents accused the builder of creating a hazard. They also accused the building inspector of improperly issuing a Certificate of Occupancy although all the work was not satisfactorily completed. The builder accused the subcontractor of failing to complete the swimming pool fence work under the terms of the contract. The subcontractor, Builder's Alliance, accused Ross Concept Living of failing to pay for work completed within the agreed to timeline. And round and round the accusations went. A typical contest of "they said-they said."

The whole mess wound up in court because of the deaths. The media had a feeding frenzy with the details, the grieving parents, and the builder's questionable operating practices. Possible payoffs to the inspector. This was not the first time subcontractors and residents had taken this builder to court. Up to now, the issues had been resolved in civil court. But the two deaths made this event a criminal matter. Four other communities built by the developer in West Central Florida experienced major structural and safety hazards. Three of the cases were resolved in favor of the plaintiffs. Cash awards. One is pending. Citing parental neglect, the court decided in favor of the defendants. The builder paid a $100,000 fine. The subcontractor was awarded his charges to complete the job, legal fees, and $50,000 for breach of contract. The building inspector was fired and is being investigated for criminal negligence. The parents got nothing. Two children dead and no one is criminally responsible.

Four pictures accompany the article: one of the grieving parents who were promising further legal action, two of the children, and one of the smiling exonerated builder, Marshall Ross. He knows there is always a need for low-income housing, so he will always make money. The net result of Liz's investigation that started two years ago includes a reprimand from the court, exchange of cash, and two dead babies. What a travesty! Not honest justice.

"Mom, will you be at our game on Wednesday? It's the last game of the season. It's at home and starts at four. We play our archrivals, the St. Thomas Aquinas 'Tommies.' Plus, and here is the best part, I will be the starting running back. Jimmy Aldridge won't be able to suit up. So, I'll get all the reps. Will you come, please?"

"I wouldn't miss it for the world. Cary and I will take you out to dinner after the game. Why can't Jimmy play?"

"Coaches are regularly notified of players who are having academic difficulties. Jimmy and two other JVs were on the list given to Coach Kelly."

"Ah, yes, the first trimester has ended. Where are your report cards?"

"Mine's upstairs in my backpack."

"So's mine."

"Please get them so I can look at them after dinner. Or, will they upset me so much I will get sick?"

"What's for dinner?"

"Sloppy Joe mix is cooking. Plus, a salad. You must eat the salad before seconds of the Joes. Now that you have made the kitchen safe for mankind, bring your dirty clothes down to the laundry room. I'm going to play loving Mom early tomorrow morning and do the laundry. Then I'll go grocery shopping for our cookout on Saturday. That reminds me, have you put your food requests on the shopping list?"

"I have. Not sure about Cary."

"Alex, you're such a weasel."

"Remember, if it ain't on da list, it don't come home from da store. Tomorrow we dine together on the back patio. Steak, corn, baked sweet potato, and salad. Dinner promptly at six. Now, what's on your agendas for tonight?"

"I'm going to the International Mall with Missy, Jenny, and Laura."

"Who's driving?"

"Missy's dad."

"Alex?"

"A bunch of us are going to the movies. We're riding our bikes."

"Both of you take your phones. When are you due home?"

"Eleven."

"OK then, my tour as Mother will commence tomorrow after my well-deserved sleep. Remember report cards and laundry before you leave."

Dinner went fast. The children call their rapid and complete eating process, "Hoovering." They appear to quietly suck their plates clean. The noise of them scrambling back up the stairs sounds like a stampede. Raising teens on her own, while maintaining the important job of Detective First Grade of the Tampa Police Department would be very difficult if her teenage children were not such good people. Two years ago, after Sandy died she set the rules of the house:

+ *Her job was to provide clothing, food, shelter, and good educational opportunities.*
+ *Their jobs were to get a good education, enjoy their teenage years, and help around the house.*
+ *They must never lie to her.*
+ *She would never lie to them.*
+ *They could ask her anything, and she would give them an honest answer.*
+ *When Alex started to date, "no" would mean "no" and "yes" would mean "no."*
+ *When Cary started to date, the <u>only</u> response would be "no."*

+ *No matter what they thought of doing that might be highly questionable or risky, she and their father had already done it and it was not as much fun as either had hoped.*

Report cards delivered, laundry deposited in the laundry room, doors opened and closed.

The teens would be gone for a few hours. The silence of an empty house is no longer depressing. For a while after the murder, she was terrified of that silence. Now it is part of life. Elizabeth washes down the last of her Sloppy Joe with the last of her beer. She will try to stay awake until her brood is home. Liz wanted the seven to three-thirty tour at TPD so she could spend time with her children, part of her life she previously shared with Sandy. When he was here, one of them was home at all times. Around nine-thirty her eyes start to close and her head nods. She fights to stay awake. Finally, she succumbs with the newspaper on her chest.

How can two young people dirty so many clothes? Multiple loads: delicates, whites requiring bleach and hot water, and colors in cool water. Time to check the shopping list, and straighten up the patio, her sanctorum. For a woman who carries a hand-held killer on her side during her day job, she relishes the non-threatening role of making a home for her family. The instinct of motherhood is powerful. An interesting confluence of conflicting forces. Either force could win on any given day. The shopping list is predictable. A bottle of wine for her would be nice. Maybe a second one for Sunday. She travels to the store between washer loads. Quick trip.

Three nice two-inch thick New York strips. She had forgotten how expensive good steak is. Chicken is cheap, because it is plentiful. Sometimes fish is less expensive than good red meat. But her brood doesn't like fish. Her police training can drive her to over think even the most mundane concepts. That's why she is good at her job. During the last load of laundry, she remembers the report cards. Each one looked like someone wrote the name of the Swedish singing group. Mom is pleased and signs the back of each card. Today, Cary is strolling the mall again. She is there to see and be seen. Alex is bike riding with his football buddies at the abandoned quarry. Nascent macho.

"How was your indoor walk?"

"Great, I bought a few small things."

"Need I ask about boys?"

"No."

Cary's grin tells Elizabeth all she needs or wants to know about the boys her daughter met at the mall.

"Is Rat Breath home yet?"

"Not yet. Why?"

"We heard there was an accident at the old quarry."

"What kind of accident?"

"Car."

"That's it?"

"That's all I know."

The fuse to parental worry burns quickly when lit by the unknown. Elizabeth's police training drives her concerns even more. She runs through the litany of what might have happened. Then, she tells herself that Alex is all right. He would have called otherwise. Someone would have called.

"What are your plans for this evening, young lady?"

"We are going back to the mall for a movie. *Games Three* is showing at eight. Hope that's OK with you."

"Need I ask about boys?"

"No."

"Wanna show me what you bought this afternoon?"

"Just some underwear and two tees; no big deal. The tees are soooo cute."

"Underwear?"

"Thongs. And, before you get worked up, all the girls are wearing thongs. So it's no big deal."

"I won't get worked up over your underwear. It's just that it wasn't too long ago that proper young ladies did not wear thongs. Bikini briefs were about as daring as young ladies got. Never thongs. I just need to fast forward to your generation."

"In the Stone Age of your youth did women wear bras? Or hadn't they been invented yet?"

"Bras, yes. Just not thongs."

The talk, bras, her first period, now thongs. Cary is growing up too fast. Enter Alex covered with dirt. Liz greets him forcefully.

"Not in the house! Take your shoes and clothes off in the garage and toss all your clothes into the laundry room. Then go upstairs and shower for dinner. Your clean clothes are hanging in your closet or folded in your bureau. Now scoot."

Dinner is nearly void of conversation except for the occasional compliment on its quality and quantity. Because teens inhale food, there is no time to talk except to ask for more. Alex eats his twelve-ounce steak, two sweet potatoes, and two ears of corn. Cary eats less starch. Liz's growing and very active teens would lick their dinner plates, if no one were watching. She watches.

"Alex, what do you know about the car accident at the quarry?"

"The police came. Some guys were dirt racing and one ATV rolled off the hill. Heard that the ATV was bumped by a car. Couldn't see if anyone was hurt. The ambulance was there in a few minutes. That's all I know."

"What are your plans for the evening?"

"More bike riding. This time the lighted park trails where we don't have to worry about cars."

"And when does the park close?"

"Ten."

"And when will you be home?"

"Eleven-thirty at the latest."

"Thank you. And you, Cary?"

"Same time."

"Thank you. Remember we will be going to the eight o'clock Mass. I will take care of clean-up."

"What about dessert?"

"The ice cream is in the freezer and the butterscotch sauce is in the fridge. Help yourself. None for me. I'll get all the sugar I need from your kisses."

Big grins all around. Rinsing the dishes, Mom receives two 'thank you' kisses. The door closings tell her she is alone. Dishes in the dishwasher. The outdoor cooker will burn off the residue of beef fat. Trash is taken care of. It is now her time. She takes a large picture album and wine bottle onto the screened-in porch beyond the patio for some bug-free, early-evening reminiscing. Tomorrow is the anniversary of Sandy's murder. He was the lead detective on a case involving a drug-dealing street gang, Los Hermanos. The department, led by his squad, was raiding a deserted warehouse, a hovel the gang called home. All was going according to procedure, when a firefight erupted. Vests and shields provided protection from the frontal response, but not enough from fire coming from the rear. The gang had a lookout on the other side of the street. The lookout had an AK-47. Sandy and two of the SWAT Team were caught in the crossfire. He was hit in the head and neck. All three died where they fell.

The jury determined that the shooter was not guilty by reason of mental defect or disease, and now resides in the State Mental Institution in Lake Worth. Three deliberate homicides and Enrique Flores gets 'three hots and a cot' until such time as a panel of state appointed psychiatrists determine he is not a danger to society. Then, freedom. Something Sandy will never enjoy. Liz still wonders how this low-life drug thug could afford high-profile lawyers and psychiatrists. The gang leaders were not so fortunate and were convicted of three counts of Murder One. They are presently appealing the verdict in a futile attempt to avoid the prescribed sit-down with Ol' Sparky.

The porch lights illuminate the album. There are several photos of Liz and Sandy on the beach. Some with dear, but seldom seen, friends. Some just the two of them. Photos taken by kind strangers. Sandy was so handsome.

Big and strong with a salt-of-the-earth look. She always felt safe in his arms. Then there are the photos of the two of them in uniform standing in front of the Tampa Police Department's Headquarters. She was a rookie, still a "uni." He had just been promoted to Detective Second Grade. Then the children. Two years apart. Pictures of both christenings. Days on the beach with small shovels and pails. In the woods on one of the numerous picnics. The two tricycles in the background.

In front of the Christmas tree, the children were surrounded by presents piled nearly as high as they were tall. With her parents. With his parents. They were a happy family. The now-three family is smaller yet still happy. Pictures with Sandy stopped two years ago. Now the book is filled with pictures of his children as they grow. He would be so proud. Night air, a full stomach, and the now-empty bottle of wine cause Liz's head to bob. The closing of the front door and dropping of keys in the dish on the small hall table abruptly lift her from sleep. Teardrop circles on the album tell her it is time to stop chewing on loving memories and retire.

Eight AM Mass at St. Regis Catholic Church is populated by people who have plans for the day, people coming home from a late last night, those who simply want to get the perceived obligation out of the way, and a mother with teenagers. The huge faux-Gothic building sits amid a modern school campus comprised of several large buildings: lower school, middle school, upper school, auditorium, and gymnasium. Most of the land for the total campus was donated by several old-line families. Their largess pressured the city to donate a few parcels of abandoned property.

Alex and Cary attend St. Regis Prep School. Their substantial tuition bill is offset by scholarships given to the children of police personnel killed in the line of duty. The balance of the yearly bill must be paid by Liz. It's tight, but she manages. Sandy's life insurance policy proceeds have been invested for college expenses.

Sandy and Liz chose their house, in part, because of its proximity to the school. They hoped that Alex and Cary could ride their bikes to school someday. Sunday the family goes to church by car. Soon Alex will drive the threesome to church.

Mass is simple and direct. Liz lights a candle for her husband. The children pray with her at the lighted sacrifice. After the service, the three drive six miles to a small private cemetery. There they stand before a headstone engraved:

Alexander C. Kimble
1973 – 2013
Beloved father and husband.
Protector of the citizens of Tampa.

Three white roses are laid on the ground. Liz whispers:

"Hey, Sandy. I miss you. Alex and Cary miss you. You would be so proud of them. They are growing into the wonderful people you and I had hoped. Alex is getting bigger each day. Soon he will look just like you. Cary is becoming a beautiful young woman. We all wish you were here with us. I will love you forever."

Silence is held for a few minutes. The family turns and heads back to the car. The children each have their own swim and cook-out parties. They claim their homework is done. She trusts them. Today will be a day for Liz...the *Times*, and three crossword puzzles. Maybe a nap.

II

"Kimble, I want you to go to the Impound Lot and help the old motorhead check out a damaged car."

"OK. What's up?"

"I just got a call. A preliminary report indicates the car belonging to a citizen may have been tampered with and that tampering caused the accident in which said citizen died. The citizen is Marshall Ross, the builder involved in the deaths of the two kids at Oak Villas. That was your case, was it not? Consider this a follow-up. Plus, the brass is becoming a pain about open cases. So, this is a chance for you to close a closely related case and thus to get them off my back and get me off yours."

"Yes, Lieutenant."

Lieutenant Manuel Gracia IV was more than his usual gruff self when he handed Liz the assignment. He was pissed about something. Ever since Liz made Detective First Grade, Gracia has treated her like a second-class citizen. He even went so far as to complain in private that Liz got her promotion because she is a widow of a fellow detective, and that the additional pay was some form of compensation for her husband's death. Gracia is old-school conservative Hispanic. He has an opinion, usually negative, about everything new in the good-old-boy department…especially an officer's gender or sexual preference. He has been heard to lament that, "It wasn't like this when my grandfather and father were on the force." His complaints are never voiced up the line. He knows better. He speaks in innuendos and codes to male members of his squad and his like-thinking peers.

The Impound Lot is twenty-five minutes east of downtown. Between two trailer parks, the police facility is protected by an electrified fence and two noisy dogs of mixed and unknown lineage.

Liz's squad car is greeted at the gate by the leaping, barking, and growling of the guardians. They truly look and act like junkyard dogs. A short stocky man dressed in mechanic's coveralls pivots from his workbench and stares at the gate. Seeing a patrol car, he whistles and calls the dogs to be quiet and to come inside the open bay doors. Then he presses the red button that opens the gate. Liz enters the compound, exits the car, and approaches the man, Sergeant Leonard Sly. He limps from two bullet wounds in his right leg acquired during a gang riot that he helped quell with force.

"Welcome to my work palace, where all the auto magic happens, Detective First Grade Kimble."

Always the same corny greeting. Always a big smile. A friend.

"Sergeant Sly, what have you got for me? I hope I didn't drive out here just to gaze upon your comely countenance."

"It's Leonard, and I have something interesting that may be pertinent to one of your cases. Let me show you. I kept the BMW up on the rack just for your arrival."

They walk through the barn-like structure. Among the various cars, vans, and pick-up trucks being examined for evidence is a crumpled late-model maroon four-door M series BMW. Very big and very expensive in its former life, it is now a mangled mass of metal, leather, and glass.

"Be careful. It would be a sad thing if you dirtied your nice clean clothes. Here we go. Notice anything special about the brake fluid line?"

"I see the hole in the line."

"Do you know what's special about the hole?"

"No, but I know you'll tell me."

"Now pay close attention. The hole was caused by a crimp in the line. See the part of the line that's squeezed. This squeezing broke the metal and created the hole. The hole was made from the outside of the line…not the inside. The fluid did not create the hole and burst from the line, it leaked through a man-made hole. When we got the car up on the lift, we noticed the fluid line was not entirely within its covered channel. The channel was hanging on to the frame by the rear bolts. Initially, we thought this was caused by the accident. Then we noticed that the bolts along the side of the channel were missing. Could have come off as a result of the accident? Not likely. You can see from the exposed metal at the bolt sights, how the bolts on the side of the channel had been removed before the accident. They show signs of being scraped.

"They were roughly twisted off, and the threads were stripped. Someone was in a hurry. A good mechanic servicing the car would not be so careless as to do that. Someone who knew where the channel was and what it held, and wanted to quickly get to the brake fluid line would aggressively twist the bolts and scrape the metal. Then this person would take needle-nose pliers and crimp the line causing a small hole. The protective channel would then be crudely and partially replaced. Fluid from the broken line would slowly drip into the channel and onto the ground where the car was parked and spurt from the line when the driver used the brakes to slow down and stop.

"Last Sunday, when Marshall Ross was on his way home from the festivities, he would use the brakes as usual. Each time he applied even a little pressure to the brake pedal, the fluid would squirt out until there was not enough fluid in the line and the cylinders for the brakes to be effective. So when he needed his brakes to slow down around a dangerous curve like the one at Malfunction Junction, they would fail him."

"Now you own my attention."

"It is safe to assume that he had a few drinks at the event. Perhaps more than a few. Alcohol would have been a substantial contributing factor. My guess is that his blood alcohol level was probably beyond the legal limit. The Medical Examiner can confirm that. Someone who knew Ross's habits was counting on him drinking too much. They also knew about the braking system of this model BMW. So, they tampered with his car and let the drunk driver do the rest. That's what the facts and my gut tell me. But remember, I'm just a mechanic at the TPD Auto Impound working toward his pension. I'm not sophisticated and intelligent like Detective First Grade Liz Kimble."

"Sandy told me many times to trust the instincts of the older guys. He mentioned you more than once as one of the oldest, and therefore wisest. So I trust what you're saying."

"Now that you brought Sandy up, Helen and I have spoken about you and Sandy man times during the last two years. He was a good man, and you two seemed so happy. I'm not sure who misses him more: Helen or me. By the way, how are Alex and Cary doing?"

"Alex has the looks of his father and will have his father's build in a few years. He is going to be quite handsome. And Cary is becoming a young woman. Both of them are doing well in school and growing up too fast…way too fast. How's Helen?"

"She's fine. Her health is good. She's beginning to make plans for our time together after my retirement. She mentioned the other day that she would like to see you and the kids around the holidays…for dinner."

"Tell her yes. That would be lovely. I'm sure the kids would enjoy seeing the two of you. I know I would."

"Then it's a date. I'll have my people call your people."

Liz extends her hand to the gray-haired warhorse and firmly grips the man's large dirty hand in friendship. His smile is avuncular.

"Thanks, Leonard. You have been a huge help."

Marshall Ross is back in Liz's life: from possible perp two years ago to real dead vic today. Back then, she and Sandy worked different shifts. These different shifts greatly limited adult-lover time together. Their joke was that this was TPD's birth control system imposed on its married officers. This time of year, with the slightest urging, her mind repeatedly wanders back to Sandy.

During the drive back to the station, Liz itemizes her next steps. She learned at the academy that every successful investigation has a plan that has an attainable goal, yet is flexible enough to adapt to new facts or events. Set the goal and start to execute the plan. But keep options open. She will work the investigation with no team or squad. There's simply not enough money to support a full police force. The city had to employ severe cutbacks in its infrastructure. Police, fire, and sanitation forces were rightsized due to dramatically declining real estate values and thus dramatically declining real estate tax revenue for the city. Some people were furloughed until each department's budget could be reinstated. They found part-time jobs working nights as security guards anywhere they could, or cashiers at convenience stores. Those not furloughed were the members of the force who had substantial seniority. These men and women were assigned a variety of cases. TPD kept Liz on active duty as a gesture of support given Sandy's death in the line of duty. She was aware that Gracia secretly resent this and thus her.

The force is now stretched thin. Specialization no longer applies to the force. Beyond the Gang Unit, homicides, burglaries, domestic violence, auto thefts, and the like are investigated by whoever is on duty. There are no homicide detectives. There are no robbery squads. There are only detectives who are required to investigate any and all offenses as they occur. The "Expansion of Comprehensive Expertise," as the city leaders called it, required some education as to procedures and forms to be completed. Retraining the older members of the force took time and slowed the investigation process. Everyone's day became overly filled. This undoubtedly was the driving factor in the number of open cases the brass is complaining about.

How ironic. First, the budget is cut, then the manpower, and now the brass complains about open cases. It's like a fisherman who overloads his boat with supplies, then complains that the boat doesn't have enough speed. The brass does what the City Council wants and the City Council members are lousy planners. Politicians usually are lousy planners because they always seek the expedient quick fix to ensure re-election. The new procedures call for the investigating detective to give the appropriate lieutenant a progress report every day. At the end of each tour or if a significant event occurred. Command and control: both online and in person. Oh, joy!

To Lieutenant Gracia, Liz relates what she saw and learned at the Impound Lot and outlines her course of action. Her first step will be to review all the files of the parents and relatives of the deceased children to see if one of them is a mechanic. She will follow up with the families, who will not be displeased that Ross is dead. But, they will be offended that they might be considered perpetrators of his death. She will visit the families before the end of her tour. No overtime is permitted by the city unless under extraordinary circumstances. These are not extraordinary circumstances. She will e-mail the Medical Examiner for Ross's tox screen information before his official report is issued.

Gracia approves the plan of action, but reinforces that this investigation will be about a suspicious death...not a homicide. Investigating is like sculpting; extraneous people must be considered then discarded from consideration until the killer is revealed. Therefore, she must start with and be gentle on non-Marshall family members and associates. If her initial work comes up cold, she is permitted to speak to the widow and offspring.

Isaac and Ramona LaRue lost Tito. Isaac is a baker. Ramona is a registered nurse working at County General. Ramona is from Guatemala and has no relatives living in the area. Isaac has two brothers and several male cousins. One brother is a priest and the other teaches International Studies at Penant High School. Nothing obvious there. Liz looks into the public records for the four male cousins; one is doing state time…eight-to-fifteen, one is in Afghanistan with the Army, one cousin lives in Texas, and the fourth works for 4UNow, a massive used car dealer in Pinellas Park. BINGO! Raphael LaRue will get a visit after Isaac and Ramona.

Jose and Yolanda Martinez lost Roberto. Jose works for Firestone as a store manager, and Yolanda teaches at Steiner Middle School. Jose is worth getting close to. No immediate family in the area. The closest sibling, a cousin, lives in New York.

Two leads.

Her tour takes a detour for two hours into the myriad forms to be completed for this case and updating the other seven to which she was assigned. Two burglaries, a stolen car, a smash and grab at a jewelry store at the International Mall, a missing child, a custody case with possible child endangerment, and a spousal abuse case with an order of protection. When the economy tanks, violence increases due to frustration.

The department's computer system has exponentially increased the speed of the form filing. That's the good news. But the bad news is that now there are many more forms to file; event forms, evidence forms, interview forms, and forms to find other forms. During these times, she feels more like a Data Entry Specialist than a police detective.

First the LaRues. The bakery confirms that Isaac worked on Sunday from three to eight PM to prep the bread, pies, and various sweets for the week. Liz calls County General HR. They will get back to her. Next the Martinez family. She calls the Firestone store. Jose says he was doing paperwork at the store on Sunday. He had to do the work then because Monday was the start of a new quarter and all sales, supply, and salary data has to be uploaded into the corporate system by midnight on the last day of each quarter. He claims to have been alone at the store from four until nine. Obviously, no one can verify that Jose was at the store because it was closed to customers. Liz will have to contact Firestone corporate offices to see when the information was uploaded.

A visit to the 4UNow car lot. The general manager confirms that Raphael LaRue is the head mechanic at the company. Raphael has had no problems during his five years of employment. No one can vouch for his whereabouts on Sunday, one of his days off. Liz gets permission from the manager to talk to Raphael. She walks purposefully into the large work area.

"Excuse me. Are you Raphael LaRue?"

"Yes. What do you want?"

"I need information and you can help me get it. Can you tell me where you were this past Sunday evening between six and ten?"

"Why do you want to know?"

"I am sorry. Let me introduce myself. I am Police Detective First Grade Elizabeth Kimble of the Tampa Police Department, and I want to know your whereabouts on Sunday evening. OK?"

"Why?"

"As I said, we are gathering information. Where were you on Sunday between six and ten PM?"

"I was over at the beach in the afternoon and then went to a few bars to quench my thirst. I had dinner at Coconuts and was home by nine."

"Can anyone vouch for you during the evening?"

"No. I was alone."

"Do you have any receipts from the bars?"

"Paid cash."

"OK. So far, so good. Is your home address, 341 Beach Cove Circle, Unit 2, Indian Rocks Beach?"

"Yes."

"Thanks for your time."

Sometimes, because she is a woman, Liz has to be brusque with perps and persons of interest in a face-to-face situation to get their attention and to catch them in a lie. The Q and A sessions are not intended to be pleasant conversations over tea. They are designed to acquire facts quickly. Facts that can be confirmed or not. She thinks she sees a large hole in Raphael's alibi.

From the squad room, Liz makes calls to confirm stories. The police axiom of "Listen and verify" applies to all persons of interest. The Firestone data was uploaded at seven-fourteen. Not enough time for Jose to get across the bay and commit the crime. County General reports that Yolanda was on duty in the ER on Sunday from noon to midnight. The manager of Raphael's apartment complex is not sure when he came back to his bungalow. She fell asleep around seven and he was not in his bungalow before then. One for three is still a good percentage.

Liz has to dig a little further into Raphael's past. No arrests. No jail time. No wants or warrants. He's a damned choirboy. Still her gut tells her something is amiss.

If one of the grieving families was going to have Ross killed, they would be careful to maintain a distance between themselves and the perp. An employee of Firestone? Another mechanic at the used car lot? A hired gun? Who in this area has a record of carjacking or tampering for profit and is not a guest of the county or state? Computer digging begins anew and produces three possibilities: Tony Arcado, Benny Rojas, and Tiffany Myers.

Telephone interviews are different from interviews conducted face-to-face. The person being interviewed on the phone is not physically on guard, because the interviewer is not in the person's face or space. On the phone, the police are almost friendly because they want simple answers to simple questions: questions of fact. On the other hand there is much less subtlety in a face-to-face interview because more, detailed information is sought. In many face-to-face interviews, the interview is held where the police want it to be held, so the interviewee knows he is a person of interest or a suspected perp. Thus, his actions and answers are guarded. He strives to protect himself with half-truths and dodges. He very often answers questions with questions to avoid answering the interviewer. This can happen whether the conversation occurs in the squad room or in a public place. Not so much over the phone. In either case, the interviewer does not answer any of the interviewee questions until he feels comfortable he has gotten enough preliminary information to move on.

"Is this Tony Arcado?"

"Yes, who wants to know?"

"Detective Elizabeth Kimble, Tampa PD. Can you account for your whereabouts last Sunday evening?"

"I was at a cookout with my brother and his family. Why?"

"Hopefully, your brother will verify your presence at the cookout. May I have his telephone number?"

"OK. It's in Orlando…407-555-4309. You never told me why you wanted to know."

"We are simply gathering information. Thank you for your time."

Liz notes to call the sister-in-law not the brother to verify. Second call.

"Is this Benny Rojas?"

"No. Who is this?"

"Detective Elizabeth Kimble of the Tampa Police. Do you know how I can reach Benny?"

"He is in the hospital…County General. His heart."

"How long has he been in the hospital?"

"He went in Saturday afternoon. Why?"

"We're doing some information gathering. Thanks for your time."

Scratch Benny's name off the list. Third call.

"Is this Tiffany Myers?"

"Yes. Who's calling?"

"Detective Elizabeth Kimble of the Tampa Police. Where were you last Sunday evening?"

"Returning from Nashville. Why?"

"What was the purpose for your trip to Nashville?"

"I was visiting a friend. Why?"

"What is your friend's name?"

"Ray Bonafiglio. Why?"

"What is his telephone number?"

"615-555-0553, why do you want to know?"

"Did you fly or drive to Nashville?"

"I flew Southwest. Why do you want to know all this?"

"We are gathering information. Thanks for your time."

The fourth call to Linda Arcado confirms Tony's story. Damn! He was telling the truth. Give it a rest. Let the facts to date percolate and see what questions or holes in statements bubble to the surface. The remainder of the shortened day is filled with more computer input. Oh, joy!

The rivalry between St. Regis and St. Thomas Aquinas High Schools is fierce regardless of the sport or level. The bitter part of "bitter rivalry" comes mostly from the parents and graduates in the stands. Both are Catholic schools; St. Regis is private and St. Thomas Aquinas is public. Societal separation. Therein the source of the friction.

The JV football game will be hotly contested. Both teams are undefeated. The winner of this game wins the District Championship. It has been a long time since St. Regis competed for a championship in any sport. The boys believe this is their year. Except that Jimmy Aldridge, the team's leading rusher will not play. In his place is another freshman – Alex Kimble.

The parking lot is packed. There are the usual banners urging teams to victory. There are also banner with the names and jersey numbers of specific players. There are also a few banners of questionable taste, which are removed once spotted. Liz shows her badge and is admitted without charge. Cary is somewhere on campus with her crew. She and Liz will find each other during the game. A cute girl from the booster club is in charge of collecting the admission charge.

"Hey, Mrs. Kimble. I understand that Alex is starting. If you see him before the game, tell him good luck from Annie."

The coquettish giggle confirms that the girl is an admirer. Certainly not a secret admirer if she introduces herself to Alex's mother. Liz works her way through the crowd and finds a seat among the blue and white of the St. Regis Bulldogs. The boys look almost grown up in their pads. Several of the JVs are much larger than Alex, number 44. Obviously, these are linemen. Teams are into their warm-ups. Players try to focus on the exercises, but many sneak a glance at the opposition. St. Regis has twenty-four players suited for the game...St. Thomas Aquinas has forty-two. The Tommies have several very large players. It has been that way for years. They view the Bulldogs as their younger, smaller, and very inferior rivals. The societal hierarchy often spews from the mouths of players. Privileged preppy is an expression often heard.

The Dogs win the coin toss and defer until the second half. The Tommies start the game from their eighteen. Two long passes dropped and a sweep that nets six yards cause them to punt from deep in their own territory. St. Regis brings the ball to its own forty-five. The first play is a handoff to Alex. He sprints off-tackle and is met immediately by a linebacker and a defensive tackle. The ball pops loose and is recovered by the linebacker. Suddenly, the bitter part of the rivalry rears its ugly head.

"What a pussy. The wimp coughed up the ball when he was barely touched. Way to stick the cream puff, Gerry. That's my boy. Hey, Regis, get a real player. Send that kid to the cheerleading squad."

The ugliness comes from the mouth of a woman, overdressed in Tommy colors, maroon and gold, sitting in the visitor section, a few rows away from Liz. Liz is torn between defending her son and the required decorum of a police officer. She stifles her visceral reaction and sits quietly. She is not one who can easily suffer in silence, but she must. The Tommies score in eight plays. The Dogs take the ensuing kick back to their thirty. The first play is another left tackle trap. This time, Alex gains sixteen yards. Gerry missed the runner at the line of scrimmage. Two complete passes and St. Regis is on the three. Back to the basic slant. Alex scores by bouncing off Gerry. After the score, the teams trade missed opportunities and punts. The St. Regis punter is also a midfielder on the soccer team. Thus, the back and forth slowly favors the Dogs. They are in scoring position as the first half is about to expire. No time for a running play from fourteen yards out. Enter the kicker. He splits the uprights and the Dogs go into the locker room leading 10 to 7.

The second half is more of the same back and forth until midway through the fourth quarter. The Tommies connect on a "Hook and Lateral" play that gets them to the Dogs' three-yard line. With the defense stacked against the run, the Tommies' quarterback lofts a balloon to the tight end in the corner. Touchdown. Score 10-14. The Dogs are in a hole with four minutes to play. They take the kickoff back to their thirty-five. On the first play, Alex goes in motion from left to right. The quarterback takes the snap and fakes a handoff to the fullback diving over the left guard. Then the QB spins and hits Alex in full stride down the sideline. Alex's strides remind Liz of Sandy. The boy is pushed out of bounds on the Tommies' thirty. Three and a half minutes to play. Lots of time. St. Regis calls a timeout. Liz can see the kids are amped.

The formation looks like it will be another left tackle trap, but the fullback carries off the right guard and gains eight yards. The Tommies are missing tackles at the line of scrimmage. The next play is a pass that sails over the receiver's head by three yards. Third and two. St. Regis uses the fullback as the decoy for Alex to run around the end for six yards. The Tommies call a timeout. Play is resumed with a minute and ten seconds to play. The QB completes a screen pass for three yards. Fullback up the middle gains four yards. Alex, head down, powers off tackle and gains five yards. Next, Alex goes in motion and takes the pass behind the line of scrimmage. He steps out of bounds on the two. What's next? The last play of the season.

St. Regis is in a spread formation. The Tommies call another timeout to regroup in the face of this new formation. Tight ends are lined up in front of wide receivers on either side of the formation. Only Alex is behind the quarterback. He's there to provide pass protection. At the snap, the quarterback drifts back toward Alex, raises his hand and waves an air pass to the receiver on his right. The ball is not in his hand. It is in Alex's hands. Alex goes from a blocking stance to another head-down run…this time off tackle where he meets and runs through Gerry. The game ends 17-14. St. Regis team, families, and friends go wild. Exiting the stands, Liz finds herself behind Gerry's Mom. Liz puts her arm around the shoulder of another St. Regis Mom.

"Ya know, if the Tommies had linebackers who weren't afraid to tackle, this might have been a different game."

She is loud enough for everyone to hear. Gerry's Mom hears and turns to the source of the smack talk. Liz offers a sardonic grin. If looks could kill, Alex and Cary would have become instant orphans. But the woman's withering glare can't erase Liz's smug smile of pride. There are times when being a Mom is more powerful than being a police officer. The hero's dinner consists of plates of barbecued ribs, sweet potato fries, and coleslaw. Alex has two orders of everything. Liz did not ask about Annie. The family drives home. Big hugs all around before bed.

III

Telephone first. A message from Emily Prentiss, one of the spouses in an ugly custody case. Mrs. Prentiss alleged child neglect and implied child abuse against her husband to gain custody of and support for the children. Today, she thinks that she is in danger because her husband is in a car parked across the street from her house. She claims this is a clear violation of the court order. But there is no court issued restraining order. Just one in her head.

"Mrs. Prentiss, this is Detective Kimble. Can you give me details of what is happening?"

"Walt is just sitting in his car and looking at the front door."

"When did this happen?"

"Half an hour ago. The kids aren't home from school yet. He's just sitting there. I'm really scared."

"Stay where you are. I'll be right over."

Fifteen minutes. Liz spots the six-year-old Mazda parked across the street from the Prentiss house. The engine is not running. She pulls in front of the parked car. Before Walter Prentiss can start the car and leave, Liz is at the driver's side door.

"Walter, what are you doing?"

"I came here to see my kids. She won't let me visit with them. The court said she had to let me spend time with them. We have specific days and times. But when I show up at the proper time, she tells me the kids are not at home. I just want to see my kids to make sure they're OK. I haven't seen them for four weeks."

"This is no way to see them. They're still in school."

"I'll wait. Why won't she let me see my kids? I make regular child support and alimony payments at the Court House. She has to let me spend time with them."

"Have you been to court to enforce the visitation portion of the separation agreement?"

"No."

"I advise you to not take these matters into your own hands. Let the court do its job."

"But that could take months."

"You could ask for an emergency hearing. The court would hear you within twenty-four hours. Or, I could take you to jail for menacing."

"Menacing? I'm not menacing anybody. I just want to talk with my kids. Will you talk to her and get her to let me see my kids?"

"Yes, now go home."

As the car roars off, Liz knocks on the front door.

"Good, you got rid of the bastard. But for how long? I know he'll be back. Then what do I do? Call you again so you can shoo him away?"

"Mrs. Prentiss, the children's father indicated to me that he has not seen the children for four weeks. He stated that when he shows up to see them, you tell him they are not at home. Is this true?"

"You know kids. Always running off to play somewhere. I can hardly keep track of them."

"For four weeks?"

"Are you calling me a liar?"

"No, ma'am. It just seems strange that for a month, Mr. Prentiss has been denied the court ordered visitation."

"What can I tell you? Kids will be kids."

"Well, I'm sure the court would not approve of this situation continuing. The court's goal is to ensure the safety and well-being of the children. Well-being in this case includes unsupervised time with their father. The court might view this last month during which their father had no visitation as custodial interference on your part. If the court finds there was custodial interference by one parent, the court may alter the entire separation agreement."

"They can't do that."

"Yes, the court can do that, because it's the court. So I urge you to be sure the children are available for time with their father. Is that understood?"

"I guess."

"OK, then have a good day."

Liz enters the incident in her case notes file to discuss with Gracia later. Check e-mail, which contains the usual assortment of department announcements and one from the Florida Department of Law Enforcement. The FDLE has taken over jurisdiction in the missing child case, and will continue the investigation in conjunction with the FBI. Tampa PD will be notified of any developments in the case. Liz assumes that the parents will be notified that the case is now in the hands of other agencies so she won't have to. Hopefully, Gracia and the brass will consider this a closed case since she and the department are no longer responsible for the investigation.

Now to the smash and grab. Many of the items of jewelry from the robbery at International Mall turned up at two pawnshops. Shop owners and the in-store video indicated the individual pawning the goods was the same man in both cases. He was visited at home and arrested when the two unies found other items of jewelry hidden between the mattress and box spring in his bedroom. Willie Davis is now a guest of the TPD awaiting trial. Another case closed. Liz is on a roll.

The pop, pop, pop, pop of the small caliber gun is covered by the roar of traffic on I-275. The shooter leans over the victim's head, opens his mouth, stretches his tongue from his mouth, and crudely saws off the tongue. The absence of a tongue is the mark of a rat: a message to all who think they can buy their freedom or earn an income by talking to the police. The bloody, dirty body is stomped. His face is kicked until an eye falls from its socket. The gunman bends over and scours the ground around the body looking for something. Then he slowly turns to the waiting car, enters and two criminals drive away...at the speed limit.

"Kimble, you're up. Body dump under I-275 at the Horatio Street Bridge. That's all that was called in. Unies are on the scene."

Liz springs into action, very willing to forego the paperwork...or in this case e-work due to the paperless environment. Her equipment for investigating a crime scene consists of a flashlight, notepad, two pens, and a digital camera. Before leaving her desk, she tucks the cuffs of her slacks into her socks. With a red, green, and blue Argyle pattern, the socks were a gift last Christmas. Walking out the door, her look from the waist down vaguely resembles that of golfers many years ago who wore Plus Fours. Two detectives sitting at their desks slurping coffee smile at her appearance. Rain last night and early this morning will make any outdoor crime scene a mess. It is cheaper to launder socks than have slacks dry-cleaned. The drive takes ten minutes.

There are already two squad cars in the area. The red and blue blinking lights of the squad cars and the ME's wagon create a stroboscopic atmosphere. High-intensity lamps are being assembled and will soon render the under-bridge cavern an area of sunlight securely marked by yellow TPD crime scene tape.

"Hello, Detective."

"Hello, Doctor. What can you tell me?"

"Well, this one is particularly nasty. Multiple gunshots to the head did him in. Somewhere during the process, he was savagely and repeatedly struck. Not sure if he was beaten before or after he was shot. Maybe both. I'll know for sure after I get him on the table. Regardless, the killer must have really hated the victim. His head and upper torso took the damage from the blows. Not sure yet what caused the blunt force trauma. In the absence of a stick or baseball bat in the area, my guess is feet inside shoes were the culprits. But, that is your area of expertise. Be careful. Watch where you walk. There is an eyeball around here somewhere. There may even be a tongue. I'll have more accurate information this afternoon."

"Has the corpse been rolled?"

"We were saving the good stuff for you."

"Why, thank you, Dr. Kovalewsky. You're too kind."

Liz turns the body to either side and checks his pockets for an ID or any clue that would lead to the murderer. Nothing. The vic's style and age of clothes indicate he was a low-life street thug. She thought there would be nothing because two of the pants pockets had been turned out. Was the killer looking for anything that could aid the investigation? Clue Number 1: the killer or killers know how the police work. Did the perp not know all the tricks of street thugs? Liz lifts up the left pant leg and pulls down the sock. Nothing. Repeat on the right side. The man's driver's license and three hundred dollars in fifties are tucked between the ankle near the heel and sock. Hector Lopez was thirty-two and lived at 245 Estrella Avenue. It is obvious from the damage done to the body that the perp was in no real hurry. Not a robbery because the perp left the money and driver's license for the detective to find. Only one conclusion; the items were meant to be found. A pro. A pro with an agenda beyond murder. Why? The perp's action was intended to deliver a message to all those who would be questioned.

She takes several pictures of the vic and the scene. There are no shell casings. The perp took time to clean up. Pros do not leave telltale shell casings with fingerprints. The gun appears to be a .25 or .22. It will be impossible to trace the gun by the slugs. They entered the head and ricocheted through the brain turning it into grits. Most likely, there will be many fragments of four slugs resting on the brainpan. Liz guesses that the pro used a gun with a suppressor. Silence is golden during the day even under a busy bridge. Thirty more minutes at the murder scene doesn't add much to her knowledge. There are no readable shoe prints in the mud and slime created by the rain. Her socks are slightly muddy, but her slacks are spotless. Now comes the part of an investigation she dreads: reaching out to Mr. Lopez's family. An immediate visit is required.

The neighborhood of 245 Estrella Avenue is modest lower middle class: the hardest hit by the recession. There are numerous porches on which men sit in the hopes that work will fall into their resting laps. In front of the target address is parked a three-year-old bright red Dodge Charger. Before the substantial body style changes. She parks in the street beside the Dodge. As she climbs the four steps to the porch, she notices three new bicycles and deduces that in this economically hit neighborhood, Hector must have been one of the few men employed...and at a decent paying job at that. Three knocks on the door result in an opening.

"Hello, ma'am. I am Detective Kimble of the Tampa Police. Are you the wife of Hector Lopez?"

"Si. I am Ysabella Lopez. How can I help you?"

"I'm afraid I have bad news. Your husband, Hector, was found murdered today."

Two simple sentences generate an explosion of wailing and flood of tears. Ysabella staggers back into the living room of the well-kept house. Liz follows, noting the plethora of religious icons on tables and the small mantel.

"Why? Who would do this to Hector? He was a good man and good father."

Ysabella falls into a new looking leather recliner and sobs hysterically. Gradually, she regains her composure.

"Mrs. Lopez, I'm going to need to ask you a few questions. I need to get some background information about Hector. This will be an important step in helping us solve the crime. Do you think you are up to answering a few simple questions?"

"Yes, I'll try."

"Where did Hector work?"

"Fairman Chrysler Dodge."

"What did he do there?"

"He was a mechanic."

"Thank you. Just two more questions."

"Do you know if anyone was angry at Hector or threatened him in any way?"

"No. Everybody loved Hector. He was kind."

"Did Hector owe anybody money? When I say anybody, I don't mean a store or credit card, I mean an individual."

"We owe nobody nothing. Hector and I pay all our bills on time. He was a good provider. He always had cash. See how good he was. He bought the new car, this recliner, and two big-screen TVs with cash a year ago. And the bicycles for the children. Plus, he would often surprise me with nice clothes."

"Thank you for your time. I am truly sorry for your loss. The department will need you to identify the body. When you feel up to it, call this number and I will escort you through the identification process."

"Maybe tomorrow."

"Thanks. Again, I am sorry for your loss."

Exiting the house, Liz sees four men on a porch looking at her. Unemployed sentinels of the block. She walks to them.

"Gentlemen, good day. Perhaps you can help me."

Silence.

"Do any of you speak English?"

"No ingles."

"I was going to give the man who spoke English and helped me twenty bucks. Sorry to bother you."

"Waddaya want, chika?"

"Now we have someone who can speak English. Do any of you know Hector Lopez?"

"Why?"

"He was found murdered today."

"Where is my money?"

"Where is my information?"

"Money first."

"Information or no money. It's that simple."

"We all know Hector. He thought he was a big shot. He bragged about his job. He never let us forget about his job at Fairman and what he got paid. He acted like he was better than us. Plus, once in a while he would flash a wad of fifties in our faces. He always seemed to have lots of cash. But he never gave me any. None for my homies neither. We were his homies and he didn't care. When he bought that car, he spent the first day and night driving it around the neighborhood to show everybody his new expensive toy. Now, where is my fifty?"

"One more question. Do you know how Hector got the wads of cash?"

"Nah, but I know it wasn't from dealin'. He was strictly against drugs. His sister OD'd and his brother was killed in a deal gone bad."

Liz pulls out a twenty and hands it to the informative neighbor.

"Thanks for your time today. I'll be in touch."

Back at headquarters, Liz digs into the information stored in various computer databases. Hector's record is spotless. Not even a juvie record and no scrapes since becoming an adult. Not even a traffic ticket. Intriguing, but not impossible. And, the information about his brother and sister checked out. Call Fairman. The general manager praises Hector's work performance. Salary confirmed. The Charger was purchased last year using an employee discount and a trade-in. Plus, Hector put down six thousand in cash. Fairman was carrying the small balance and deducting the payments from his pay. Hector checks out. Where did he get the six large?

Tomorrow's agenda: go back and talk to Hector's homies and dig into Raphael LaRue's timeline on Sunday. For now, start the process of digging into Firestone employee banking activity. The vast majority of employees in the Firestone store have their pay electronically deposited. The territory manager for Central Florida e-mails Liz a list of store employees, as well as bank names. She tells Liz only two employees of that particular outlet do not have their pay electronically deposited. Both of these people joined the company within the last month. Establishing the electronic deposit process takes three bi-weekly pay cycles.

The six banks will send the past two monthly statements of seventeen Firestone employees based on an official request from the TPD. Ever since 9/11, banks have been quite cooperative. The multiple pages are downloaded for review and inclusion into the case file. The review of sixty-plus pages of data is painstakingly tedious and reinforces the need for Liz to have her eyes checked. Undoubtedly, she will need reading glasses. She is looking for any unusual deposits. She doesn't care about spending patterns, although she is struck by the number of times some people use the ATMs for cash, and how often the amount withdrawn is forty dollars. Many at the same ATM. She recognizes the address of the ATM…an adult entertainment establishment. Then an entry leaps off the screen. Robert Thomas deposited twenty-five hundred dollars in cash two weeks ago and then again on Monday. Another person of interest. A call to the store confirms that Robert is off today, but will be working tomorrow. He warrants a visit.

To check Tiffany Myers' travel on Southwest Airlines requires several calls to find the person who can release the information and then an e-mail request for it. After forty-five minutes, the airline confirms that Tiffany Myers flew to Nashville on Tuesday and returned to Tampa on Saturday afternoon. Time enough to do the job on Sunday. But, for whom? As a former suspect in numerous offenses, Tiffany's personal information is in the police department database. A call to her bank garners her account's activity. Liz notes a deposit of five large two weeks ago. The cost of the contract?

She reviews her case work with Lieutenant Gracia, noting four persons of interest in the car tampering; Tiffany Myers, Robert Thomas, Raphael LaRue, and Hector Lopez. She is trying to link technical expertise, extra money, and motive. He agrees she is on the right path. Liz heads home.

Bay Times Police Blotter

The body of Hector Lopez was found beneath the I-275 Horatio Street Bridge. According to Tampa Police, Mr. Lopez had been shot multiple times. Mr. Lopez, an employee of the Fairman Motor Group is survived by his wife and two children. Tampa Police Department spokesman, Robert Davies stated, "We are pursuing this violent murder with our full resources. We urge anyone with any information about the murder to contact the Tampa Police Department."

"Kimble, you have another follow-up. It seems Brenda and Willie Collins got into it. The unies are already there. Brenda is asking for you. You're very popular this week."

Another domestic violence case. This time, the court determined that husband and wife should have contact only under police supervision. As Liz pulls up to the small apartment complex, she sees two patrol cars and an ambulance. She grabs her notepad and heads toward the commotion. Just inside the door, she sees Willie on a gurney. He is on his right side. His shirt shows a blood pool on his left shoulder. The emergency bandages have been applied beneath the shirt.

"Willie, this is Detective Kimble. Do you remember me?"

"Yes."

"What happened?"

"I came by to pick up some clothes I had left in the house. I called Brenda yesterday and again this morning and asked her to leave the clothes in a box outside the front door. She agreed. That way we would not have any contact like the court ordered. When I got here, there was no box outside the door. So I called her and she said the box was inside the door and that it was too heavy for her to lift. She would open the door so I could come inside and get the box. When she opened the door, I saw she had a big kitchen fork in her hand. Before I could reach inside to get the box, she stabbed me. All I wanted was my clothes. I wasn't going to touch her or hurt her. Why did she stab me with a fork?"

"I don't know, but I'll find out."

Liz turns to the paramedic.

"How is he?"

"The fork penetrated about two inches. I don't think it hit anything vital, but they'll determine the full extent of the wound at the ER. We have to go now."

Liz beckons one of the uniformed officers to her side.

"What statements do you have?"

"Willie told us much of what he just told you. Brenda claims Willie came banging on the door demanding to be let in. When she opened the door, he lunged at her but tripped over the box of clothes. She ran to the kitchen counter and got the big fork for protection. When he got up from the floor, he came at her while she was in the kitchen. That's where and when she stabbed him. She claims she was in fear for her life."

"Who called it in?"

"A neighbor who heard a commotion. She saw Willie on the floor by the open door. Does not know what happened before she looked into the Collins' apartment."

"Where was Willie when you arrived?"

"He was on the floor by the door. See the blood stain on the carpet. My guess is that he had been in the same place since the stabbing."

"Thanks."

Brenda Collins was sitting on the living room couch, a paramedic was examining her.

"Brenda. Are you OK to talk?"

"Yes. I want that bastard arrested for violating the court order and attacking me."

"Tell me what happened."

"I was asleep when Willie came banging on the door demanding to be let in. When I opened the door, he lunged at me but tripped and fell to the floor. I was afraid for my life. I ran to the kitchen counter and got a big fork for protection. When he got up from the floor, he came at me. That's when I stabbed him. It was in self-defense. He has no business being in my house. I want him arrested and thrown in jail."

"Where were you when you defended yourself?"

"I was near the kitchen counter. Here."

Liz does not see any blood drops between the kitchen and the front door.

"Are you sure you defended yourself when you were standing in the kitchen?"

"Positive. Are you calling me a liar?"

"What is in the box by the door?"

"Just trash I want to throw out."

Liz goes to the box, opens it and withdraws a man's blazer.

"Whose clothes are these?"

"I guess they're Willie's. The stuff is trash like him."

"Brenda, may I see your cell phone?"

"Sure, why?"

"Curiosity."

The last call the phone received was from Willie's phone. Thirty minutes ago. The call lasted forty-five seconds. He was probably asking about the box of clothes.

"Brenda, we are going to take Willie to the hospital, and you to jail for assault."

"Bitch, you can't do that. I'm innocent. Willie lunged at me. He slapped me."

"Where did he slap you?"

"On my face."

"I see no marks on your face, but I'll have the paramedic take a look."

"The redness and swelling have gone down since he slapped me."

The paramedic carefully examines Brenda's face and shakes his head. No injury. No slap.

The apartment is now a crime scene and will be designated so with the usual yellow tape. Brenda's protestations are loud, disjointed, and not very ladylike as she is handcuffed and placed in the squad car.

More forms to be completed.

IV

Tiffany Myers works at La Belle Boutique, an overpriced, quite chic clothing store in south Tampa. Liz arrives promptly at ten to speak to this person of interest.

"Good morning, is Tiffany here?"

"Yes. She's in the stockroom pulling inventory for our clearance sale this week. I'll call her."

"That's not necessary, I'll find her."

Twenty-five steps and through the curtained doorway is the stockroom. There is Liz's target loading a rack with hangers of blouses.

"Tiffany Myers. I need a few minutes of your time."

"Who are you?"

"Police Detective Elizabeth Kimble. We spoke the other day. I need to clarify a few points concerning your whereabouts and timeline of events last week."

"OK. What do you want to know?"

"When we spoke on the phone, you said that you returned from Nashville on Sunday. And you gave me the telephone number of the man you were visiting, Mr. Ray Bonafiglio. After dialing the number you gave me and contacting Southwest Airlines, I learned you told me two lies. You returned on Saturday afternoon, and the telephone number you gave me is not a working number. So, now is your chance to set the record straight."

"OK. You must have transposed some numbers. The number Ray gave me was 615-555-5350. That's the number I gave you. What did you write down?"

"615-555-0553."

"You transposed some numbers."

"Let me check that here and now."

Cell phones and the calls from them can be effective interrogation tools when used in front of a perp or person of interest. It makes them uneasy. That normally leads to slips.

"Hello. May I speak to Mr. Ray Bonafiglio? Are you sure? Thanks for your help."

Liz feels she is closing in on a true suspect. She assumes an aggressive posture.

"I just spoke to a nice lady that answers the phone at Build With Us lumberyard. There is no Ray Bonafiglio working for the company, and she does not know such a man. Can you explain the lie you just told?"

"615-555-5350 is the number Ray gave me. See, he's married, but he is leaving his wife for me, because he loves me. Until the divorce papers are signed, our relationship has to be kept secret."

"How does he reach you if he wants to talk?"

"He calls me."

"Then you see the number from which he's calling. What is that number?"

"Every time he calls, it shows up "unknown number" on my display. So all I know is the number I just gave you."

Liz knows the unknown number display is that of a disposable phone. A "burner": a phone purchasable in many convenience stores. It can be used for X number of minutes then discarded.

"OK, what about the discrepancy between the day of your return to Tampa? How do you explain that?"

"I was scheduled to fly back home on Sunday. But Ray thought his wife was getting suspicious about his absence from their home. So, I left a day early. I have my original itinerary in my purse. I printed it from my computer. It will confirm my original departure day was Sunday."

"Get it for me."

Sure enough.

"What did you do on Sunday?"

"Did a little housework, shopped for groceries, and cooked a few meals for the week."

"Can anyone verify your activities?"

"Yes. My neighbor, Mr. Russell. He's in a wheelchair and has a tough time getting to the store. So, I always ask him what he needs when I go. He gives me a list and cash, and I get his items. For my Sunday dinner, I cooked paella with hunks of grouper, shrimp, clams, and yellow rice. I took Mr. Russell a covered dish of the meal around six. I ate alone and went to bed around nine. I was tired. If that's all you need, I must get back to work."

"One last question. You recently deposited a substantial amount of money into your checking account. Please tell me the source of the funds."

"Commission on my sales. I make ten dollars an hour plus commission. The commission check comes to me at the end of each quarter. You can ask management. They'll confirm what I'm saying."

"I will. Thanks for your time."

The manager of the boutique confirmed the policy of quarterly checks for sales commissions. Mr. Russell, Jack, confirmed the grocery shopping, dinner, and the fact that Tiffany's car never left the driveway after her return from the food store around four. Tiffany is clean.

Analyses of the bank records for Isaac and Ramona LaRue, and Jose and Yolanda Martinez reveal nothing out of the ordinary; no major cash withdrawals that would be necessary to pay for the "accident." No way to check any investments…for now. On the surface, neither couple appears to have paid for the death of Marshall Ross. Two more dead ends. Robert Thomas has no criminal record. Liz needs to determine the source of the substantial cash deposit. This requires a face-to-face. Call. He is working today. Across the bay to the Firestone store.

"Mr. Thomas, good morning. I am Detective Elizabeth Kimble of the Tampa Police. Is there somewhere we can talk?"

"Sure, let's go into an empty office. How can I help you?"

"Just a few questions. Can you account for your whereabouts Sunday a week ago?"

"Why?"

"We are gathering information."

"About what?"

"About your whereabouts. Where were you and what were you doing?"

"Let me see…Sunday. I went over to Orlando to see my folks."

"At what time were you with your parents?"
"I got to their house around ten in the morning and left

after dinner around eight later that day. Now what's all this about?"

"Information gathering. Thanks for your time. I hope I didn't cause any inconvenience."

A quick call to Mr. Thomas's mother confirms her son's arrival and departure times. Two down and two to go. Hopefully, another face-to-face with Raphael LaRue will fill in the apparent blanks in his Sunday. Or lead to more questions. Liz is already across the bay from Tampa, so this visit will not take long.

"Mr. LaRue. Detective Kimble. I just need a little more of your time. I need to ask you a few more questions."

"Why are you harassing me?"

"This is not harassing. If you want see harassing, I will pull you from your job in front of all your pals and take you to the TPD Headquarters for interrogation. Do you want to do that?"

"No."

"Good, let's start over. Where were you two Sunday's ago?"

"I told you. I was at the beach, hit a few bars, ate dinner, and went home to sleep."

"What time did you arrive home?"

"Between eight and eight-thirty. I remember, because when I turned the TV, the Rays game was in extra innings. But, they lost in the thirteenth."

"Can anyone verify your story?"

"Yeah, Jenna is a waitress at Coconuts. I always sit at her table. Talk to her. I tip big. She likes me."

"One last question. Recently, you made two substantial deposits into your checking account. What is the source of the money?"

"You can't dig into my bank account. That's illegal."

"The police can investigate every person of interest. You are such a person. What is the source of the money?"

"My family is helping me buy a house. I need the money to complete the down payment. What concern is it of yours?"

"No concern, just curiosity. It won't be necessary for me to talk to the server at Coconuts; you've given me all the information I need. Thanks for your time."

Back into her car, she hurries over to Coconuts.

"Good afternoon. I'm looking for Jenna."

"Who are you?"

"Detective Liz Kimble of the Tampa PD."

Flashing her badge to garner respect is always effective and it never gets old.

"Just a minute. I'll get her."

Two minutes later, a skinny woman, body has been ravaged by sun, smoking, booze, and miscellaneous recreational drugs, slithers to the hostess station.

"Waddaya want."

"I want you to answer a few simple questions."

"Like what?"

"Like, do you remember serving a Raphael LaRue dinner in the past two weeks?"

"Not sure."

"Well, maybe if we had this discussion at the Tampa Police Department offices, you might be sure. Waddaya think?"

"Hold on. What does this Raphael guy look like?"

"He has black hair and blue eyes. Stands about five-nine and weighs about 220. And he wears a lot of gold jewelry."

"Yeah. Now I remember. He was in here two Sunday's ago. He ate dinner and flirted with me. What a cheap bastard. He left me two bucks on a twenty-dollar tab."

"What time was he here?"

"Not sure when he came in, but he left around eight."

"Thank you. You have been a big help."

"That's it?"

"That's it."

On the drive back to Tampa, Liz feels a little depressed. No direct leads. Tomorrow, she will go back and speak to Hector Lopez's homies. Today, Liz will escort Ysabella Lopez to the morgue for identification of her husband's body and completion of the forms for release of his body.

The ME's file on Marshall Ross revealed that his blood-alcohol level was 0.35. Liz wonders how Ross was able to drive from the event to the Interstate before he crashed. The file on Hector Lopez revealed a substantial level of opiates in his system. They had been injected. The ME indicated the entry point for the needle to be on the right side of his neck. There were no tracks on either of his arms or injection sites anywhere else on his body. Strange. Why would a first-time drug user shoot up in his neck? Any use of drugs runs counter to what his homeboys told Liz. The front desk announces Ysabella Lopez.

"Mrs. Lopez. We are sorry that you have to go through this, but the law requires that we have a sworn statement that the body in our morgue that we assume to be Hector Lopez is, in fact, Hector Lopez. That's why we need a relative to identify the body. Please walk with me to the elevator."

Ysabella forces a weak smile, and the two women ride the elevator to the first floor. They exit the car through the rear and enter a large brightly lit room. The smell of antiseptic is heavy. Down the long center hall, they come to a closed door. Liz uses her key card to open the door. They walk down a short, narrow hall and turn in front of a large single-pane window with a venetian blind on the inside. Neither woman has spoken during the trip from Liz's desk to the viewing window. Liz taps on the window. The blind is raised half way to reveal Hector's face and shoulders. Ysabella grabs Liz's hand and squeezes firmly. From deep within her soul, Ysabella emits a soft, deep whimper.

"Si. Mi Dios. That's Hector."

The whimper becomes a moan, which becomes crying, which becomes sobbing. The process lasts two minutes.

"When can I take him to the church?"

"Once the form of identification is completed and signed by you and the mortuary, we will release the body to anyone you designate in writing."

"We can go now. I have seen enough."

On the way back to her desk, Liz marvels at the way Hector looked. Ysabella did not see the battered corpse. She was spared that horror. Dr. Kovalewsky's crew did a masterful job hiding the bruises and the empty eye socket. Hector looked like he was sleeping peacefully.

"Here is the form I mentioned. Just have it completed and sign here and here. I'll make you a copy. Then you need the mortuary or funeral parlor to sign the document for the body to be released. I need to ask you a few minor questions, if you're up to answering them."

"Si."

"Just a piece of information for our files. When we spoke originally, you mentioned that Hector was a good provider for you and your children."

"Si. He was always surprising us with gifts. Clothes, toys, the bicycles, and the two big-screen TVs."

"Did he ever mention where the money to buy these things came from?"

"No, and I never asked."

Ysabella's tone had switched from bereaved widow to protective spouse. She knew something, or suspected something about the source of Hector's sudden windfalls.

"I want to go now."

"Yes, Mrs. Lopez. Again, when you have decided on a funeral parlor, have them complete their portion of the form and be sure that you sign it. Both you and the funeral parlor should keep a copy. They need the completed form to retrieve the body. Then, call the telephone number on the bottom of the form and Hector's body will be made available for your designated third party."

"Thank you."

"Thank you for coming in today. Again, we are sorry for your loss."

At the door to police headquarters, the women shake hands. Ysabella's hand is cold and clammy. As soon as Mrs. Lopez is in her car, Liz walks hurriedly to her desk and grabs the keys to the squad car. She heads to the Lopez neighborhood.

The same four characters are sitting on the same porch. It looks to Liz as if they are waiting for someone to stop by and offer them work or maybe they are protecting the neighborhood against some evil happening. She scans the group and focuses on the man she spoke to previously. He seemed to be some type of leader. Or, maybe he just wants everyone to think that.

"Good afternoon, gentlemen. I need a few more minutes of your time. I have a few follow-up questions."

"You got money, chika?"

"I am not your chika. I am Detective Kimble. And, I have no money for you, but I have the authority to detain you for hindering a lawful police investigation."

"Whoa, pretty woman. Slow down. I was just messin' with you."

"And me arresting you would be me messin' with you. So, how about a nice informational sit-down on your porch? All four of you."

"OK, chika. I mean Detective Kimble. I will talk with you. These others. Ingles no good."

"What is your name?"

"Umberto Rosario."

"Well, Umberto, the other day you mentioned that occasionally Hector would have a substantial amount of cash. And that he would make you aware of his money."

"Si, he would wave the wads of fifties in our faces."

"How often did he have a large amount of cash?"

"Maybe three or four times a year."

"How many years did he insult you this way?"

"A few years. He was a real asshole."

"Did you ever see how much money he had, or was it just in a folded wad?"

"It was folded over. And the wad was more than an inch thick. That's a lot of money."

"Do you recall the dates that he flashed the wads of money?"

"No dates. But, I remember last year he had wads of cash in late February, early June, and August. Also, two years ago about this time, he had a bigger wad of cash, and I mean a really big wad. Maybe twice as big as he had before or since."

"Did he ever mention where he got the money?"

"No, but one time I joked with him that he must be on the police payroll."

"What did he say to that?"

"Nothing, he just went silent and glared at me. No bragging about the money. No nothing. And that was strange for Hector because he was always happy and was always talking about baseball, cars, or his money. This time he just went silent, looked angry, and walked away."

Saturday, a day at the beach: no kids, no work, no worries. Sun to tan and a crime novel in which Liz can lose her everyday thoughts. She has the third installment of the Tony Sattill series. The first two installments reflected the fact that the author had very little police training. Whatever he knew, he learned during ride-alongs on the third tour. Gathering information from a friendly patrolman during the quiet hours…from eleven to seven. The author put the limited information into the soul and mouth of the main character. Liz wondered what it would be like to be a Manhattan Police Detective: all the glamour and excitement along with the dirt and daily violence. Tampa is just fine. Alex and Cary are at parties, and thus, in the charge of other parents. On days like today, she remembers the Zen command: "Be. Here. Now." She will follow the directive after she slathers SPF 30 sunblock on her exposed parts.

The first flock of snowbirds has arrived for the warm winter season. Their pale skin and flat Midwestern accents are obvious clues as to the origins of these beachgoers. Minnesota, Wisconsin, and Michigan are all represented. The Canadians have a pleasant lilt to their conversation. Beach towels, chairs, and coolers mark each specific territory on the sand. There are no food or drink vendors allowed near the water. A little ordinance passed at the insistence of the restaurants on Gulf Boulevard. There is ample public parking, but meters require feeding every two hours. That's long enough for Liz to stay in the sun.

Two chapters into the book, sweat begins to trickle down the back of her neck and down the front into her cleavage. Time for a dip in the Gulf. As she stands and adjusts her suit, she thinks how fortunate she is to look younger than her age. Not much younger, just younger. She has a body that can wear a brief two-piece suit. Not a thong. The sand is hot going the fifty yards to the water's edge. The Gulf is cool. Ten minutes is enough. Back to her towel and the retired Manhattan Police Captain that married his lover and produced three children. What would it be like for her to have a third child? Loving and frightening simultaneously. Four more chapters and her skin is quite hot from the sun in the cloudless sky. Time to shower and wash off the sand that has adhered to the sunblock. Then something to eat. Her kids know that she will not be cooking today. The public shower water is tepid. She finds clothes for the restaurant in her beach bag. The shorts and halter top sit atop her badge, gun, and phone.

The open-air restaurant is jammed. Groups of four and six waiting to be seated clog the entrance. Excusing herself, Liz slides between two couples complaining about the cost of owning two homes, particularly on the Gulf Coast, where insurance rates have increased 300% in three years, and real estate taxes on their second home have increased 250% in four years. Liz thinks that the financially fortunate will always find a reason to complain about how expensive it has become to live in this once inexpensive idyllic environment. Second home, notwithstanding. Liz finds a seat at the bar.

"How can I help you?"

"Coors Light draft and a menu, please."

The bartender's name tag says Robby.

The beer arrives and she orders a grilled grouper sandwich with coleslaw and macaroni salad. Scanning the patrons, she sees a wide spectrum of ages...couples and families. The cold beer tastes good. It cuts through the film of saliva in her mouth and throat with just enough sting to confirm the alcohol content. Two sips from the plastic cup before the fish sandwich arrives. Until then, she had not realized how hungry she was. She is cautious not to Hoover her drink and meal. Robby appears.

"How is everything?"

With a mouth partially full of food, she can't answer. So she nods her head.

"Great. The gentleman over there wants to buy you a drink. What will you have?"

"The offer is very nice, but I have to respectfully decline. Thank the gentleman for me, would you?"

Robby, the messenger, disappears. Liz finishes her sandwich. Two swallows of beer remain.

"Why did you refuse my offer?"

She turns and sees that the voice belongs to the gentleman from across the bar.

"I came in here for a beer and sandwich. I can't stay much longer than that takes."

The guy is a beach lothario: trim, tan, wearing the latest fashion in swim trunks, a bright floral shirt, opened to display his freshly shaved chest, and two gold chains that direct the looker to his rock-hard six pack and below. He is a too-obvious hunter.

"You can stay as long as you like. Then we could have a drink together."

"Thank you, but no thank you."

"Is it me? Do you not find me handsome?"

"It's me. I have family obligations."

"You are here alone. You have no family with you."

"And I'm leaving alone to be with my family."

"One drink?"

"Here, let me show you a picture of my family."

Liz reaches into her bag and withdraws her badge and reveals her gun. The lothario's smarmy smile disappears and is replaced with a look of respect bordering on fear.

"Oops. I hope you're not frightened, sir. Both of us must be going: me to my home and you to your barstool."

Liz pays Robby and heads for her car. In the parking lot, she feels the icy glare of the spurned lounge lizard. Suddenly, she turns and spies him staring. She offers a palm-open, finger-folding, dismissive wave good-bye. Going over the bridge, she realizes that was the first time some guy has hit on her in two years. The realization produces conflicted feelings; on the plus side, she is pleased to be noticed, while on the minus side, she is not pleased to be noticed by a beach bar hustler.

V

The initial leads in the suspicious death of Marshall Ross have gone nowhere. Nothing from the families of the dead children, nothing from the known hired guns, nothing from some second- tier family members or friends, and nothing on the money trails. Nil. Zero. Zip. Nada. One more possibility to get more information about the non-murder… is the widow, Allison Ross. Time to pay a visit. The drive to Indian Rocks Beach takes about an hour during mid-morning. Liz pulls up to the gate at 21212 Gulf Boulevard and presses the button on the box.

"Who is it?"

"Elizabeth Kimble, Detective with the Tampa Police Department. I would like to speak with Mrs. Ross. Is she available?"

"Yes, please pull up to the front door."

The squawk box, the male voice at the other end, the electronically controlled gate, the circular driveway, and the massive doors at the house's entrance all speak of a life with more money than Liz could earn in her lifetime.

"Welcome. Mrs. Ross will see you shortly. Please wait in the library."

The handsome, young man, tan, trim and muscular is dressed in a bright yellow polo shirt, khaki shorts and Top-Siders. He ushers Liz down the wide main hall. The marble floor, as far as she can see, is strategically decorated with oriental rugs and potted blooming plants. The man leads her through two pocket doors and into a room with massive windows looking onto the Gulf. The natural light of the sun streaming into the library is home for the numerous plants that adorn the room – African violets, miniature roses, a flowering bonsai, a peace plant, and a bird of paradise. Liz feels a twinge of envy. Her horticultural ventures have failed miserably over the past ten years. She has little long-term success with plants from a big-box store that are programmed to die within six months of purchase. She notes a desk with a telephone and laptop. Several stuffed chairs are covered in a bright Key West floral print. There is a huge TV on the wall, but there are no shelves and thus no books. Odd for a room called the library.

Just then, she hears the click-click-click of strapless high-heeled shoes on marble. Allison Ross's entrance is as dramatic as her brilliant floral-print wrap that flows to her side and behind her. Her body is tanned and barely contained by the brief bikini top and the small triangle of fabric that magically covers her lady parts. A thong! Her blonde hair is neatly coiffed. Large-lens dark glasses cover most of her cheeks and eyes. She has a half-empty wine glass in her right hand at nine-thirty in the morning. Her smile is barracuda-like. Liz guesses that Mrs. Ross was at least fifteen years younger than Mr. Ross and twenty years older than the man who met Liz at the door. The widow does not appear to be the grieving type. She is a cougar that keeps her prey close.

"Good morning, and who might you be?"

Condescension and annoyance coat her words and drip from her lips.

"Good morning, ma'am, I am Detective Elizabeth Kimble of the Tampa Police Department. I would like to ask you a few questions, if you have the time."

"I do. Proceed."

"First, let me say that we are sorry for the loss of your husband."

"Thank you. Now what do you want to know?"

"Did your husband have any enemies?"

"Enemies? No. Fractious business relationships? Yes."

"Do you know of anyone who would want your husband dead?"

"Are you saying he was murdered?"

"No, ma'am. What I am asking are standard questions that pertain to anyone who is involved in an accidental death. We have to rule out many factors to conclude that the individual, in this case your husband, died accidentally. So, let me repeat. Do you know of anyone who would want your husband dead?"

"No, I don't. Marshall was a loving husband and father who donated much time and money to philanthropic endeavors throughout the Bay Area."

"Where were you on the Sunday of his death?"

"Now you're accusing me. How dare you."

"I am accusing you of nothing. I merely asked your whereabouts."

"Well, if you must know, I had a small gathering of my friends here. Would you like their names?"

The tone of her voice had progressed from disdain to arrogant anger.

"That won't be necessary. I have all I need."

"Then we're done?"

"Yes, ma'am."

"I'll have Lance show you out."

"That won't be necessary. I can find my way."

On her way to the front door, Liz notices pictures of two young men at various stages of their growth. She pauses to get a closer look.

"Those are Marshall's sons from his first marriage. James is a sophomore and William will be a freshman. Both at the University of Florida. They live with Marshall and me. Their natural mother is dead."

"Thanks for your time today. I hope I didn't inconvenience you."

"Not at all. I'm always willing to help a civil servant."

Snotty bitch were words that popped into Liz's mind. The boy toy, Lance, is appropriately named for his duties. Like someone named Sunny who is always happy. Liz wants to take a look at Marshall's will. Follow the money. Other avenues to explore will appear along the way. Now to Dr. Lang.

Her sessions with Dr. Bernadette Lang started the month after Sandy's death. Seeing a psychiatrist has helped Liz sort through the emotional trauma created by the abrupt loss of her husband. The doctor has been proactive in her approach, not passive like many psychiatrists. As Liz poured out her feelings of dread, sadness, and anger, Dr. Lang helped guide her to the underlying causes of each powerful emotion and gave her advice on how to address the feeling. Today will be her last visit.

"Welcome."

"Thank you, Doctor."

"What shall we talk about today?"

"As we both know, this will be my last session. That's making me nervous. Sort of like a bird leaving the nest or a child leaving home for college."

"You should not fear being on your own. It's a natural state. During the past two years you've made substantial progress in dealing with the emotions associated with losing a spouse. Particularly losing a spouse to violence."

"I know. But what will I do if a crisis overwhelms me?"

"Refer to your journal. Remember the written record of your feelings and our sessions. Use it to work through any issues that confront you. It contains much good advice from its author."

"There is one thing that has been on my mind of late. I have strong feelings for adult male companionship. Sometimes the feelings are cerebral and other times they are physical. But I still love Sandy and want to remain faithful to him. Therein, is the conflict."

"Of course you have strong feelings for your husband. Through no fault of yours or his, he is no longer your mate and all that it entails. What is natural is your fear that if you find another man you could love, you would be unfaithful to your husband. But, since he is no longer with you, infidelity is not a real issue. Is there any particular man that interests you?"

"No. I miss a man's loving and supportive nature. I enjoyed that with Sandy and I want it from another man."

"What about sex?"

"I have been taking care of that by myself, but it's not enough. I miss interacting with a man…the intimacy."

"I suggest, in the parlance of today, that you put yourself out there. Let it be felt by those around you that you're looking for a special someone. I am not suggesting that you wear a badge with that announcement or that you flirt with every man you meet. What I'm suggesting, again in the parlance of today, is for you to send out good vibes. Think about another man and what you want from him often enough in public and someone may sense your desires."

"No. I'm afraid that I might wind up with a series of meaningless affairs: nothing enduring, just one-night stands. Plus, what do I tell my children?"

"Well – first, you're smart enough to be aware of the potential pitfalls of indiscriminate dating and sex. So I trust you won't cruise the hotel bars at night or frequent noisy saloons at happy hour. But if you do what I suggest, and use good common sense, you will find the right man. Maybe at the grocery store. Maybe at a school function. Maybe on the job. Who knows? But if you don't try, you'll never know. Where any relationship goes after a few dates is up to the couple. I'm confident you could successfully deal with a pleasant dinner or a movie with a man and anything after that. Second, you might be underestimating your children. Do you honestly think that they think their mother will never have feelings for a man other than their deceased father? They will, no doubt, understand your desire to move on as long as you don't forget their father."

"Maybe you're right."

"It is safe for me to assume that you have not discussed your thoughts about dating with them."

"Yes, never."

"That's the first step. But, and here is the big but, you must not seek their approval, just their acceptance of your actions. Remember you are the parent. Write in your journal and hold the information to your heart. Is that it?"

"Other than thank you, that is it."

"You are welcome. If at any time you feel overwhelmed, call and set an appointment. The nest is always here."

They shake hands and Liz leaves feeling lighter.

Finding Marshall Ross's will was as difficult as Liz had thought. About a dozen phone calls to various City Government offices and Clerk of the Courts, as well as several high-powered attorneys, lead her to the offices of Dwayne Ragsdale, Esq.

The visual experience upon entering Suite 300 of 25 Water Street is designed to do more than impress. Liz's reaction is the proper one – awe. The oak desks and paneling, original oil paintings, the royal blue carpet, dimmed lights, and the prim, middle-aged receptionist create the image of success, power, and wealth.

"Good afternoon, how may I help you?"

"I am Detective Elizabeth Kimble. I called about a brief meeting with Mr. Ragsdale. He said he would make time in his schedule. Please let him know I'm here."

"Mr. Ragsdale, Detective Kimble is here to see you. Yes, sir. Detective, Belinda Harter will be out shortly. She will take you to see Mr. Ragsdale."

"Thank you."

Three minutes pass and a young woman enters the reception area through one of the wall panels.

"Detective Kimble, I'm Belinda Harter, Mr. Ragsdale's senior executive assistant. Please follow me."

Two women walk a long hall to its end. The large office space is eerily quiet. Liz hears an occasional muffled voice. She sees well-dressed, very serious men and women working diligently in their cubicles. There are four offices to the left of the hall and an open door revealing a conference room at the end of the hall to the left. To the right at the end of the hall, there is another large oak door. Closed. Ms. Harter knocks.

"Come."

The invitation is more like a command. The office beyond the door is richly simple: a small oak table that functions as a desk, a large round oak table and five chairs function as a meeting space. Two wall-to-wall and floor-to-ceiling windows provide light and offer two expansive views of the harbor. On the other two walls hang oil paintings; one is of the men of the first Continental Congress and one is of the U.S. Supreme Court Building. Belinda, after opening the door and ushering Liz in, departs.

"Welcome, Detective. How may we help you?"

"We are investigating the suspicious death of Marshall Ross. I say suspicious, because there are factors surrounding Mr. Ross's death that have raised questions and thus need clarification. Because we must account for all details, regardless of how minute, we need information about Mr. Ross's will."

"Well, as I am sure you are aware, the details of the will fall under attorney-client privilege. So I am duty-bound not to reveal them."

"We are not looking for specifics. We need your guidance. For instance, in general terms, how large was Mr. Ross's estate? I don't need the composition of the estate, just its general value."

"As of last year, Mr. Ross's estate was valued in excess of ten million dollars."

"Thank you. And who are the beneficiaries of the estate?"

"His sons from his first wife will receive the majority of the value, while his present wife will receive a yearly stipend from a trust."

"Will his children receive their share of the estate immediately upon his demise?"

"No, the boys' shares will come to them upon their respective twenty-fifth birthdays."

"Until then?"

"Mrs. Ross is the unpaid trustee of the entire estate with discretionary powers until the boys reach their twenty-fifth birthdays."

"What is meant by discretionary powers?"

"It means that Mrs. Ross has a hand in managing the estate. She can divest the estate of Mr. Ross's business and any investments. She can alter the investments in the estate's portfolio. She can do almost anything that she deems appropriate with the money within the due diligence strictures of her trusteeship. I can't stress the due diligence aspect too strongly. The bank holds the money and it audits the estate as a way of monitoring her discretionary activities. A very solid check and balance system."

"And the boys have no say in these matters until each reaches the age of twenty-five."

"That is correct. But, if the bank spots activities of Mrs. Ross that are not in the best interest of the estate, they would notify the boys and me."

"What would fit the definition of 'not in the best interest of the estate'?"

"If Mrs. Ross were to transfer amounts of money in excess of her stipend to her personal accounts, she would be in violation of the trustee agreement."

"Then what?"

"We determine the proper course of action to stop or remedy any such activities."

"I guess that's it. Thank you for your time. You have been most helpful."

"I am happy to have helped. I'll have Miss Harter walk you to the receptionist."

Liz has uncovered a tenuous link to Allison Ross's killing of her husband. Money is the motive. How does she get her hands on more money than she is due? How is boy toy involved? If Allison gave Lance the details of Marshall's whereabouts that fateful Sunday, he had the opportunity. But does he have the auto mechanic skills to sabotage the car? Liz must have a sit-down with Lance.

The first blow from a baseball bat to the back of his head stunned the brown-skinned man. He yelped like a dog. As he turned to find the source of the blow, he felt a second strike to the side of his face. He screamed. A third hit, again to the back of his head, crumpled the man to the ground like wet paper. He twitched and moaned as strikes from two baseball bats and a pry bar rained down on his body. His feeble attempt to protect himself with upraised and crossed arms was futile. The pry bar crushed the humerus, ulna, and radius in both arms. His moans became whimpers. Whimpers went silent. With no energy to escape, he lay on the grease-stained concrete floor, filthy with age. The blows went from the man's head down to his rib cage. From there, the hips and legs were savagely struck. Many bones were broken. Then the blows stopped. The breathing of the brown-skinned man was so shallow as to be inaudible. But he was not yet dead.

Six hands grabbed the limp body and dropped it onto a tarp. The tarp was rolled, carried outside the building, through a fence, and thrown into the bed of a pick-up truck. The three men didn't bother to wash away the blood on the floor. It seemed to blend in with the years of grease and dirt of the unused building. The man's jaws and teeth had been broken, and his finger-tips cut off using a tree trimmer. Police identification would be difficult, if not impossible. The men covered the tarp with broken cinder blocks and concrete-covered bricks. These were thrown viciously onto the rolled tarp as final humiliation. The forty-five minute ride from the beating site to the dump site caused the tarp and its contents to bounce. The brown-skinned man did not notice the uneven ride. Finally, the destination – the city and county garbage disposal site. Upon a cursory peek at the pick-up's bed, the truck is waved through by the security guard at the gate. The pick-up truck drives to the rear of the public dump. Three men unload their cargo, making sure to cover the tarp with the construction materials. Done, they leave and head to a drive-thru car wash. Mission complete.

Today, Liz will attempt a meet and greet with boy toy, Lance. She employs a pop-a-squat maneuver. Parking her unmarked car near the entrance to 21212 Gulf Boulevard, she waits for the manservant to leave the castle. She doesn't have to wait too long. The gate opens and out drives Lance in a new Mercedes convertible…top down. He heads to the bridge and the mainland. Shopping is a duty far beneath his benefactor. He pulls into the Gulf Side Plaza. Liz is two cars behind him. As he exits his convertible, she approaches him.

"Lance, may I have a little of your time?"

"You're that cop that came to the house yesterday. Your questions upset Allison, I mean, Mrs. Ross. What the hell do you want now?"

"I want to see your driver's license. You made an illegal lane change a few blocks back. I will also need to see your registration and proof of insurance."

"Here's my license. The insurance card and registration are in the car. I'll get them."

Liz sees that Lance R. McMullin is twenty-three years old. His residence is listed as 629 Sandy Beach Path in St. Petersburg. She notes these in her book. Lance returns with the insurance card and registration.

"Here."

The car is registered to Allison Ross, as Liz expected.

"All this seems to be in order. Next time, be careful changing lanes. Cars behind you and beside you can't read your mind. Let them know when you want to change lanes. Thank you for your cooperation. Have a great day."

They part ways. Liz has some digging to do when she gets back to Headquarters.

"The crows and buzzards were swarming way more than normal. They were real close to the landfill and many of them landed. There must have been thirty or forty of the birds…all in one place. They normally soar a couple of hundred yards above the heaps of garbage. But these birds were swarming about twenty feet above the area where construction materials are dumped. So I went to look and this is what I found."

The tarp was bloody and ripped where the birds had pecked and clawed their way to their meal…a battered corpse. Police had responded to a call from Conrad Winds, the Superintendent of the City and County Refuse Disposal Site. Detective Archie Leach caught the case.

Liz discovered that Lance McMullin had no criminal record whatsoever. He was a graduate of a community college outside of Atlanta. There is nothing in the public records to indicate what he has been doing since graduating three years ago. Most likely, he took his good looks and charm to the beaches of Florida where he could bartend a little and hustle a lot. He appears to have found his big score in Allison Ross. Liz wonders how long the relationship has been going on. Obviously, it didn't start two weeks ago. He is, no doubt, good with his hands, but does Lance have the skills of a mechanic?

Liz also did some digging into the pedigree of Allison Ross and unearthed a past checkered with legal issues. Born Allison Rabonitch. Since becoming an adult, she's been arrested for solicitation, forgery, and petty theft. Her pimp, when she was arrested for solicitation in her twenties, was Robert G. McMullin. Liz checks out this new player. Deceased while a guest of the state four years ago. Survived by a son, Lance R. McMullin. This trio adds new meaning to the phrase, keeping it in the family. Allison has also been a party in three landlord/tenant lawsuits. It seems she doesn't like to pay rent. She has been a guest of the county twice for a total of eight months. Her aliases have been Sally James, Amanda Prince, and Billie Jean Winters. All contact with law enforcement ended ten years ago…right before she married Marshall Ross. While this is not enough to make her a suspect in her husband's murder, it paints a picture of the non-grieving widow sufficient to pique Liz's interest.

VI

Bay Times Police Blotter

The body of a man was discovered at the City and County Refuse Disposal Site on Tuesday evening by employees of the sanitation department. Police report that the man's head and body suffered such severe trauma as to render identification impossible. Police are asking anyone with knowledge of the crime to call 813-500-5555.

"Leach. Kimble. In my office. Now."

Lieutenant Gracia had assumed his mantle of aggressive leadership.

"In the past weeks, we've caught three major cases, three murders. Yes, I'm designating the Marshall Ross suspicious death a murder. You two are responsible for solving all three. The most recent city dump murder will be handled by Detective Tony Dannello. So before the city fathers start raising a stink and department brass are all over me like flies on road kill, I want you two to open your case files and share all information about the three cases regardless of how trivial it may appear on the surface. A fresh set of eyes on each case may help both of you. When you're done with this step, I want you two to sit with Dannello and review his files and he yours. With the work of you three, we will get to the bottom of this mess. This many homicides within such a short period of time is, I'll bet, not serendipity. It's hinky. A little voice in the back of my brain keeps whispering that the murders are connected. If that's true, we need to get in front of this mess before the newspaper and TV do. I want a status report of your efforts by the end of your tour tomorrow. Most important, I want to be able to report up the line that these damned cases will be solved very soon. Take Interview Room 4 and play nice. Am I clear?"

Liz and Detective Archie Leach take their laptops into a windowless, dusty, twelve-foot by twelve-foot bare room. The process of exchanging case files begins. After the downloading, they discuss each fact in each file. They note comments and questions and put them in a separate general file for review later with Gracia. This process will take all day because it requires attention to detail and dialog.

Detective Leach has just three more years until retirement. He has held on to his job in the face of budget cuts because of seniority. The fact that he is the brother-in-law to the Watch Commander may have had some influence on the decision to keep Leach. Archie is five-ten and weighs about 240 pounds. His attire is like that of a tourist: light ill-fitting khakis, floral shirts that are never tucked into his waist band and white sneakers or "tennies" as he calls them. Overall, he would blend in with the attendees of any early bird special or mall walk. He sweats a lot and shaves on alternate days. Unfortunately, to cover the odor associated with sweat, his body reeks of too much cheap cologne. Sandy never wore cologne. That could be a problem for Liz in this closed room. Archie is cordial and soft-spoken. Plus, his work is thorough but most times slow.

"How was school today?"

The opening question at the dinnertime roundtable. Like a volley across a ship's bow, the question commands attention.

"Great. The baseball sign-up sheet was posted today. I'm psyched. Practice for pitchers and catchers starts next week. The rest of us start before Christmas break. We'll have practice over the break."

"Varsity or JV?"

"JV. There are a lot of really good upperclassmen ahead of me. Guys who will play in college. So, I'll use this year to hone my skills for three years of greatness."

"Anything else."

"Yes. On the sports bulletin board there were pictures of our win over the Tommies. They even had one of me scoring a touchdown. I got alotta attaboys for that."

"What about real schoolwork?"

Another shot, but closer to the target.

"I am keeping my academic prowess under wraps until it's shown to the world in all its glory with the second trimester report cards."

"Young man, your modesty is overwhelming."

Smiles all around.

"Cary?"

"Nothing worth reporting."

"Don't consider this reporting. Consider this time to share with your family."

"I have a history paper due before Christmas break; compare and contrast the root causes of World War I and the present crisis in the Middle East. I don't know where to start."

"What do you know about World War I?"

"Very little."

"Start there. What about the winter musical?"

"Practice. Practice. Practice. And then more practice. We're talkin' practice. My life is getting squeezed."

"No doubt, your plate is full."

"I just don't know if I can handle it all."

"Sure you can. You're Cary Kimble."

"That's easy for you to say."

Cary's harsh response is accompanied by her eyes tearing up. This triggers an instinctive and protective, yet inquisitive response in Liz's brain. Something other than the pressure of academia and the theater is bothering her daughter. But Liz knows better than to dig deeper at the dinner table. An hour after kitchen clean-up, Liz heads upstairs. She pauses and listens at Cary's door. Silence. She knocks softly.

"Yes."

"It's Mom, honey. Do you have a minute?"

"Sure, come on in."

Cary's on her bed staring at the ceiling. Her eyes are red and swollen.

"Sweetheart, something is bothering you. What's wrong?"

The silent pause lasts for nearly two minutes...an eternity.

"You can tell me. Whatever's wrong, we can work through it together. Tell me."

More silence.

"Is it something at home? School? Whatever it is we can talk it through."

More silence. Tears run down Cary's cheeks. Sobbing starts. Then blubbering as Cary looks into her mother's eyes.

"It's the girls at school. Missy, Belinda, and Jenny are teasing me real hard."

"Why would they do that? They're your crew."

The next silent pause felt like it lasted for an hour.

"Because I told them I'm a virgin. They started to call me Mary."

Liz was stunned...seventh graders discussing virginity and all the emotional entanglement that goes with losing it. She wants to know more, but must tread lightly.

"How did this start?"

"We were discussing boys and I said I thought Jimmy O'Brien was cute. Missy said that if I felt that way, I should let him know by doing something about it. She asked if I would like Jimmy to be my boyfriend. I said sure. She said I would have to do more than pass him a note. I would have to let him kiss me. And maybe more, because Jimmy is one of the Big Dogs. Big Dogs are guys in a secret club who think they are big deals at school. They dress really neat. They're all athletes. They're all good looking and they know it. The Big Dogs are cool and the cool girls hang with them. The Big Dogs call these girls, Big Bitches. If I wanted to be a Big

Bitch and hang with Jimmy, I would have to do something special for him.

"I kinda knew what she meant, but asked her to tell me more. Then she went into detail about a special way to use my mouth. It was disgusting. I told her I would never do that. Then she asked if I was still a virgin. I told her yes. Then she said that I should give it up to Jimmy. I should… you know, Mom. That would make me a Big Bitch. I would be Jimmy's Bitch.

"I told her definitely no. I would not do that just to be part of some stupid secret club. That's when the three of them started to laugh at me and call me…Virgin Mary. It was devastating. I thought they were my friends."

"I think I understand your reaction. I don't quite understand theirs. First and foremost, you are too young for sex or sex games. Second, it is your body and you're free to do with it as you deem appropriate. This fact should be guided by your good sense. Your good sense is the basis of healthy self-respect. You're smart enough and you have a good soul to know what is right and what is not right. Having sex to be accepted into a phantom organization is not right at any age…whether you're twelve or my age. Told to have sex to be accepted is peer pressure. Peer pressure normally comes from people who are weaker than the one being pressured… you. They want to bring you down to their level, so in their eyes you won't be superior to them. I mean by that, they have low self-respect and want everyone to feel like they do. Does this make sense to you?"

"Yes. But I'm afraid if I don't do it, I'll lose Missy, Belinda, and Jenny as friends."

"If they don't want to be your friends because you won't have sex with Jimmy O'Brien, it seems to me that their friendship is based on them controlling your life. It is your life to control as you see fit. If you lose them as friends, the loss will be temporary. You will always find friends. Some you will keep for a long time and some will be friends for only a short time as distance separates you. If you lose your self-respect because of something they want you to do, the loss will be permanent. My advice is that you don't do what they want you to do, but do what your good sense tells you is right. And you know what is right."

The room is silent. The tears have stopped. A glimmer of relief has returned to Cary's face.

"Thanks, Mom. You're the best."

"Honey, you're the best."

Liz heads back downstairs to finish the newspaper. Her heart is racing, but she must maintain the aura of calm. She is angry that someone is badgering her baby. She is happy that her baby shared her pain with her mother. She tries to recall the circumstances surrounding her one- night event with Jerry Jackson. Twenty minutes of fumbling with clothes and to find a comfortable position in the back seat of his father's car. Then twenty seconds of awkward intimacy. He was finished before she started. That night, she felt anxious and bewildered. The next day she felt sore, embarrassed, and betrayed. Her self-recrimination finally gave way to acceptance. She has always believed that Jerry was embarrassed that his part in the event was over so quickly and clearly demonstrated how little experience he had. Fortunately, he never mentioned the evening.

Hell, as high school sophomores, what experience with sex did anyone have? Today, seventh graders are pushed into having sex. What about Alex? Should she buy condoms for both of them, or just for Alex? Would that signal to him that she approved of him having sex? Or, would it signal to him that if he were going to have sex, it must be safe sex? She is uncomfortable with either option. Often being a parent of two young teens demands choosing the lesser bad option. That scares the crap out of Liz.

"Well, what have you two learned? Archie?"

"We have a sketch of the poor bastard who got his head kicked in. It's rough, but I think the unies might be able to get an ID if they distribute the flyer with the sketch and usual reward wording. That's my case. We can't go too far until we know the name of the vic. We have a lot more to chase in Liz's cases. First, Hector Lopez was right-handed. The ME confirmed it. The needle entry is on the left side of his neck. It would be awkward for a righty to inject something on the left side of the neck. Plus, talking to Hector's homies, Liz learned that he never did drugs. Highly unlikely that a first-timer would inject himself in the neck. Therefore, we conclude that the dope was used to make Hector docile so his captors would have no problems with him. Liz?"

"Umberto Rosario, one of Hector's homies, remarked that Hector would periodically flash large wads of cash. We are confident that Rosario either knows more than he is saying or he knows more than he realizes. Plus, Hector bought a new car with a substantial cash down payment. The cash is a big unknown. Who? Why? When? These are the questions that must be answered as we proceed. I think this will lead to the reason he was killed.

"As to the murder of Marshall Ross, the wife has a motive…a ton of money…and possible means…her boy toy, Lance McMullin, who just happens to be the son of Allison Ross's former pimp. Hell, Lance may even be her son who is now sharing her bed. How bizarre would that be? We have to pursue Lance and any associates who have the skills of a mechanic."

"LT, Liz and I would like to flip-flop our duties on these cases. I'll pursue Lance. A new cop just may shake the boy toy's confidence. I will also re-interview Allison Ross. That ought to shake her, too. But, given her privileged ego, this tactic may lead to her calling someone at the top of our department and screaming harassment. So, I will have to be my usual demur self. I'm giving you a heads-up in case the brass comes down on you. Liz will continue to talk to Umberto as part of the Hector Lopez investigation and take over securing an ID of the mutilated body. We can get all this done quickly and report back to you tomorrow."

"Sounds good. Archie, be very careful when dealing with Mrs. Ross. Because of her husband, she has many friends in high places."

Leach views Liz's role in this new team as subordinate. Distributing the flyer to precincts. Big damned deal. It's a job for a uni, but she is a team player. She's amazed at the sketch developed by the police technicians. The ME stitched up the man's face and covered the cuts and abrasions with makeup. Then the Photoshop crew went to work to make the guy look alive. The printer produced one hundred copies of the mystery face: a black man between the ages of twenty-five and forty. He has a small, well-tended moustache and goatee, and angular features. According to the ME, the man was six-feet tall and weighed approximately 190 pounds. No tats. She grabs the copies and heads to the Fourth Precinct Station. She explains the picture and what help she needs from the lieutenant in charge. Liz leaves fifty copies. Then she drives to the Sixth Precinct Station and repeats the process. Archie calls.

"Hey, Liz, I think we are on to something with this Lance character and his sugar momma. She claims to have met him while they were both shopping for a Mercedes. They struck up a conversation…blah, blah, blah. I'm headed over to the Lockney dealership now. How you doing on the wallpaper?"

"Just dropped off bundles at the Fourth and Sixth. If we don't get a nibble there by end of tour tomorrow, I'll repeat the process the day after at surrounding precincts. But, I am confident that someone in one or both of those neighborhoods will recognize our man. I hope to hear something soon. I'm headed to Umberto's neighborhood. Let's touch base before the end of this tour."

"You got it."

As she turns the corner on to the street toward the Lopez house, she spots Umberto and his crew. He smiles.

"Umberto, mi amigo, I need a few minutes of your time."

"This time, my time will cost you."

"This time, like all times, your time is my time. Or, you'll do three-day jail time for hindering an official investigation."

His smile dissipates.

"What do you want?"

"I want to solve the murder of Hector Lopez and I need your help. For this help, I will give you a special 'get out of jail free' card. You can use it if you ever run afoul of the law. This is a magic card. It will vouch for your valuable service to the Tampa Police Department, so if you get picked up, you'll be free to go home. Is that clear?"

"Si."

"Now, what more can you tell me about Hector's wads of cash?"

"Not much more than I already told you." "Did you ever see Hector talking to people who don't live in this neighborhood?"

"Twice I saw two big white guys drive up to Hector's house, get out and talk to Hector on his porch. One of them handed Hector a small envelope that looked full."

"Do you remember when you saw these events?"

"The first time was about two years ago. The second time was last August. I think those were the times. I am not sure of the dates."

"Do you remember what these men looked like?"

"Big guys. Big bellies. Short-sleeve shirts and baggy pants."

"What about their faces?"

"Nothing special…just white guy faces. They all look alike to me. Wait. One guy had a handlebar moustache and a mullet haircut. You know short in the front and long in the back. The other guy had no face hair and was bald."

"That's great. If you looked at some photos, would you be able to identify the two guys?"

"If they're there, si."

"I'll need you to come down to police headquarters and look at mug shots."

"Police headquarters? I don't know, chika. That will look like I am being arrested or ratting out someone. Both of those would not be good for my rep here in my hood."

"I'll pick you up in an unmarked car tomorrow morning at eight. You will be safe and secure. I'll bring you home before noon."

"Better. I'll meet you outside Café de Cuba. You know where that is? After we are done at the police department, you can take me back there. That way no one has to know what I am doing. OK?"

"OK. See you tomorrow at eight."

Liz heads for headquarters. Her spirit buoyed.

Her desk phone rings.

"Liz, we are getting somewhere. It turns out that Lance was not looking to buy a car. He was a sales booster. Lockney Motors hired him to walk the lot and look for women who were shopping. He would tell them he was also shopping, but couldn't make up his mind which car he liked best. The general manager told me this is a common problem with women shoppers; they want to buy, but don't know which car they like the most. So any female he met on the lot would understand his dilemma. From this, empathy and trust would develop, and he would guide the shopper to the most expensive of her alternatives. Then a salesman would arrive and help her with the purchase. Neat, eh?

"The GM told me Lance was paid a commission on every sale he worked. Further, the GM was introduced to Lance by one of the mechanics at the shop…a Wilton Burbiski. So, we now have motive, means in Burbiski, and with the wife's knowledge of Ross's whereabouts that Sunday, comes opportunity. Can you look up any files on Mr. Burbiski? According to the GM, his home address is 629 Sandy Beach Path in St. Petersburg. I won't be able to make it back to the station before the end of my tour, so I'm going home. We can review whatever you find in the morning. Thanks."

Archie hung up before Liz could answer. Yes, she would be able to access any files. No, she doesn't work for Archie Leach. She checks her notes. The address Archie just gave her triggers a gut reaction. She digs. Wilton and Lance shared an address. What else did they share? She inputs the data and an arrest record pops up. Wilton Burbiski has been arrested twice for check forgery and once for the sale of stolen merchandise – a BMW. All three cases were dismissed after he made restitution. There were no others arrested with him. Where did a lowlife like him get the money to make restitution? Does he have a sugar daddy or sugar momma too? Is his sugar momma the same as Lance's? Is Liz getting closer to some real answers to big questions? A visit to Mr. Burbiski is called for tomorrow. Tonight, Liz wants to be with her babies.

VII

Seven fifty-five. Liz pulls into the parking lot of Café de Cuba. She settles in to wait. Confidential informants and snitches are notoriously late. They fear showing themselves without determining the meet will be unencumbered by intruders. She waits. At eight-fifteen…no Umberto. At eight-thirty…no Umberto. Liz leaves. Disappointed that she has been stood up, she will go to his neighborhood after meeting with Archie. For now, it's back to headquarters.

"Kimble, nice of you to make it in today."

"Sorry, LT, I was attempting to meet with a person of interest who could provide valuable information. He never showed."

"Would Umberto Rosario be the person of interest?"

"Yes. Do you know where he is?"

"On his way to the morgue. His body was discovered around six this morning. He had been shot and dumped in the parking lot of the art museum. Interesting thing about Umberto…he lost his tongue. Just like Hector Lopez. So we may have a killer who enjoys mutilation."

"Is there an indication of the size of the gun that killed him?"

"Initial reports indicate a big gun…a nine millimeter or 45 caliber. You need to get in front of this before it hits the media. That will happen by noon."

"Excuse me, LT, but the murders were committed with two different gun sizes. So I think this may not be the work of the same killer. Umberto may have been killed by a copycat."

"Maybe. Or the same killer with two different weapons. Why were you going to meet with Umberto?"

"When I spoke to him yesterday, he remembered some details about the wads of cash Hector received. He remembered seeing two guys meet with Hector on his porch. One of these guys twice gave Hector a filled envelope. A day after each time Hector received the package he would flash a wad of cash in front of his homeboys. I convinced Umberto to come to the station and look at mug shots today. My gut tells me one or both of the two guys he saw with Hector became aware of Umberto's friendly relationship with me and my plans, and short-circuited them. Plus, the tongue removal left a message for others not to cooperate with the police. We have to go back and find someone else in the neighborhood that saw the two men and the envelope exchanges. Crap!"

"Yesterday, did Umberto give you a description of the two guys?"

"No. He said thought he could identify them. He was going to tell me when we looked at the mug books."

Liz's conscious decision to lie was based on her desire to keep some information in her pocket, for now. If the information proves to be true, it could always be introduced later. Maybe her deception was based on her lack of total trust in Gracia. She is beginning to get spooked by her boss, a man she doesn't like.

"His murder appears to be somehow related to the Hector Lopez murder, so this one is yours, too."

Detective Leach is sitting at his desk.

"Liz, what did we learn about Burbiski?"

"It's in the file. Nothing spectacular, except that he was able to make restitution for his crimes to avoid prosecution. My question is: how was a lowlife drifter able to make restitution for five thousand dollars in bad checks and eighty-three hundred dollars for a stolen BMW? Bottom feeders don't normally have access to that kind of money. Someone was bankrolling him and did not want him left out there to snitch on them. A silent partner?"

In this instance, her speculation that the silent partner could be Lance is best kept in her pocket. Something else for later.

"Good work partner. You can check into it while you're confirming Wilton's whereabouts on the night of the murder. Perhaps a nefarious partnership has existed for some time. I want to chase down that lead. Let's meet here at the end of our tour and bring LT up to speed. See you around three."

Liz is slightly annoyed by Leach's condescension. She does not work for him. She works for the citizens of Tampa. Archie runs away to the other side of the bay, while Liz returns to the neighborhood of Hector and Umberto.

As she turns down Estrella Avenue, she senses something is amiss. There are no children playing in or near the street. The neighborhood sentries are nowhere to be seen. Then she spies a curtain moving and the vague image of a face peering out at her. Something or someone has spooked the good people of the hood. She stops in front of number 380, exits the car, and approaches the house. As she is climbing the steps to the porch, a teenage girl comes out of the front door and stands at the last step with her arms akimbo.

"Whatchu wan?"

"I want to talk to your mother."

"Waddabout?"

"I will discuss that with your mother."

"Me first."

"It's about Umberto."

"Whaddabout Umberto?"

"I need to talk with your mother."

"Umberto was my husband. Talk to me."

Liz is stunned. The woman has the appearance of a young teen…maybe Alex's age.

"Can we sit on the porch?"

"Come inside. It's safer."

Safer? Whoever is looking already saw Liz. The young woman leads the way inside.

"Now tell me."

"I am saddened to tell you that your husband was murdered."

No response. No tears.

"Who did it?"

"That's what we are trying to find out. Do you know if anybody was angry at Umberto? Did he owe anybody money?"

"Money? That's a joke. Umberto never had any money. That's why I work. There were people who were angry at Umberto. He was always putting his nose where it didn't belong. He thought he was a big shot in the neighborhood. But he was nobody, especially since he left his friends."

"What do you mean since he left his friends?"

"He used to be part of Los Hermanos. They did stuff together. And, they provided for their wives and children. When he left Los Hermanos, we moved out of the old neighborhood to this place. He said it was for a fresh start. I think he was running away like a puta."

"Do you know if Hector Lopez was a part of Los Hermanos?"

"Si, but he left them before Umberto."

"Thank you for your time. We need you to identify the body. When would you like to come to the morgue?"

"Never. But, I guess I have to. Give me the weekend to make arrangements for the funeral. I'll come on Monday. How soon after I identify him will you release the body?"

"Within one hour of completing the appropriate forms."

"Fine."

"Here's my card. Call me before you come down to police headquarters. I need to prepare the forms for you to sign. Again, we are sorry for your loss."

"Sure."

The file on Los Hermanos is rich with history and incidents. As Liz digs into particulars, she is troubled by the memory of Sandy. The dilapidated warehouse where

Sandy was murdered was the hangout for Los Hermanos. The gang's main source of income came from drug dealing, but they also dabbled in extortion and car theft for resale out of state. In this situation, they were just one part of a large ring. She must be careful to keep her personal feelings in check and be guided by facts to solve the Lopez and Rosario killings. There is a substantial part of her that's not sorry these two reformed thugs are dead. Karma has a way of catching up to bad people when they least expect it and biting them in the ass.

Los Hermanos, once the biggest and baddest bunch in town, has been reduced to a few young punks whose incomes come from small-time protection and burglary. The halcyon days of fear-based power are over. So, what is the connection between the two deaths and the new gang? She calls Detective Bob Dover to get the current gang intel.

"Hi, Bob, this is Liz Kimble. I've been looking through the Los Hermanos file and I see that the last entry was six months ago. I'm calling to see if there is anything new you might know or something that has yet to make the official file."

"What's this about?"

"As you may know, Hector Lopez was recently murdered. And Umberto Rosario turned up dead this morning. Since they both had been part of Los Hermanos until a few years ago, I am looking for a deeper connection."

"This ancient history may be what you're looking for. Before the shootout two years ago, Hector left the gang. There was a widely held suspicion that he had been looking to go straight well before then. There were also rumors that he had turned and was a CI. So, his departure was no big loss or surprise. He moved his wife and kids to Estrella and a safer neighborhood. Umberto Rosario is another story. After Hector left the gang, Umberto was pushed out of the gang by the young up-and-comers in a power struggle. There's a group of about a half-dozen or so that tried to fill the vacuum of leadership when all the former leaders were either killed or sent to the State Prison at Starke a few years ago. Today, the two major players are Roberto Ricardo and Jose Hernandez. The gang has kept a low profile for about a year. But I think they're working to return to their glory days. I've heard from my CI that the young bucks have a goal to run the drug business in the city within two years."

"Can you think of a reason they would want to kill Hector or Umberto?"

"Out with the old and in with the new. Maybe they're cleaning the streets of old garbage. Recent rumblings indicate that the new Los Hermanos is ruthless and quite vicious. The initiating beat-in takes ninety seconds, not the usual thirty of other gangs. And there is no getting out of the gang except through death."

"According to the file, the gang hangs out above a bodega at the corner of Platt Boulevard and Plant Street. Is this still the case?"

"Yes. But if you are going to pay them a visit, do it during the day. At night, that corner is not safe unless you have an entire squad and an armored personnel carrier. Those sonsabitches have no fear of TPD. They may be and act like teens, but they are stone-cold thugs."

"Thanks for the intel and heads-up. I'll keep you in the loop."

The post-tour update with Gracia reveals that although Archie is not ready to stop looking at the Allison/Lance/Wilton triumvirate for the murder of Marshall Ross, each new lead stops at a large wall. Nonetheless, Archie likes working on the beach. Liz will work downtown and pay a visit to the Los Hermanos hangout on Monday.

On the drive home, Liz can't get Los Hermanos out of her mind. The removal of the tongues of both victims is a clear sign of hatred for a snitch. Did her conversations with Umberto get him killed? She must not let any feelings of responsibility muddy her police thinking.

"What would anyone like to do tonight after dinner?"

"I'm going to the movies with my crew."

"Who is driving?"

"Laura's older brother Jacob. He's a senior."

"Is he cute?"

"Mom!"

"Sorry I touched a nerve. How about you, Alex?"

"Nothing. Stay home and watch TV."

"Then you can be my date."

"Date?"

"Date…not in the social convention of today. Just two people hanging out doing nothing together."

"Well, I'll be your date if you order pizza."

"Bribery of a law enforcement officer is a crime and punishable by many noogies."

"Yeah, if you could catch me, the star running back, you might be able to give me noogies."

"On my slowest day, I can outrun you."

"A race. You're on. Cary, you be the starter. We'll run in the backyard. The neighbors can't see over the stockade fence and see you making a fool out of yourself, old lady."

"I will ignore that feeble attempt at smack talk. Since you got the racetrack, I get the distance. Fence to fence to fence three times. Each runner must touch each fence or he will be disqualified. Like a relay handoff."

"Or she will be disqualified. Let's do this."

"One more thing, any interference with a runner is cause for immediate disqualification. And the disqualified runner or loser, that's you, will have to do the household laundry and cleaning chores for a week."

"I look forward to no cleaning and no laundry. Are you ready for double duty?"

"I want to change into running gear. Give me ten minutes."

Absent the herald of coronets, the three of them walk through the porch onto the field of testosterone. The backyard is bordered on three sides by a ten-foot stockade fence. Max is at Liz's heels. He thinks he is going outside to run or relieve himself. He likes the outside. Cary stands at one fence, the contestants stand at the other. The distance between the fences is approximately seventy-five feet. The race will total one hundred and fifty yards with multiple turns. Alex and Liz go through their stretching routines. They are ready.

"Runners take your marks. Set. Go!"

Alex breaks with the command and is two steps ahead of Liz before she starts. A short-lived lead. Her distance running through high school and college produced in her a long graceful stride. This may not be a big advantage in a sprint, but every little bit helps. Alex runs like his football training has taught him...short powerful piston strokes; this could be an advantage in the backyard dash. But does he have the necessary stamina? His normal football runs are five to ten yards. At the first fence touch, they are neck and neck.

Max has joined the fun and runs with the two humans. He barks and jumps for joy occasionally near the humans. He never jumps onto either runner. This is a game he has never seen, but he likes it. He will not win the race because he does not know it *is* a race. All three make the turn. Max's turn is wide and behind the contestants. He is not sure of the rules of this new game. So sometimes he runs ahead, sometimes he runs with, and sometimes he runs behind the human runners. Halfway back, Alex's youth and power begin to show as he pulls ahead by a full step. They turn again. He barrels ahead while Liz lopes about two feet behind him. They turn for the third time. Alex is beginning to lengthen his lead. At the fourth turn, he slips. Liz does not. Neither does Max. Now all three are even. At the final turn, Liz begins to feel her lungs burn and her legs weaken. She must not falter, and with one last burst, she finishes...a very close second. Max is third. He continues to leap and run in esses and circles with an occasional jump, not realizing the new backyard game is over.

"Not bad for an older person. Mom, you did real well."

Even gasping for breath, Alex's competitive spirit drives him to squash the loser.

"Mom, that was amazing. You almost beat him."

"Thanks, Cary. Guys, I need to shower after I order the pizza. You too, champ."

She hugs her son with all the love within her.

"Mom, you're slow but strong."

Alex finally gives up a compliment.

"Mom, Laura just called. They're on their way."

"Gimme a kiss. What time will you be home?"

"Eleven."

"If something happens and Jacob does not want to be a chauffeur, call me."

"We'll be fine. Love ya."

"Backatchya."

Pizza ordered, Liz stands directly beneath the shower head. Her pulse rate has finally slowed to normal…the low 60s. Hot water and shower gel will make her feel like a woman…different than a Mom who dared her son and lost. When she and Sandy would go for a Saturday run, he would let her take the lead until the last mile, and then he would roar past her to finish well ahead. After the run, they would shower together and he would seduce her amidst soapsuds and warm water. They would make long languorous love. If memory serves her, Alex was conceived on such a Saturday afternoon.

She closes her eyes and a hand massages her areolas and pinches her nipples, while a hand traces her taught stomach and touches her mons. The fleshy protuberance is caressed. She sees Sandy's face as his chimerical body presses against her. Her hands are his. She opens her mouth to kiss him and her pulse quickens, while her breathing becomes deep and slow. She feels herself melting into his embrace. The caressing of the button of joy causes her whimpers to transform into moans. The pleasure pulses and radiates throughout her body. Suddenly, her body becomes tense and she begins to tremble. Her eyelids flutter. At nirvana, her legs buckle and she nearly falls. The process of reaching a happy ending takes about three minutes. Release and relief. No guilt because she was with Sandy.

She knows that two slices and a beer will fill her up and knock her out. She will miss most of the multi-segment TV program about WWI. Big whoop! She will be with her son.

Cary's keys hitting the dish by the door awaken Liz and tell her it's time to go to bed.

VIII

Bay Times

Three Bodies in Two Weeks
by Harold Shade

Within the past two weeks, Tampa Police have discovered the bodies of three men who were brutally killed. Hector Lopez was found beneath an I-275 bridge, Umberto Rosario was found in the Tampa Museum of Art parking lot, and an unidentified male was discovered at the City and County Refuse Disposal Site on Tuesday evening by sanitation employees. Both Mr. Lopez and Mr. Rosario had been shot multiple times. The unidentified male had been beaten to death. Mr. Lopez and Mr. Rosario were once members of the Los Hermanos street gang. But their affiliation with the gang, known for drug distribution and merchant extortion, ceased within the past two years. Because of dissimilarities in the three murders, police speculate that this is not the work of a serial killer.

Mr. Lopez, an employee of the Fairman Motor Group, is survived by his wife and two children. Mr. Rosario leaves a wife. The Tampa Police are asking the public for help in identifying the third victim. Police spokesman, Robert Davies stated, "We are pursuing these currently unconnected violent murders with *our full resources. Anyone with knowledge of the crimes or identification of the unknown victim, please call 813-500-5555. A reward of $5,000 is offered for information leading to the arrest of the killers."* This is an ongoing story. As this reporter learns more, we will inform you, our readers.

The drive to work is the same as it has been since Sandy and Liz bought their home. It takes twenty-five minutes before seven in the morning and thirty-five minutes in the late afternoon. Turn left at the end of Oakmont, then four miles and eight traffic lights to Rose then turn right, then four miles and eight lights to Bridge, then left and two lights to the department parking lot. Today, Liz thinks she sees something strange; a gray sedan appears to be following her. Always two cars behind and in the lane different from her minivan in a feeble attempt to hide, it slows down when she slows down and makes the same turns that she does, except into the parking lot. By the time she turns in to the restricted lot at police headquarters, the gray sedan is no longer in her rear view mirror. Coincidence or was she being followed? Why would she be followed? Did the follower want her to see that she was being followed? Does this connect with Umberto's murder? Hector's murder? Ross's murder? If so, which one or ones? How does it connect? Is she becoming paranoid? Then she remembers, "Just because you're paranoid doesn't mean they aren't following you." She smiles.

"OK, people, we are now under the microscope of the public. The *Times'* article, which mentions a reward, will cause a flood of calls from concerned citizens who want to do their civic duty and collect the money. We've set up a phone bank with volunteers who will take the calls and distribute the information to Detectives Leach and Kimble. They have been given the green light to use the rest of you as resources. I can't stress enough the pressure the brass is feeling from the Mayor and City Council. The pressure to quickly solve these murders has been intensified and placed onto my shoulders. So, because I'm a great leader and your best friend, I will share that pressure with you. I want everyone to pitch in on this. I know this is above and beyond, but that's why they pay us the big bucks."

The squad braces for a few hectic days of calls with tips based on psychic readings, dreams, and grudges. Some of the callers will be known to the department as busybodies looking for a payday. Everybody wants the fame of solving crime. Most of all they want the money. Some want the reward before the arrest. If history is any indication, the callers crawl out of the woodwork to get the cash.

"Liz, I'm going back to see Mr. Burbiski. What about you?"

"Pay a visit to a bodega at the corner of Platt and Plant, the clubhouse of Los Hermanos, to learn more about Umberto, Hector, and the gang's new regime."

"Should we reconvene at two?"

"See you then."

It's a nice day with temperatures expected to reach the low seventies. Liz decides to walk the twelve blocks to the bodega. She also needs to walk out the stiffness in her legs caused by the backyard race. She passes small shops: merchants ready for the day of commerce. The bodega is an unassuming structure. She notices there are children playing in front of every store except this bodega. There are three young males all dressed in a similar style – black pants, oversized white T-shirt and a green bandana – standing by the entrance. They close ranks as she approaches. It is as if they are blocking her path.

"Excuse me; I'd like to go into the store."

"There is nothing in there for an Anglo like you, chika. Maybe you would find what you need at the Shop and Save a couple of blocks over. Why don't you go there?"

"But, I want to go inside this store."

"The store is closing. You're too late."

She pulls back her jacket to reveal her 9mm Sig Sauer on one side of her belt and her badge on the other.

"Please move so I can enter."

"We didn't know. We were just protecting the store like we protect the neighborhood."

"That's very honorable of you. Now move."

The three men move aside giving Liz barely enough space to squeeze between them. As she does, she feels a hand clasp her left breast from behind. Immediately, she grasps the offending appendage and spins to face the offender. Twisting the hand in a reverse and backward direction, she causes the young tough to scream out like a baby and fall to his knees.

"Would you like me to break your hand for assaulting a police officer?"

"OK! OK! OK! I'm sorry. But you are so beautiful, I couldn't resist."

Liz applies even more twisting pressure and lifts the hand higher as she forces the offender's face to the floor.

"Kiss the floor, my friend. I could arrest you, but I won't because it's too much paperwork for me and too little jail time for you. So, I'll cut you a break. Do you understand?"

"Si, chika. I'm very sorry."

"OK. Now get up and put your hands against the door. You two, stay where you are. Do you have knives or needles or anything sharp that might hurt me when I frisk you? Are you carrying any drugs?"

"No needles and no drugs."

The pat down is brief and uncovers nothing of interest. His wallet contains a driver's license. The grabby weasel is Roberto Ricardo. He is eighteen and lives a few blocks from the bodega. She hands him his wallet. Something about his name that sounds familiar.

"Stand where you are, while I pat down your buddies."

Liz turns and glares at two grinners. She puts her face within three inches of one face and whispers in a threatening manner.

"Do you have knives or needles or anything sharp that might hurt me when I frisk you? Are you carrying any drugs?"

"No, chika."

"My name is Detective Elizabeth Kimble…not chika. Comprende?"

"Si."

The pat down of grinner number one uncovers no wallet. But, she is able to confiscate a box cutter and a small bag of marijuana.

"That's for my personal medical use. I am fighting glaucoma. The box cutter I use to open big packages at the store."

"It's very proactive of you to start fighting a condition that doesn't appear until an individual is in his sixties. I'll just keep the dope and the box cutter as evidence of possible illegal activity. If I have to come back here for whatever the reason, and you are involved in the reason, I will arrest you. Got that."

"Si, Detective."

"Now you, smiley."

The pat down of grinner number two also uncovers no wallet. But she is able to confiscate a switchblade.

"The same goes for you. Now, all three of you leave and stay away."

The three semi-toughs skulk down the block. Their macho huffing and puffing has been called by a woman. As Liz turns to enter the store, she catches a glimpse of a gray sedan about half-way down the block on the other side of the street. She thinks she recognizes the cracked windshield and the rusted spots on the hood. Too many coincidences for one day? Then she remembers that in detective work, there are no coincidences. How did the driver know where she would be?

"Good morning. I am Police Detective Kimble. Do you mind if I have a look around your store?"

The young woman behind the counter nods her head to give permission.

At the rear of the store, Liz spies a doorway covered by a curtain. Standing inside the bodega's entrance, she can see a back storeroom filled with dry goods and boxed food. There is another door at the rear of that room to the right.

"What's behind the door?"

"Nada."

"Do you mind if I look?"

"OK, look."

Liz walks through the supplies of boxed food and dry goods and opens the door to reveal stairs.

"Where do these stairs lead?"

"To more storage upstairs."

She peers up the dark, narrow path up to the second floor. Some of the wooden stairs are cracked and all are crooked. Clicking on her LED penlight, she begins her cautious ascent. Fourteen delicate steps later, she is at the top landing. Yes, there are boxes of dry goods along one of the long walls. But there is also a table and four chairs in the middle of the room. She sees an ashtray with a few doobie butts. The windows have blinds and curtains so the room can be darkened and lights can be turned on without anyone on the outside knowing. No scraps of paper. No evidence of any crime. She heads down the rickety stairs.

"Senorita, do you know Roberto Ricardo or Jose Hernandez?"

"No."

"Well, if you do happen to see one or both of these men, please have them call me. I'd like to talk to them."

Halfway back to headquarters, she realizes she had Ricardo in her grasp. And that the woman in the store had lied to her. A survival action. Damn! She turns quickly and heads back to the bodega. Half a block from the store, she sees the three amigos.

"Roberto Ricardo and Jose Hernandez – stay where you are. I want to talk to you. All of you stay put."

She turns to the third member of the trio.

"What's your name?"

"Benito de Vila."

"Benito, how old are you?"

"Twelve."

"Be careful Benito or you won't see your sixteenth birthday. And by careful, I mean stop hanging out with street thugs like these guys and start hanging out with your classmates at school."

"Chika, watch what you call me. Waddaya want now?"

"Remember, that's Detective Kimble. I am not your chika. I am the law. Allow me to show you my badge and gun again. I want to know what you three know about Los Hermanos."

"Nada."

"Now, Roberto, we both know that's not true. Los Hermanos used to run the streets of downtown, and I am given to understand that the gang may still be a force to be reckoned with. It's just the shot callers have changed from Hector Lopez and Umberto Rosario to Roberto Ricardo and Jose Hernandez. So, now that we have established that you and Jose are the leaders of Los Hermanos, what I want to know is what you know about the murders of Hector and Umberto."

"Nada."

"Are you aware that they were murdered within the past few weeks?"

"Si."

"See, you do know something about the murders after all."

"OK. But we did not do those terrible things to the two OGs."

"These two original gangsters were out of the life. Maybe you were afraid they would talk to the police. That's why you killed them."

"We had nothing to do with them after they left the organization."

Liz knows it's foolish to ask for alibis for the dates of the murders. Their alibis would be iron clad and vouched for by at least two non-gang members.

"Before I leave, I want each of you to write your name, home address, and telephone number in this book. That way, I can reach you 24/7. That's it for now. Benito, be very careful in choosing your friends. Adios, my new Hispanic BFFs."

She has met the enemy and they know her. Liz noticed that Benito was fidgeting when she spoke to him. His eyes were darting left and right and up and down. He may be guilty of something or know something that she wants to know. He may just be a kid not yet hardened by the street life. He could crack with another visit or a trip to headquarters. She needs more intel. When back at the office she will call Bob Dover.

"Kimble, I can tell you that Los Hermanos is recruiting younger boys and girls to be part of the gang. As young as ten, but mostly early teens. They serve an apprenticeship. Do favors and odd chores for the shot callers. The younger ones are the ones who mule drugs and carry weapons. The shot callers know the system is powerless to prosecute the apprentices as adults, because of their age. My guess is that this Benito kid is one of the apprentices. I wish I could tell you that we have extensive intel on the gang. But we just don't have the resources to make them a high priority. If you have any reason to sweep them up, I will be glad to do it for you."

"I think Benito will come unglued if we…I mean you…were to lean on him."

"If you really think so, I will get him and his mother into our offices tomorrow. What do you want to know?"

"I want to know what he knows or has heard from other gang members about the murders of Hector Lopez and Umberto Rosario."

"That's it?"

"I'll be behind the glass when you talk to him. I will hear him and watch his reactions to your questions. Thanks."

"Archie. What did you learn about Burbiski?"

"LT, he has an alibi for the time of Ross's murder. He was with several friends at an all-day backyard cookout. They confirmed his presence from noon to ten. So he is off our list. I also learned that he and Lance have been friends since community college. That pretty much sums up the totality of my knowledge about Wilton Burbiski. Just another dead end. What about Los Hermanos? Kimble?"

"I met Roberto Ricardo, Jose Hernandez, and Benito de Vila. Roberto and Jose are shot callers, while Benito is a wannabe. The gang unit is bringing Benito in for a friendly chat. I think he could tell us a great deal about Los Hermanos."

"Let me know what you learn."

"Damn, Archie, I thought we were onto something with the Lance/Wilton connection. I still think the non-grieving widow had something to do with her husband's murder. I just can't seem to connect her to anyone who could have altered the braking system. I want to let that case alone and just let the facts percolate in my subconscious. Sooner or later an epiphany will flash and I will see the right path. Gawd, that sounds strangely evangelical, doesn't it? I have to take another call."

"Noon today? Great."

"Archie, do you want to sit in on the interview with Benito de Vila?"

"Nah, I'll leave that exciting task for you, while I work on my three other open cases."

Three cases? Who the hell is Archie's Rabbi? That's such a light load. Has he been given a soft schedule because of his age or as a form of payoff for previous services rendered? Liz is feeling frustrated, paranoid, and a little pissed. Her attitude is being distorted by regular monthly hormonal changes. The curse is definitely not a blessing. File updates require her attention for the next three hours. Data Entry Specialist Kimble reluctantly reports for duty.

"Benito and his mother are here."

The clarion call to leave the mundane, and move to a learning session.

"We appreciate you taking time from your busy life to bring Benito. We need him to help us by answering a few simple questions. First, rest assured that Benito is not under arrest. He is here as a concerned citizen. There is no need for a lawyer. We will be brief and you will be on your way shortly."

"Bueno."

"Benito, we learned that you have been hanging out with Roberto Ricardo and Jose Hernandez. Is that right?"

"Si."

"Are you aware that they are jefes of a street gang known as Los Hermanos?"

"Si."

"Benito, mi niño, why do you do that? It's dangerous."

"Yes, why do you hang with two shot callers?"

"I get respect from people in the neighborhood. Just like they get respect."

"That's not respect, mi niño. That's fear. Your father, God rest his soul, knew Los Hermanos. He knew of their drug dealing and the money they earned from making storeowners pay for protection. Los Hermanos is muy malo."

"Benito, you can be a big help by answering a few more questions. What do you know about the murders of Hector Lopez and Umberto Rosario?"

The boy sits stone still and looks down at the small table in the interview room. Suddenly, the boy's mother calls out.

"Benito, answer the policeman."

"Well…I don't know for sure, but I heard that Los Hermanos did not kill those two guys. They were killed by somebody else."

"Who told you that?"

"I heard Roberto talking to Jose last week. They were upset because they knew Los Hermanos would take the heat for the murders. They said that the last thing the organization needed was to have the police blaming them. Looking at them too closely. They did not say for sure who killed those two guys. But they thought it might have been Muy Loco. Muy Loco has been making moves to expand into our neighborhood…selling drugs on our street corners and demanding money from shopkeepers in our neighborhood. Their move started a few months ago and has been very slow. Los Hermanos does not want a war, but Muy Loco will not take a sit-down."

"So your shot callers think Muy Loco killed two Los Hermanos OGs and is moving into your territory, but they won't do anything about it? That shows me that the two at the top are weak. Do you think they are weak?"

"No."

"Then why won't they do anything to avenge the death of two OGs and the loss of power over their neighborhood?"

"I heard Roberto say that they have been told help is coming. So they must sit and wait."

"Help? What kind of help? Who?"

"I did not hear what kind of help or who the help is."

"Benito, mi niño, you must be honest. Tell the policeman everything you know."

"I did tell what I know. That's all I know."

"Thank you, Benito, for your honesty. And thank you, Mrs. de Vila, for bringing Benito here today. We are done. You may leave."

The three exit the interview room and Dover escorts the mother and son to the building's front door.

Liz is waiting for him in the interview room.

"Kimble, did that help your investigation? I'm not convinced he told us everything he knows about the murders and the conversations between Roberto and Jose. I think he told us just enough to get us off his back."

"Benito introduced an invisible force outside the gang. Tough to find invisible forces, but not impossible if they are real forces just hidden from view. Maybe the mention of Muy Loco is simply a way to push us away. I think we… er, you should have a sit-down with Roberto and Jose tomorrow. I'll silently observe again."

"Thanks for bringing this to our attention. We will schedule two sit-downs for tomorrow. I'll let you know the time."

"OK."

IX

"Liz, this is Leonard Sly. I think you should pay me a visit as soon as possible. Like right now."

An ominous message left by a friend. If the purpose of his call is police related, he would have gone through Lieutenant Gracia. This must be personal. Liz takes a ride to the Impound Lot.

"Leonard, what's going on?"

"Come with me."

They exit the work area filled with numerous vehicles and several technicians and walk through the back door of the massive garage. Leonard leads the pair along a narrow, partially overgrown path to a small block building at the edge of the property. The small one-story structure looks vacant. The windows are intact but filthy and the front door is surprisingly clear of the vines and growing plants that appear to be enveloping the outer walls of the structure. Leonard leans against the door and it begrudgingly opens. He enters first.

The single room looks to be thirty-by-thirty. The sun struggling to shine through the windows provides enough light that Liz can see metal racks that act as shelves. On the shelves are boxes and bins of all shapes and sizes. This is the tool and parts storage room for the Impound Lot. The place has a slight, yet distinguishable, odor of human waste.

"Be careful where you step. This is a crime scene."

"Crime scene?"

"Yep. See the brown pool-like mark on the floor?"

"Yes."

"That's blood."

"It looks like a dirt and grease mixture."

"Take this paper towel and dab it in the middle of the pool."

She obeys and holds the paper up to a window to examine the dark red moisture.

"It is blood. How did it get here?"

"They're back and they must have killed somebody here in my domain."

"What? Who's back?"

"The Street Cleaners."

"OK. You have my complete attention. Who are the Street Cleaners? Why would they have killed somebody? And why here?"

"Street Cleaners are members of the police force who belong to a very secret society. The aim of this society is to rid the city of undesirables who have avoided the law or have managed to avoid prosecution."

"You're making this up."

"Listen carefully to what I'm about to tell you. The Street Cleaners came into existence about seventy years ago – during the Bolito Wars. Back then, they were referred to as *limpiadores en la calle*. References to them were always whispered. All the members were of Spanish descent. Back then, several rival gangs fought street battles or wars for control of the very lucrative Bolito Lottery. In this lottery, an entrant picked five numbers from one to one hundred. Each ticket cost a dime at first and within ten years, a quarter. Everybody could afford small bets so they made multiple bets. The payoff started at twenty and grew to five hundred dollars. The payoff was miniscule relative to the intake of cash because everybody wanted to play. The enterprise was very profitable for those who ran this illegal lottery. Just like the statewide lottery run today; small bets, many players, and a limited number of relatively large payouts. But unlike the statewide lottery, the Bolito Lottery was secretive, not sanctioned by any government, and localized to one city... Tampa.

"After five years of fighting and random beatings, the wars intensified and got really ugly. Bodies began piling up in the streets in front of restaurants and shops. Certain members of the police force decided that legally permitted police efforts and the court system were failing the city and its decent citizens. So, these police lieutenants and captains formed *limpiadores en la calle* or Street Cleaners to rid Tampa of this cancerous crime wave. As the name Street Cleaners clearly states, this organization was collecting and disposing of the trash. To do so, they would be the judge, jury, and executioner as to what or who constituted a crime and therefore trash. On the side, this righteous organization made a ton of untraceable cash. They extorted money from criminals they could threaten rather than kill.

"They started small. Legend has it there were only five in the original group. At first, they would give an offending miscreant a severe beating...broken leg or broken arm. They didn't start to kill until these tactics lost their impact. Not mass murders, but an occasional murder and many, many disappearances. Occasionally, a body would be found in front of a known gang hangout or in the city dump. The message was clear and received. Stop what you are doing. One of the warring gangs would temporarily convert to non-combatant status. This continued for more than a decade. The Street Cleaners had given notice that gang activity would be tolerated only if it were minor, sporadic, and did not threaten the citizens. Gradually, the Street Cleaners went underground. Over the years, if real gang activity became obvious to the media and citizenry, the Street Cleaners would re-institute a program of swift and aggressive pacification. Over time they morphed from a group trying to stop the Bolito Wars to a group of self-righteous vigilantes seeking to right any wrongs against society that due process can't. And their efforts lined their pockets. I think what we have here is an indication that the Street Cleaners are alive."

"How do you know this?"

"I am an old-timer. But, I can assure you I am not a Street Cleaner. I heard much talk about them as I was coming up in the ranks. Hell, I think I even knew a couple of them but could never prove it."

"How did you discover this murder scene?"

"I came to the storage house to see if we had any parts for a job we were doing. This is what I discovered."

"Who are the Street Cleaners today? Certainly, they can't be the original group. They must all be dead by now."

"Legend has it that the right to be a Street Cleaner is inherited...passed from father to son from the 1940s to today. It is still a small group, but as generations expand so did the group which now may number twenty or more members of the force. And we can't forget the wannabes.

Men who do not enjoy the lineage of Street Cleaners, but who can earn their way into the cabal by doing jobs like beatings, extortion, and even murders at the request of the organization. There may be ten-to-fifteen or so wannabes. And more each decade as they learn about the spoils of this illegal enterprise."

"Who are they?"

"No one ever says. It's very secret. They would make the inner circle of the Masons look like chatty Kathies. The members may know one or two more of their brethren, but no one knows all of them and no one outside of the group knows anyone in the group."

"That's not very helpful. What happened here?"

"They brought someone into the Impound Lot. They came the back way and entered through a hole in the fence. Cops know of the hole. I doubt if any civilian knows of it. Then they killed the guy."

"Who did they kill? Why did they kill him?"

"I'll bet the *who* you can answer by checking the DNA on that paper towel with the DNA of recent murder victims. Like the body found at the dump. The *why* is also a mystery for you to solve. But be very careful with whom you discuss this. You can never be sure who is a Street Cleaner. They can be very brutal, because they don't want their organization and activities known to the good citizens of Tampa. More importantly, they don't want their money stream cut off."

"How about the Internal Affairs Bureau?"

"IAB will dismiss your accusations as an unfounded myth and squash your inquiry. Or just lose the paperwork. It's very possible that one of the Street Cleaners is a high-ranking member of the rat squad. Maybe even the one to whom you report your suspicions. If they know that you know, your life would be in danger. No, you have to follow this investigation on your own.

"Holy crap!"

Liz is stunned. Digesting what Leonard has told her is like swallowing an entire T-bone steak – meat and bone. On the way back to police headquarters, she tries to formulate a plan but has great difficulty because of the enormity of the situation…crime sanctioned by police vigilantes and murders by cops. She pulls off the road to think with a clear mind. Slowly, the plan comes to her. First, any of today's Street Cleaners will be ranking senior officers and not unies, or very young sergeants, lieutenants, and above. Second, today's Street Cleaners are the grandsons, grandnephews or even grand cousins of the men in the first group. She must learn who on the force fits this type of legacy. That would take digging through personnel files. Impossible to access those files. Wait!

What about the celebration a few years ago, entitled Seventy-five Years of Service? The department threw a big picnic and the newspaper took lots of photos of officers and their families celebrating the heritage of a few families whose members had been on the force for at least three generations, some four, and a few families served five generations. It's the perfect place to start. The large photo and commemorative plaque hang in the lobby. Third, to clear up this quagmire while remaining safe from retribution, she will need help from someone not possibly associated with the maleficent group. Outside the force. But her first stop is the ME for DNA comparison.

"We went over the vic's body, and checked his tats against those on the bodies of known bad guys in our system. We found Eduardo Montenegro. We discussed our findings with Detective Dannello, who told me that Montenegro had a minor record of robberies and extortion. His last arrest was five years ago. A jewelry store robbery. But, he was never tried or sent to prison. He seems to have been off the radar after the file entry. Why do you want to know? Mr. Montenegro's murder is not your case."

"Doctor, I got a tip on the murder, and I want to follow it unimpeded. If the tip proves accurate, I'll share my intel with Dannello. If not, then not. I want to know if the blood matches. Get back to me with any new information about the vic. Do not report this to Dannello. I'll take care of sharing details with Dannello. OK?"

"OK. But keep me out of this scheme."

"Hey, Kimble, did you hear?"

"Hear what, Archie."

"Assistant District Attorney Lembetick announced his retirement. His last day is Friday. The announcement said he had decided to explore opportunities in the private sector after thirty years in the DA's office. His real plans for the future most likely include fishing, boating, and painting beach scenes. So, we can deduce that he was asked to retire. Out with the old and in with the new. I think DA Block is cleaning house for some major push like his re-election. I understand that they've already hired a newbie, Marion Morrison. His bio is impressive, if you belief half the bullshit they say about themselves. Graduate of Florida and Florida Law. Clerked for Judge Skiggs in the Appellate Division. Spent some time as an attorney with Fleder, Nelson, Bainro and Morgan. They protect the rich and famous. The guy starts Monday. He has big lazy shoes to fill. Lembetick did whatever the minimum was to not look like he was asleep. I think he could doze off with his eyes open. Never took a risk or exploited the power of his office. Coming from a well-connected local family was his security. I don't think Morrison has that luxury. His family comes from Fort Myers."

The professional paths of Liz and ADA Lembetick never crossed. The last time she had anything to do with the DA's office was the trial of Marshall Ross. So she feels no need to comment on this changing of the guard in the District Attorney's office other than a big whoop.

The lobby of police headquarters contains numerous pictures and plaques commemorating meritorious service, various phases of the building's construction, and the prize she sought. The big picture of the event depicts approximately forty men and women standing on bleachers. The officers have been grouped by family. Sometimes the original member is noted as deceased. All are in uniform. Some are smiling. It reminds her of a high school class photo for the yearbook. The photo has been blown up to four feet by three feet. The names of the honorees are listed by row below the photo and on the bronze shield beside it. Liz holds her cell phone up to the photo and snaps a shot of the names. Damn! The glare of the ceiling lights bounced off the glass and obscured many of the names. She slightly changes her angle. First to the right. Then to the left. One more straight on. Bingo! She has her prize. Now to blow-up the three shots to make the names readable. This is a job for Kwik-Printz...away from prying eyes. Her lunchtime prep for work at home...also away from prying eyes.

"Thanksgiving is next week and I have the day off. I invited your Aunt Shannon for the day. She will arrive from Jacksonville on Wednesday evening so we have time to prepare the feast. The meal will be served in the dining room at 1:00 PM regardless of what football game is on. And, like every year, I have invited two members of our military who are stationed at McDuff. This year Staff Sergeant Brendan Davis and Lieutenant Alice Rettan will be joining us for the holiday, since they have no family in the area. They will be arriving around ten in the morning, or as they say ten hundred hours. Just like your father, his father before him, and my father, we will treat our guests with the honor they deserve for service to their country. We will not bicker and squabble like family. And, all of us will dress in clean, proper casual clothes. No T-shirts, running shorts, or flip- flops. Collared shirts, khaki slacks or skirt, and loafers or sneakers constitute the uniform of the day."

"Mom, what if we have plans for the afternoon?"

"Cancel them."

"Mom!"

"Easy, Cary. Don't argue with me on this one. The soldiers must feel lonely on a day they used to spend with their parents and siblings like you and your brother."

"Alex, maybe you can learn some manners from them."

"OK. This dinner is over. Bus all the dishes. I'll scrape and clean. And, while you're in the kitchen, be sure to write any special requests for Thanksgiving food on the list. Shannon and I will do whatever we can to accommodate your requests. Now don't you two have homework?"

With Alex and Cary upstairs, Liz sits at the big kitchen table and unrolls the enlarged photos. On a legal pad, she lists the names of present day captains and lieutenants whose police force lineage goes back at least five generations, then those with four, and finally three. Liz excludes any officer whose lineage started with a female. Back in the day, women would have been excluded from this special boys club. Women were crossing guards, secretaries, and file clerks. She also excludes any present-day female captains and lieutenants. All four of them. Meticulously, she completes her list, double checks it, and then triple checks it. The final tally is twelve names of possible Street Cleaners.

Oachoa	*Winters*
Brawley	*Schliemann*
Gracia	*Antes*
Mettle	*Montoya*
Hernandez	*Fernandez*
Qito	*Salvatore*

Liz stares at the Gracia family names. It bothers her but may explain a great deal. Now what? Who can she tell of her hunch? Who will help her root out this evil? Something to sleep on.

Third Body Identified
Harold Shade

Police have identified the third man discovered in the recent flurry of brutal murders as Eduardo Montenegro. Mr. Montenegro's address is listed as 765 Poinsettia Street. Police records reveal that he is a native of El Salvador, has no known employer, and leaves no immediate family or other relatives living in the Tampa Bay Area. Mr. Montenegro is known to police to be a member of the Muy Loco street gang. Police say that Muy Loco has been in a power struggle with the remnants of the Los Hermanos gang for control of illegal enterprises in Hillsborough County and his death may be a consequence of the struggle. A spokesman for Tampa Police stated, "There is a possibility that the recent murders are related to the struggle for dominance that has escalated in the past year. We will investigate and continue to report on this threat to tranquility in our city. We urge anyone with information to call the Tampa Police Force tip line, 813-500-5555. A reward of $5,000 is offered for information leading to the arrest and conviction of the killers."

"Ricardo, you are not under arrest. We are asking for your help getting more information about the murder of Hector Lopez. Is that clear?"

"Si."

"Do you know Hector Lopez?"

"Si. He was in our organization until he decided to leave a few years ago."

"Did he leave your organization on good terms?"

"Si, after the blood out, he was free to go whereever he wanted."

"Blood out?"

"Blood in and blood out is the Los Hermanos way. He took the beating like a man."

"Was he involved in fighting the police at the Los Hermanos hideout two years ago?"

"No, I think he was out of the life by then. But he still had friends in the organization."

"Who were his friends?"

"I don't know all of them. I do know that Enrique was a friend of Hector."

"Enrique who?"

"Enrique Flores."

"Anyone else?"

"Nah."

"Now let's change subjects. What do you know about the murder of Umberto Rosario?"

"Only what I read in the paper."

"Do you know who killed Rosario?"

"No."

"Do you know why he was killed?"

"No."

"Who was Umberto to you?"

"My cousin and a former member of our organization."

"Was he in your organization when he was killed?"

"No."

"Did he blood out like Hector?"

"No, he was a puta, and ran before we could talk to him."

"Running away. Is that against the rules?" "Si."

"What does your organization do to runners?"

"Nothing more than to be sure they never come back to the neighborhood. We keep tabs on runners. Someday a puta slips up. Then we catch him and give him a dos equis."

"Dos equis?"

"Si, twice the beating he would have gotten earlier."

"Why wouldn't you kill a runner?"

"A killing brings the cops. A beating does not."

"OK. How about Eduardo Montenegro? What do you know about Eduardo Montenegro?"

"He was a lowlife Muy Loco. A bottom feeder. A weasel. He was a wannabe."

"Wannabe?"

"Yeah. He tried to join our organization, but we turned him down. He was a purse- snatcher and small-time stick-up guy. Los Hermanos do not do crime. We protect our neighborhood. We wanted nothing to do with him. Muy Loco took him in. They deserved each other. They're all low lifers. Scum."

"What do you know about his murder?"

"Nothing more than what I read. But I can guess that the Muy Locos figured him out and decided to get rid of him."

"You think Muy Loco killed Eduardo?"

"Not us, for sure. But it wasn't us. That's all I know."

Liz is standing in the observation room, mutual for both interrogation rooms. The setting is functional, two large panes of one-way glass, four chairs, a door, and a wall. Someone in the observation room can hear the interviews of two people at once. Perfect for today. Bob Dover is with Ricardo, and Lieutenant Eddie Flom is with Jose Fernandez. Each interviewer asks the same set of questions in the same order. This procedure is based on the proven concept that two partial statements will make a complete disclosure of the facts or reveal any inconsistencies and lies. Liz must note any discrepancies in the responses of the two gang members.

"Jose, you are not under arrest. We are asking for your help getting more information about the murder of Hector Lopez. Is that clear?"

"Si."

"Do you know Hector Lopez?"

"Si. He was in our organization until he decided to leave a few years ago."

"Did he leave your organization on good terms?"

"After the blood out, he was free to go wherever he wanted."

"Blood out?"

"Blood in and blood out is the Los Hermanos way. He took the beating like a man."

"Was he involved in fighting the police at the Los Hermanos hideout two years ago?"

"I am not sure."

"What do you mean?"

"I mean, I don't know. I think he was out of town at the time of the raid, but I can't be sure."

"Out of town?"

"Yeah, I think he had gone back to Honduras to visit. I think I remember his papi was very sick and about to die."

"Anything else?"

"Nah."

"Now let's change subjects. What do you know about the murder of Umberto Rosario?"

"He was a piece of caca who deserved what he got."

"Do you know who killed Rosario?"

"No. But whoever did it did us all a favor."

"Why do you say that?"

"Umberto was always complaining and scheming. He was a double-dealer that was always looking for an angle, and he didn't give a damn whose toes he crushed trying to get ahead."

"Did he crush your toes?"

"Twice, but I did not kill him. Killing is not the Los Hermanos way. We are protectors of our neighborhood."

"Do you know why he was killed?"

"No."

"Who was Umberto to you?"

"A bad member of our organization."

"Was he in your organization when he was killed?"

"No."

"Did he blood out like Hector?"

"No, he was a puta, and ran away before we could talk to him."

"Run away? Is that against the rules?"

"Yeah."

"What does your organization do to runners?"

"Nothing more than to be sure they never come back to the neighborhood. We keep tabs on runners. Someday a puta slips up. Then we catch him and give him a dos equis."

"Dos equis?"

"Si, that's twice the beating he would have gotten earlier."

"Why wouldn't you kill a runner?"

"A killing brings the cops. A beating does not."

"OK. How about Eduardo Montenegro? What do you know about Eduardo Montenegro?"

"He was a lowlife El Salvadoran Muy Loco. Someone who would rat out his own mother for a payday. A weasel. He was a wannabe."

"Wannabe?"

"Yeah. He tried to join our organization, but we turned him down. He was into real petty shit like purse-snatching and robbing shop keepers. Los Hermanos does not do those things. We protect our neighborhood. We wanted nothing to do with him. Muy Loco took him in. They deserved each other. They're all low lifers."

"What do you know about his murder?"

"Nothing more than what I read. Maybe the Muy Locos figured him out and decided to get rid of him."

"You think Muy Loco killed Jose?"

"Not us, for sure. That's all I know."

The responses by both men are strangely similar. Almost as they were rehearsed...scripted like the questions. But they revealed one major flaw. Liz knows that Hondurans and Salvadorans do not join the same gangs because of blood feuds that go back generations in the Central American countries. Montenegro was from El Salvador as are most of the Muy Locos. Most of the Los Hermanos are Hondurans. Another reason for Los Hermanos to reject Montenegro. Why would he try to join a gang of people who hate him and his lineage?

X

"Alex. Cary. Shannon is here."

With these words, the holiday begins. The teens come bounding down the stairs yelling their greetings before they come face-to-face with their aunt. Hugs, laughter, and high-pitched yelling fill the house with familial love.

"Holy crap! Look at you two. Cary, you've grown a bunch since I last saw you. And, if you don't mind me saying it, you are filling out nicely. How beautiful you are. And Alex, you're huge. No longer the cuddly little boy. You are soooo handsome. Do you have a girlfriend? Do you want an older girlfriend? Of course not. I'm sure you have many girls chasing you. Cary, have you started to date? I'll bet your Mom is petrified that day is here or right around the corner. Because the day you start dating will mean there are two women in the house. Not a woman and a little girl. I want to know all about your lives. We have two days for that. Will that be enough? Let's start now."

"Shannon, we want to know all about your life, too."

"Catchin' bad guys. Puttin' them in jail. Makin' the streets safe for the citizenry of Duval County. Just like your Mom in Tampa."

"But you work undercover in a narcotics unit. That must be exciting."

"Dirty and dangerous. If that's what you mean by exciting. That's enough about me; let's talk about you. Liz, will you excuse us while we catch up. We will go food hunting and gathering in an hour. OK?"

Liz smiles as the three of them leave for the patio. The Q and A session between aunt, niece, and nephew commences in earnest. The normal conversation is broken by what can only be whispering. Kitchen cleaned, Liz is ready for grocery shopping.

"OK, guys. Shannon and I are off to kill a turkey and harvest the vegetables for tomorrow."

"Mom, remember no chewy cranberries in the cranberry sauce. Just buy the canned stuff. It's smooth and sweet. Also, let's try cornbread stuffing. And sweet potatoes, not regular. Most important, lots of succotash."

"I am holding your list. No need to reinforce the written word. See you two in about an hour and a half. Love ya."

"Back atchya."

Two police detectives head out to patrol the aisles of a huge grocery store crammed with panicky last-minute pre-holiday shoppers.

"Liz, how go the battles? Are you winning the war?"

"Work is work. Understaffed and overloaded. City bosses want more results faster with fewer people. So it trickles down to us. Like tying the hands of a swimmer and demanding that she win the half-mile race to the island in the middle of the lake. But we manage. They can't find others to do what we do for so little money. I guess my situation could be considered job security."

"What about your cases?"

"A surprising number of recent murders. I think they are somehow related. I just don't have a good handle on the minutia and the nuances therein. How about you? How's the narco squad?"

"Made a buy-and-bust-and-climb-the-ladder last month. I was the hooker jonesing for a fix. You should have seen me. I had a blonde wig, huge platform shoes, a halter-top that barely covered my girls, and cut-off jeans that showed two inches of my butt cheeks. The dealer wanted to give me the heroin in trade. He was drooling. After he was busted, he started to cry like a baby. We flipped him and went right up the ladder to a master distributor who was holding twenty keys. He will go away for so long that he'll probably die in prison. The twelve street dealers in his organization were also busted. They'll each get a minimum of ten years. Hopefully more."

"Weren't you afraid you could be beaten or killed?"

"There were four of Duval County's finest hiding in doorways and parked cars thirty feet from me. These guys are the biggest and meanest on the force. Their job is to make sure I go home at the end of my tour. They are my protective pit bulls. I was safe."

"Safe, if you assume that they can get to you before the bullet does."

"Now you're talking like a Mom and not a cop."

"I am a Mom *and* a cop."

"Don't worry about me, Liz. I am, and will be, fine."

"Social life?"

"The job is my life just as yours is yours. One or two nights a month I go on dates. Nothing serious and all more or less work connected. As for the sheet-sweating stuff, I do what I need to do on an ad hoc basis. When I feel the urge that I can't satisfy, I cruise the bars in the better hotels. It's very easy to find a traveling business man who wants company for a night. It's a win-win. Often I even get dinner. How is *your* love life?"

"Aren't you worried that some guy is into something very kinky or will try to hurt you? My love life...I still miss Sandy. And I am afraid to start over at my age. Plus, the children."

"The guys I pick up are not looking to attack me. Their egos are inflated when they think they are so smooth as to get someone as good-looking as me...for no charge. I see your point about age. You are not as attractive as your younger sister. Your body is not as firm yet supple as someone eight years younger. And you miss Sandy. Maybe you should wait until you're in your seventies to start over. By that time, your lady parts will be withered and non-functional and your girls will sag to your waist. But you'll probably find someone with whom you can hold hands, share denture cups, and reminisce about days gone by and opportunities squandered.

"Jaysus, Liz! Sandy died two years ago. You've used his death as an excuse for so long that you actually believe you have no chance at an adult female life. I think it's time you get back on the horse, or rather find some horse to get back on you. Of course, you love and miss Sandy. But, he is not here and he is not coming back. It's time for you to move on. Put yourself out there for the eligible male beasties to see, admire, and lust after. You won't find Mr. Right sitting at home and you won't find him immediately, but you will find a lover and maybe love."

"Shannon, I think that's enough on that subject. You take a cart and this part of the list. I'll do the rest. Like Mom used to say shopping is a divide and conquer indoor sport. We'll meet during our travels and figure out what we couldn't find. Ready? Go."

Liz buys a twenty-five pound bird. For ever-ravenous teens there will be lots of leftovers and some for the freezer. The rolls have been squeezed and tossed back into the bin like dead carp. She decides on two loaves of seven-grain. The pumpkin and mince pies look fresh. Hell, with vanilla ice cream, everyone will love it. Beyond the bird, bread, and pies, Liz's part of the list contains mostly the elements for weekday meals. Shannon bumps her cart into Liz's and they both giggle. Memories of shopping with their mother bring out the child in both detectives.

"Shannon, what are we missing?"

"Alcohol."

"There's a liquor store through the door near the entrance. We'll stop there before we check-out the groceries. The crowd is beginning to play on my nerves. If we're done, we should leave. My treat."

"OK. Then I get the booze."

The check-out takes a long time. Several customers forgot items. One man doesn't seem to have enough money. He looks like he's down on his luck. His clothes are ratty. He needs a shave. He is putting items aside hoping that he can afford what remains when Liz approaches and hands him forty dollars.

"Ma'am, what's the money for?"

"Consider it a Thanksgiving gift."

"I can't accept this. That's way too much money. I don't know you. I can't pay you back."

"That's the beauty of a gift. Once the money leaves my hand, it's no longer a gift, it's yours to do with as you see fit. No strings attached and no repayment required. The money is a gift pure and simple. You need the money, and I have the money. How convenient. Enjoy your Thanksgiving."

"Bless you."

"You're welcome."

The shoppers who see the physical and verbal exchanges smile and nod approval. One of them applauds. Then two. Ten. Then all the people at the registers. Liz is an unknown hero to a group of shoppers. She starts to get teary-eyed out of embarrassment and nods acknowledgment of the kudos. She has to find one last item…flowers. Several big bunches of flowers. Her house must be home for her guests. As Mother used to say, "At home for guests, set a nice table and have fresh flowers to show your love."

"Liz, are you ready?"

Shannon appears from the liquor store carrying a large fabric wine bag with the store's logo on it.

As they walk to the car Liz catches a glimpse of a big man with a big belly, baggy pants, a handlebar moustache, and a mullet. He is standing in front of the trunk of a gray sedan facing the sisters. The car has a cracked windshield and rusted spots on the hood. He looks familiar. From where?

"Jaysus, Shannon, how much wine did you buy?"

"Two for us tonight and three for four adults tomorrow. Plus, I bought a little surprise beverage for my sister and me…a nice bottle of Cognac. You can never have enough good spirit."

"Does Cabernet or Pinot Noir go better with putting away groceries and getting the kitchen ready for duty tomorrow?"

"Cab. Let's save the Pinot for the turkey."

"Alex. Cary. Come down here and help."

"Liz, that's the biggest bird I've ever seen."

"I agree with Aunt Shannon."

"Alex, we will have enough for a few meals beyond Thanksgiving."

"About a month's worth, I'd guess. A month of eating turkey. Oh, joy."

"Cary, we will not be eating turkey every night for a month. What you fail to realize is that we have two adult guests tomorrow. Plus, you and your brother eat a great deal at every meal. I'll freeze most of what we don't eat tomorrow so we can have it whenever we want…like when I don't have time or the inclination to shop. Consider the turkey as meal insurance. Alex, please get me the big tub from the garage. Shannon, pour me a glass, please."

Thus begins the preparation for tomorrow's roasting. Over the next three hours, the bird begins a night of soaking in brine and poultry seasoning, side dishes are prepped, the table is set, and flowers arranged. Alex and Cary are responsible for the table and flowers. Cary finds the Irish linen tablecloth and six matching napkins in the massive chest.

"Mom, the tablecloth shows its fold marks. I'll iron them out. Can't put our best china, glasses, and silverware on a wrinkled surface."

"Thanks, Cary."

"I'll take care of the flowers."

"Where did you hide the candelabra and candles?"

"Look in the closet by the front door, Alex."

The queries, responses, and commands bounce from kitchen to other rooms for about an hour until the teen's duties are complete and it's time for inspection. Meanwhile, wine is steadily sipped by the adults cleaning vegetables and making ready for final cooking tomorrow. The bottle has been emptied. Liz and Shannon wash and dry their hands for an inspection of the house. All is as near perfect as can be.

"Great job, you guys. Now one last simple item for the each of you. Dust and vacuum the downstairs."

Tasks complete, the siblings demand to be compensated.

"If you touch any of the food for tomorrow, Shannon and I will have to kill you. And you know we both have guns. As your reward for doing a good job, I offer you fruit, cheese, and crackers."

The children smile broadly at their mother's faux threat. They each take a plate of reward to their room.

"Liz, they are wonderful. You've done a remarkable job with them."

"Not so much me as their genes get the credit. They are intrinsically good people. I simply guide them."

"But, what about you?"

"What do you mean?"

"They love you and you love them. But you're an adult woman. You should have more. You should have an adult male to love."

"Let's not go there again. I'm not ready. Besides, I have my job."

"Most married people have jobs. Jobs and mates. Has Cary or Alex ever broached the subject with you?"

"Never. As teens, they have their own issues about the opposite sex. OK! That's enough. This subject is officially off the table."

"You can't stop me from asking."

"Yes, I can. My house, my rules. This subject is closed for discussion. Got it?"

"Got it."

"Pour me another glass while I take out the trash. And open the door for me."

"I'll have to open a second bottle. It seems I bought a bottle that had a hole in the bottom."

Two large trash bins are parked to the left of the driveway entrance: one for recyclables and one for garbage. Heaven forbid a homeowner should mix garbage with paper, plastic, and cans. Such a heinous transgression warrants a stern form letter from the cartage company. As she approaches the two bins, she sees a car parked across the street three houses down from hers. Liz thinks it's odd because the Browns have been away for a week. Why would a car be parked in front of their house? She stares at the gray sedan, trying to see who is in the front seat. Suddenly, the engine starts. The car pulls into the Brown's driveway, backs out, and drives away from Liz's prying eyes. Is it the same car she saw in the store parking lot? Is the wine making her paranoid? Are her confusing cases and their unknowns playing mind games?

The day for giving thanks is here. The doorbell rings at ten-oh-one. Military precision beats socially acceptable late arrival.

"Shannon, please slice and season the sweet potatoes with olive oil, cinnamon, salt, and tarragon. I want to welcome our guests."

"Hello and happy Thanksgiving. I am Liz Kimble. Welcome to our home."

"Good morning, ma'am, I'm Staff Sergeant Brendan Davis."

"I'm Lieutenant Alice Rettan, ma'am. Thank you for inviting us to share your holiday."

"OK. A major ground rule…no formalities. No uniforms. No ranks. No titles. I am not ma'am. I'm Liz. For this day, this is your home and we are your family. My children, Alex and Cary, will join us momentarily. My sister, Shannon, is in the kitchen. Please come in and make yourself at home."

"Shannon, our guests are here. Come and say hello to Brendan Davis and Alice Rettan."

Suddenly, the clump of teenage feet on the stairs nearly shakes the house.

"Alex. Cary. I am pleased to introduce Brendan Davis and Alice Rettan."

Greetings all around. Excitement covers the faces of the siblings as they meet real life members of the military. Not action figures. The reaction is the same each year.

"Here's another rule. You are not allowed in the kitchen to help with anything. This is our day to serve you. Guys, grab a plate of appetizers, offer our guests a drink, and show Brendan and Alice the patio. We dine about one. Shannon and I will join you shortly."

The conversation among the six runs the gamut from home to military to school. Finally, the inevitable.

"I am a Detective with the Tampa Police Department. Shannon is a Detective with the Duval County Sheriff's Department."

"Alex, Cary, you must be very proud of the dangerous jobs your mother and aunt do day in and day out."

"The work they do isn't nearly as dangerous as yours."

"Alex, your mother and aunt have jobs much more dangerous than ours. We think about using our weapons only when ordered. Your mother and aunt must think about using their weapons every day they are on duty. We normally know the location of our enemy...they don't jump out of a doorway and fire at us. Our missions are well planned and the duration is known. Their missions are nearly spontaneous every day. Their careers are more dangerous than ours."

"Thanks for the kudos. I believe it's time for the bird to serve us. I'll let it sit for thirty minutes before carving."

The meal is served and consumed with gusto. Conversations bounce to school, sports, roles in various combat missions, original hometowns...Bozeman, Montana and Lancaster, Pennsylvania. Plates are cleared and stacked in the kitchen, dessert and coffee are served, and the last of the third bottle of Pinot poured. Talk focuses on plans for the future. Around four-thirty Liz senses the departure of her guests is approaching. Mother's instincts are never wrong.

"Liz, this has been fantastic. Way better than eating on base...better food and nicer dining company. But, this Staff Sergeant and Lieutenant must be returning to base. We are on alert at eighteen hundred hours. I don't know how to thank you and your family for making us feel at home."

"No thanks are necessary. Shannon and I thank you for your service."

Goodbyes are said at the door.

"OK, Alex and Cary, your KP begins now. Dishes get scraped and put in the machine. Silverware gets washed and dried immediately by hand. No spots. Uneaten, untouched food goes into storage containers. When I inspect your work, I'll tell you which container goes into the fridge and which goes into the freezer. In advance, thanks for your help. Shannon and I will retire to the porch to enjoy the fresh evening air."

The bottle of Calvados is opened and the brown ambrosia is eased into two snifters. The sisters settle in for relaxation.

"I'm not throwing you out, but when do you have to leave?"

"Tomorrow afternoon. I pulled the eleven-to-seven. We are making another buy-and-bust. So we can drink and laugh to our hearts' content. How about you?"

"I report at 7:00 AM. So, a hangover is not an acceptable way for me to start my tour."

"You are still the goodie-two-shoes."

"No, I'm a police officer who is raising two children on her own and trying to solve a series of complex seemingly intertwined cases."

"That sounds like someone throwing their own pity party."

"Jaysus, it does, doesn't it. How do you deal with pressure without whining?"

"I hold firm the belief that I am making the streets safe for the citizens and that job requires an occasional sacrifice on my part. If truth be known, occasionally I take out my anger and frustration on a perp. A not-so-gentle interrogation in an alley gets answers I want and relieves my pent-up emotions. Plus, they're all too embarrassed to complain that they were tuned up by a female. So, it's a win-win for me and the department. And I have a few evenings at the hotel bars."

"I can't do that."

"Then get to a gym and hit the heavy bag. Better yet, find a man and get laid, for gawd's sake!"

XI

Liz checks her gym bag: sneakers, socks, shorts, official TPD T-shirt, underpants, sports bra, shampoo, body wash, deodorant, hair brush, toothpaste and brush, and towel. Everything's there. The bag is tossed onto the minivan's passenger seat. After the backyard race fiasco and yesterday's holiday drinking, she has to recommit herself to being in better physical shape. The fact that Shannon's figure is trim is another reason for Liz to regain her body's health and vitality. Looking at Shannon, Liz felt like a female version of the famous doughboy. Competition between siblings is very strong. Starting today, she is on a path of physical redemption…Monday, Wednesday, and Friday, noon to one.

The gym at headquarters is always busy. In the absence of mirrors, men and women preen and strut around the large room seeking human admiration and validation of their bodywork. Is this a place to "put it out there" as suggested by Dr. Lang? She is almost embarrassed to think about that. Liz's routine is simple: run thirty minutes on the treadmill; twelve-minute miles at a six percent grade and fifteen minutes on the weight-machines; abs, arms, and shoulders. Showering and dressing for work leave no time in her lunch hour for lunch. She will have to eat two pieces of fruit, an energy bar, and a plain yogurt at her desk. Gracia does not like people eating at their desks. Big whoop! Her workout program demands it.

The first mile on the treadmill strains Liz's breathing; she gasps for breath. Mile two is slightly easier. She finally hits her rhythm in the last half-mile. Sweat is pouring off her. Water and a brief rest. To the machines. A medium weight at a slow pace is the surest way to strengthen and build muscles. Crunches on two different machines. Liz will be sore the day after tomorrow. She can't help but notice the young men and women who are very muscular...some are too muscular. These are bodybuilders, not body re-claimers like her. These young studs, male and female, eye each other as casually as they can. Their glances are somewhere between envy and lust. Do they eye her?

Workout complete, getting ready to return to work requires that she share a locker room with women, some of questionable femininity. They don't stare at her and she doesn't stare at them. In the shower, the answer to the big question about seeking help comes to her. She must go outside the department for help in coming to grips with today's activities of the Street Cleaners. Someone untainted by the past, and with no blind allegiance to the force. What about the new ADA, Marion Morrison? He has no link to the corruption and he might welcome the opportunity to make his bones. Is that enough leverage? The next question is how to alert him without revealing what she thinks she knows? Anonymous letter. Letters are opened by administrative assistants. A card. It looks personal and congratulatory, so it will reach Mr. Morrison unopened. She'll buy it, write the message, and drop it in a mailbox before she gets home. Liz feels physically energized from her workout and emotionally energized by her course of action. She knows fatigue will hit hard immediately after dinner.

Dear ADA Morrison,

Congratulations on your appointment. What do you know about the Street Cleaners? Check the files from the 40s and 50s. I'll call Thursday, and we can discuss the present-day situation.

All the best,
Beatrice Potter, a concerned citizen

Liz tells Gracia that she thinks she has a lead on more information about the Hector Lopez murder. She wants to drive to the State Mental Institution at Lake Worth and talk to Enrique Flores.

"Let me remind you that Enrique is in a mental hospital because he suffers from diminished capacity. Any new information you may get from him must be viewed in this context. Besides, the trial got all usable information from him before he was institutionalized. You'll be wasting your time."

"It is never a waste of time for me to talk to my husband's killer. If I leave now, I can be back to close out the tour at my desk."

Reluctantly, he agrees and volunteers to call ahead to facilitate her entry into the facility.

The drive across the peninsula takes a little under ninety minutes. The building is simple, large, and formidable. The only windows above the first floor appear to be small slits. She parks, enters the sunlit but sterile lobby, and announces her reason for being there. She fills out the visitor log with name, badge number, date and time. In five minutes, a man appears from a side door. Orderly? Nurse? Doctor?

"Good morning, Mrs. Kimble. I'm Ralph. I'll walk you to the interview room where Mr. Flores is waiting."

They are buzzed through the side door and walk down a hall that takes a circuitous route to the rear of the building. The hall is brightly lit. The doors along the hall walls are closed and labeled with names of what or who is beyond them. The floor is beige and the walls are eggshell. The entire look is non-jarring and non-threatening. Almost calming. Other than the gentle footsteps of Liz and her escort, there is no noise in the hallway. The visitation room is painted in the same bland colors.

"Here we are. I must warn you that Mr. Flores may be unresponsive or he may slur his speech. He took his meds about an hour ago and their initial impact is still in effect. So I advise you to speak slowly and softly. And be patient. He is cuffed and secured to his chair and his legs are shackled, so he can't hurt you. You'll be safe. If you need assistance, I will be at my desk just outside that door. Simply call out and I'll be at your side in a few seconds. Enrique, this is Ms. Kimble, she wants to talk to you."

Ralph exits the visitation room, which is a roughly ten-by-ten square space with two small, thin, horizontal windows near the ceiling. The limited natural light is augmented by fluorescent tubes in two panels nestled in the white ceiling. The table is dark green metal and the two chairs match. They are bolted to the floor and have no padding. No one is to change the seating arrangement or to stay seated for a long time.

"Good morning, Enrique. How are you today?"

His eyelids are drooping, his head nods, and spittle is visible on his lips.

"My name is Liz. I'd like to talk with you today. Is that OK with you?"

Enrique raises his head and offers a small subtle smile as he nods agreement.

"Did you bring cookies? I like cookies. Chocolate chip. I like all cookies. Especially chocolate chip cookies."

"Sorry, I have no cookies."

"That makes me sad."

"I'd like to talk about your days in Tampa and your friends, Los Hermanos. Do you remember the men in that group?"

A series of small nods.

"Do you remember someone named Hector Lopez?"

Enrique offers a blank stare as he searches his fog-shrouded brain. Then he nods and grins.

"Hector is my friend. He helps me. Is he here with you?"

"Sorry, he could not join me on this visit. How does Hector help you?"

"He gives me money and stuff when I need it. He gives me cookies."

"Is there another way Hector helps you?"

Enrique stares straight ahead as if in deep thought.

"He warns me about the police."

"What does he tell you?"

Liz leans into Enrique as if to get inside his scrambled brain and find the truth.

"He tells me when the police are coming."

"Where are they coming to?"

"To our special place. He tells me the police are coming to our special place."

"Is Hector at your special place?"

"No, he is far away."

"How does he warn you?"

"He calls me on my phone."

"When he warns you, does he tell you anything else?"

"He tells me to get my gun and be ready for war."

"Do you do what he tells you?"

"Yes, I shoot at a cop or two."

"Thank you for telling me that. Now, I have two more questions."

"I'm very tired. They gave me a shot. I only get a shot when I have been acting up, as they say. The shot makes me sleepy. But, I wasn't acting up. I was quiet. Why did they give me a shot?"

"Just two more questions. I'll be brief. Do you know Umberto Rosario?"

"He is a friend of Hector, but I don't know him."

"Do you know Eduardo Montenegro?"

"No."

"Thank you for your time today."

"Do you have a gift for me?"

"I didn't bring a gift, sorry. Maybe next time."

Enrique's smile goes away. Liz slowly rises from her chair and calls for Ralph. He escorts her to the lobby where she signs out. Seated in the squad car, Liz is trembling. Her mind is whirling as if it is in a waterspout. Her brain is covering the events surrounding Sandy's murder, creating non-stop confusion and anxiety. Hector knew of the raid because someone told him did the police tell Hector to tell Enrique did Hector tell Enrique to get his gun and station himself on the opposite side of the street from the hangout did the police set all this in motion to be sure that all Los Hermanos OGs would be killed was Sandy's death collateral damage or was he a target what did the police have against Sandy this never came out at the trial because Enrique confessed and was protected by lawyers and doctors the police had their killer so they did not push the issue...

The little voice of survival whispers in her head, "breathe, Liz, breathe." She stops the mental and emotional hurricane and takes five slow, deep breaths. During the drive back to Tampa, Liz churns all these thoughts trying to find the answers. She's not thinking like a rational objective police detective, because Sandy is involved. She is thinking like an angry and confused widow. Her visit to Enrique has re-opened an old wound and poured the pain of iodine into it.

"Mr. Morrison, you have a call from Beatrice Potter."

"Thanks, I'll take it."

"Ms. Potter. I'm glad you called. How can I help you?"

"Mr. Morrison, did you dig into the archives and review the information as I suggested?"

"Yes, I did, although I'm not sure what that piece of history has to do with Tampa today."

"I will tell you what I know and what I think when we meet."

"OK. When can you come to my office?"

"Not in your office. There are spying eyes all over the city. Let's meet at a discrete location. Say, Cady's Grille on 4th Street in St. Pete. Do you know the place?"

"No, but I'm sure I can find it."

"Good. Is tomorrow, that's Friday, at four suitable with you?"

"That's fine. How will I know you?"

"I'll recognize you. See you then."

Marion Morrison hangs up and grins. Is this the mystery that may further his career? Or are these the whisperings of a delusional paranoid who is trying to suck him into her fantasy? Or is this a trap set by someone who thought he should have gotten Morrison's position? Will this crush his career in Tampa before it gets started? What the hell, one visit can't hurt.

"Damn, Liz, I don't know why you dragged me into this mess."

"You are the corroborating third party. No axe to grind and the only historian I trust."

Leonard Sly is nervous. Did he kick the hornet's nest in an attempt to help a friend? Will the hornets swarm back on him? He's resigned to the gambler's code of *in for a dime, in for a dollar*? Are his hands clean enough for restaurant eating or is the grime under his nails and in the folds of the skin on his hands from his work obvious? Is his nervous sweat obvious?

At four-ten, a well-dressed, well-groomed man enters the dining room. He approaches the booth where Liz and Leonard are seated.

"Beatrice Potter?"

"Yes, Marion Morrison?"

"Yes."

"Please be seated. Allow me to make formal introductions...I am Police Detective Liz Kimble and my friend is Sergeant Leonard Sly. We are both members of the Tampa PD. Here are our IDs. May we see yours?"

"Sure."

The confirmation is necessary for the safety of everyone.

"After our conversation, were you able to further review the DA files from the 40s and 50s?"

"Yes, and I made copies of all documents in which the Street Cleaners were mentioned. Not that many pages. There were more innuendos and allegations in the newspaper clippings than facts in the formal files of our office. I surmised that the Street Cleaners were a minor factor in local politics sixty or seventy years ago. Then, they were either disbanded or simply dissolved as a group. They have been non-existent since the 50s. So, now that's out of the way. Why the clandestine meeting, Detective Kimble? And why is Sergeant Sly here with you? He can't be your protection."

"Leonard has critical knowledge about the subject at hand...present-day actions of the Street Cleaners, while I have a bunch of seemingly disconnected theories about their activities. We came to you to see if you can help us find answers to our questions."

"First, let me say that any illegal actions on the part of any member or members of the police department are within the purview of the Internal Affairs Bureau, not the District Attorney's office. So, you have brought to my attention something that may be way beyond my scope of influence. Any investigation must be conducted by the police."

"We came to you and not IAB because we are concerned that the present-day Street Cleaners have influence within IAB. From what I've learned about the vigilante organization, one of their present-day members could be a ranking officer in IAB."

"Let's assume for the moment that the Street Cleaners have remained dormant for a long time, and did not just cease to exist. Why would they be resurrected now?"

"Sir, the Street Cleaners have never been dormant. They've just stayed under the radar, invisible to the public. Other members of law enforcement have turned a blind eye toward the corruption. They started by being a silent force against evil. Gradually, they morphed into a vigilante organization that set its own rules for right and wrong, good and evil. The violence they inflicted became partially visible to anyone who could read a newspaper or watch a TV news show. So to avoid deeper public scrutiny they went underground. Their acts of violence were kept out of the public eye. The deaths were ascribed by the department to gang activity. Bodies were buried not dumped. Gradually, original members of the gang retired. Before they retired, they inducted their sons into the gang. This process went on for three or four generations. Tampa became a safe city, so the need for vigilante justice was no longer a priority. Within the past ten years the new Street Cleaners have been promoting gang corruption that is besmirching the image of Tampa. They want Tampa to be restored to its former brilliance as a very safe city. This gives them the reason to make a lot of illegal money. They control the gangs by taking extortion money to let the gangs operate. So on one hand, the police cry out against gangs and with the other hand they take their slice of all illegal activities of the same gangs."

"All of this paints an interesting conspiracy theory because it might contain a few grains of truth. Just grains. I need more than a conspiracy theory to embark upon an investigation that will piss off the police department and the Mayor."

For the next hour, Liz and Leonard reveal what they know and what they think about the murders of Hector Lopez, Umberto Rosario, and Eduardo Montenegro. The blood in the storage building at the Impound Lot. Enrique Flores' conversation about the raid and Sandy Kimble's death. Los Hermanos and Muy Loco. ADA Morrison takes copious notes. Finally, Liz hands the ADA the list of names of possible present-day Street Cleaners.

Oachoa	*Winters*
Brawley	*Schliemann*
Gracia	*Antes*
Mettle	*Montoya*
Hernandez	*Fernandez*
Qito	*Salvatore*

"This is all very interesting. What you have given me is a large splattering of points, dots if you will, with no logical or provable lines connecting the dots. Assume for the moment that I believe what you have said and what you have shown me. Before I go forward with a full-scale investigation, I will have to do much more homework. Whatever I do...whatever *we* do from now on, must be done in secrecy until we are ready to announce our findings or simply and quietly stop our investigation. Over the next week, I may call upon you for information or confirmation of facts. How can I reach you without getting others involved?"

"Call me on my personal cell. Here's the number."

"Call me at the Impound Lot. The call does not go through the police phone system. And there are no big ears or prying eyes there. When you call, please do not use your name or title. Refer to yourself as Mr. Potter, Beatrice's husband."

"OK, then let's plan to meet in my office one week from today after five. Most people will be heading home by then so we should have privacy. Is that agreeable?"

Two people nod. The three shake hands as confirmation of their pact.

"Hey guys, we need to talk about Christmas. I was thinking we should do something special. Just the three of us. I was thinking we could go to the Keys. Take the ferry from Fort Myers. Two overnights then the ferry back for the drive home. We'll do it between Christmas and New Year's. Waddaya think?"

"Fantastic."

"I like it. It will mean no baseball practice but for a second-team member, that's not a problem."

"The trip will be a large part of your gifts. Mrs. Santa may be able to scrounge up a few little items for her favorite teens. So, are you still good to go?"

"Mom, that is so cool. My crew will be jealous."

"Can we snorkel while we're there?"

"Sure, Alex, why not?"

"If we're all in, I'll start to make the reservations."

"As I mentioned on Friday, I have to work today because I took Thursday as PTO. Sunday is a great day to get all the forms completed and calls to other voicemails asking for information. I'll be home by four. We'll have dinner at six."

Liz spends three hours as a Data Entry Specialist and the rest of her time at a crime scene…sorting through the details of Willie Collins' murder. He and Brenda got into it and she repeatedly sank a ten-inch, heavy-duty carving knife into his chest, neck, and face. The parking lot of their apartment complex was alive with unies, squad cars with blinking lights, and Detective Kimble. The yellow tape around the crime scene created a little island. The ME confirmed TOD and the fact that the blade entry points slashed several arteries and vital organs. He did note that two of the entry wounds appeared to be post-mortem. There were no hesitation marks. All the stabbing was done with substantial force, apparently driven by deep-rooted anger. Liz deduces that Brenda's rage continued after Willie was on the ground. Brenda is not crying. She is stoic. She knows what she did to relieve her rage and is no longer angry.

Forms filed, Liz heads for home to wash off the stink of the day.

"Mom, there was a guy here today looking for Dad. This guy knocks on the door and asks to speak to Dad. I told him that Dad died two years ago. He was not surprised. He said that police work is very dangerous, and that all policemen and policewomen should be careful. He apologized for the intrusion. I asked for his name, but he said it didn't matter. Then he turned, walked to his car, and drove away. It was all weird."

"What did the man look like, Alex?"

"He was a big man with a big belly, baggy pants, a handlebar moustache, and a mullet. You know one of those haircuts hockey players have."

"What did his car look like?"

"It was a gray four-door with cracks in the windshield and rust spots on the hood. A real clunker. Who was he?"

"I have no idea. My guess is some misguided stranger. Now, let's get dinner ready. No turkey."

"Huzzah."

Liz stands very still. The hair on her neck is prickly tall, and there is a growing knot in her stomach. The blood rushing through her system is pulsing loudly in her ears. Her pulse rate quickens. Breathing is short and shallow. Nervous sweat starts to form on her upper lip and in her armpits. Someone is watching her and they want her to know they are watching. They have involved her children. The visit to her home is not an accident. The message is clear…Sandy is dead and she could be next. They must have an idea that she is looking into their activities. Are they tracking her every move? This is now war. She must tell Leonard and ADA Morrison about the man in the car.

XII

"Kimble and Leach, in my office, now."

It's Gracia-gruff Monday.

"Where are you on the various investigations? Leach?"

"On the Marshall Ross murder, we are back at square one. All the leads have come up empty. I still think the non-grieving widow is culpable of something. Maybe, she is guilty of just being selfish, but not the death of her husband. That said, I'm not convinced she's totally innocent."

"Nicely ambiguous. Kimble, in your report you noted that she said her husband had no enemies, but he had 'fractious business relationships.' Well, maybe fractiousness became anger and hatred. Leach, look into all people and companies that sued Ross and/or his company in the past five years. Look for any settlements that were way lower than the amounts stated in the initial lawsuits as well as suits that were dismissed. Getting cheated big time or several times may be reason enough to kill. Kimble, what about the murders of Lopez and Rosario?"

"There appears to be a tenuous connection between the two. I have multiple theories of the crime. Number 1: Los Hermanos may have tried to rid itself of the stink of two OGs. Theory Number 2: just as Los Hermanos shot callers claim, the deaths of two OGs are on Muy Loco. I understand they are worried about Muy Loco encroaching on their territory. The murders could be a signal to Los Hermanos that Muy Loco is the new Big Dog. Theory Number 3: the murders may be a way to deflect police interest in Los Hermanos and onto Muy Loco. As with theory Number 1, Los Hermanos did the crime."

"Jesus, you've got multiple suspects and too many conflicting theories. Very ambiguous. I need clarity not fog."

"Wait, there's more. Benito de Vila said he heard Roberto say not to worry about Muy Loco encroachment; he was told that help is coming. So they must sit tight and not react to Muy Loco's moves. That leads to Theory Number 4; the help is coming from outside the city. A rival gang may be moving in, will absorb Los Hermanos, and eliminate Muy Loco. I want to go back and talk to Roberto Ricardo, Jose Hernandez, and Benito de Vila. The first two gave us just enough half-truths to lead us down wrong paths. Their stories were close but didn't quite match. I have more digging to do."

"Two bodies and three possible killers. Two gangs hate each other so their involvement is to be expected. The third possible killer is an unknown, uncorroborated force outside the city that may or may not be involved as support or to swallow up one of the gangs. Holy crap! I need a scorecard just to know the names of the players. You'd better settle on one theory and solve the crimes, quickly. The brass doubts our ability to serve the public. The Watch Commander referred to my squad as clowns in the car. That's not good for me. And, more important, it's not good for you. I'm sure you like your job and don't have a burning desire to go back to uniform-duty patrolling the streets, if you get my drift."

"I understand, sir."

"Where is the murder of Eduardo Montenegro in all these theories?"

"Montenegro was a Muy Loco. Los Hermanos claims he tried to join their gang, but they rejected him, so he joined Muy Loco. I find that line of reasoning not credible, because Montenegro was from El Salvador as are most of the Muy Locos. Most of the Los Hermanos are Hondurans. Why would a Salvadoran try to join a gang of his historically sworn enemies? I suspect that Los Hermanos killed Montenegro to send a message to Muy Loco to stay away. Or this new, outside force did the killing for them. I will follow up with Dannello. I think there is a strong connection between the Montenegro murder and the others."

"Jesus, I can barely follow you. So, I'm sure the DA's office won't be able to. And thus, no arrests, no grand jury, no trial, no conviction. What you have so far is a big mess. Clarity, Kimble, clarity. What about your visit to Enrique Flores?"

"No help whatsoever. He is an over-medicated, drooling mess. When I saw him, he could recall nothing. Absolutely, no help."

"I told you he would be no help. Work closely with Bob Dover. He knows the gang activities throughout the state. That's it. Let's close the cases before Christmas, if you please. That would be a present the entire city could enjoy."

A police axiom is that building a solid case is like building the Great Wall of China using only a child's small plastic blocks; each small block attaches to and builds on another that builds on another that builds on another, until finally the Great Wall is built. There are not instant walls. Liz must spend a day finding the small blocks and seeing if they can be used to build a big wall. Dover is jammed and will have a sit-down with her tomorrow. Dannello is out for the day. Message left. This is a workout day. A day to loosen stiffness and strengthen sore muscles. Oh, joy! Then more data entry and archive digging. Oh, joy! Oh, joy! It's great to be a detective and solve major crimes!

Bob Dover tells Liz he is not positive of any gangs in the state presently making moves on Tampa. But, he would not totally discount Orcas from Orlando. They're getting squeezed by the local Gang Task Force, and may have plans to get out of Orlando and move into the Gulf Coast territory. Liz tells him that she is going back to talk to the three Los Hermanos that were at the bodega, and asks Bob to keep her looped into any chatter he may pick up on gang activity in other parts of Florida.

She fills in Tony Dannello and asks if she could talk to the shot callers of Muy Loco about any involvement in the Lopez and Rosario murders, as well as the murder of Montenegro. He agrees to arrange a sit-down. He will get back to her this afternoon.

Liz walks to the bodega at the intersection of Platt and Plant. There they are: her best Hispanic friends. They do not smile as she approaches.

"Buenos dias, mi amigos."

"Very good, chika, your Spanish sounds almost natural. Maybe you have some of our blood."

"How quickly you've forgotten. It's not chika. My first name, and you can all me by my first name, is police. My second name is detective. I need to ask you a few follow-up questions."

"Sorry for the disrespect. Are we under arrest? Will you put the cuffs on us and drag us down to police headquarters?"

"No, Jose. No arrests and no cuffs. Just a few friendly questions and answers among compadres. I walked here, so there is no squad car for you to alert the neighborhood. I came alone, so you have nothing to fear. I am one police detective in search of clarity, and you can give me that clarity."

"I doubt it."

"Jose, two years ago during the raid on your old hideout, where was Hector Lopez?"

"Don't know. Do you guys know?"

"No."

"No."

"Was he here in Tampa or was he out of town?"

"He was in Tampa. We don't know where because it was before we were told such things. That information was for OGs only."

The problem with lying is that the liar must remember every detail of the lie, as well as know the truth. In this situation, Roberto is the liar.

"Was Hector a friend of Enrique Flores?"

"I think they were cousins. Not close cousins. I think their families came from the same village where everybody is related. Hector was older."

"So as an older cousin, Hector looked after Enrique. Is that correct?"

"Hector took care of Enrique. Enrique is slow. Hector watched out for him. Making excuses for his screw-ups."

"Do you think Eduardo Montenegro could have killed Lopez or Rosario?"

"No way, Detective. This I know for real. He was a coward, like all Salvadorans. Not brave like us... Hondurans."

"Do you know a gang called Orcas from Orlando?"

"I heard of them. They are a mixed gang of black and white street hustlers. No big deal."

"Do you know they are planning an expansion move into Tampa?"

"No way, Detective. We will defend our neighborhood and the people who live here against any gang, anytime."

"Do you know Orcas have formed an alliance with Muy Loco to take over the city?"

"That's caca."

"I'm just repeating what I heard from our Gang Unit. You guys are in trouble of becoming useless, obsolete, and forgotten like old women. I think that's why your little group killed Montenegro. To send a message of strength. To tell Muy Loco and Orcas that you are the top dogs in Tampa, just like you were three years ago, before the police destroyed your gang."

"We do not kill, because killing brings publicity and cops. Things we don't want. Nobody can destroy Los Hermanos. We have adapted to the new world without the OGs. We are the new leaders that will bring Los Hermanos back to the top."

Jose's voice is loud and strident. He is obviously shaken by Liz's assertions.

"OK. That's it for now. If I need to talk to you again, I'll just walk to your corner."

Tony Dannello is a fifteen-year veteran of the force, dealing exclusively with the issue of gangs...from street crime and extortion, to robberies, and murder. He was a friend of Sandy's.

"Liz, let me do the introductions. Be cautious of what you say and how you ask questions. Muy Loco members live up to the gang's name. To say they are volatile is an understatement. They can fly off the handle at any perceived slight, regardless of how insignificant you may think a comment or question is. Treat the two men we'll meet with respect."

"Are you telling me how to get information from a gang member...a criminal? Are you telling me to treat thugs like upstanding citizens?"

"No, I was just trying to give you a heads-up about these two guys. I have been working them for three years. I have their confidence. They're open with me. And I want them to be open with you."

"Got it."

Liz is aware that Tony tried to get close to her after Sandy was murdered. Too close. He offered comfort... and dinner. She was not ready for a new adult male in her life and took offense at Tony's thinly veiled attempt to bed her. But, she won't let his faux-protective instinct or carnal desires interfere with her investigation. She will use the time-honored "good cop-bad cop" procedure. Let him be the silent good cop. While she is the questioning bad cop. Tony has arranged the sit-down at a small patch of green in Muy Loco territory. He feels it is safer if they are all in view of the public.

"Good afternoon, Geraldo. Good afternoon, Alberto. Permit me to introduce Detective Liz Kimble. She is the one who requested this sit-down. Liz, I am pleased to introduce Geraldo Jimenez and Alberto Cosmarti."

His cloying deference is unnerving. He is acting like some low-level official at the Court of St. James. These guys are street thugs. They deserve no such niceties. No one shakes hands. The two police sit at a concrete table facing Geraldo and Alberto. Liz takes control.

"Thank you for seeing me today. I would like your help in clearing up a few issues on which the police force is working."

Geraldo and Alberto turn their heads. Liz can't see their eyes behind the black aviator glasses. But she knows the two are not looking at her. They are sending a clear message; Liz is not there. She is insignificant. Their way of showing disrespect to this woman. She'll put an end to their grab for power at her expense.

"What do you want?"

The question from Geraldo was directed at Tony. A less-than-subtle slap in Liz's face.

"It's not what I want…it's what Detective Kimble wants."

"We don't know her. Who is she anyway?"

"I am the police detective who needs your help, just like Detective Dannello needs your help from time to time. I am a representative of the same police force as Detective

Dannello. So you can help us or not. It's your call. But, if you don't help us, we won't be able to help you when Los Hermanos tries to take over your territory. Now, take off your glasses, and look at me when we speak."

The glasses are not removed.

"That bunch of Honduran pickpockets can't even keep their neighborhood safe. What makes them think they can move on us?"

"They have the backing of the Orcas from Orlando. The two gangs combined create a mighty force. Strong enough to push Muy Loco out of the picture forever."

"Caca. Orcas would never hook up with those putas."

"I wouldn't bet on that."

"I would."

"Who killed Eduardo Montenegro?"

"Los Hermanos."

"Not likely. Would you kill one of your own to throw suspicions onto Los Hermanos?"

"Not Eduardo. He was a good member of our organization."

"We are aware that Eduardo tried to join Los Hermanos but was rejected. Then he joined Muy Loco. Why would you take in a second-hand reject?"

"Salvadorans stick together."

"He tried to reject his Salvadoran heritage by joining a Honduran gang. And still Muy Loco took in the traitor."

"He never spoke to those putas. He was Salvadoran all the way."

"OK. If he was such a good member of your organization, and a true-blue Salvadoran, why have you not retaliated against Los Hermanos for killing him?"

"Killing brings you people. You are here now asking foolish questions about his death."

"You're correct, he was killed and we are here now. But my questions are not foolish. Would the Orcas join forces with an organization that can't protect its members or seek retaliation for the murder of a member? I doubt it. I think Orcas see Muy Loco as a minor group to be eliminated. They want to move into Tampa and join with Los Hermanos. They keep the strong and get rid of the weak, that's you. That's Muy Loco."

"Chika, we are done."

Alberto is talking to Liz as Geraldo stares straight ahead pursing his lips. Tony is no longer a factor in the conversation.

"Al and Gerry, we're done when I say we're done. And when you speak to me refer to me as Detective. I am not your chika. Who killed Hector Lopez and Umberto Rosario?"

"Not Muy Loco. Los Hermanos were cleaning house. Getting rid of the stink of two OGs."

"Would Orcas have killed them?"

"No. It was Los Hermanos."

"Are you sure it was not Muy Loco?"

"Damn, chika, you are not listening. It was Los Hermanos."

"Damn, Al you're not listening. I am not your chika. When you speak to me refer to me a Detective. If you want me to respect you, you'd better respect me. I have the power and authority to make your life a living hell. Think of that and me over the next few weeks. Well, thank you for your time today. If I need any more information, I'll reach out later."

The two police detectives get up from the table, while the two gang members remain seated and stare in their direction. People near the table had stopped to listen to the loud voice of the interviewee responding to the soft voice of the interviewer. Sandy told her once to never lose your cool during an interview. Maintain well-modulated tone, soft volume, and a gentle but firm demeanor. Let the perp be the one to lose his cool and raise his voice. Speak softly, but carry a big stick...the stick of arrest. It makes the perp vulnerable to the truth.

"Jesus, Liz. You came on really strong with those guys. Maybe a little too aggressive."

"Tony, I have multiple murders on my plate. I don't have time for niceties with street thugs. These guys made it obvious from the beginning that they did not respect me. They acted as if I weren't even at the table. So I made sure they knew that I am due their respect. I am the detective asking the questions. I am in charge. They must understand that I am the detective who could ruin their life. I thought our good cop-bad cop scenario went well. My guess is that the next time you're in touch with Alberto and Geraldo they will be cooperative because they know how beneficial cooperation with the good cop can be. Plus, I'll bet they don't want to see me again. But, I'll tell you this, if I want to speak to them again, I will. With you or not. Is that understood?"

Back at headquarters, Liz and Archie begin to review and codify their knowledge and assumptions.

"Kimble, I found some interesting information about lawsuits against Marshall Ross and Ross Concept Living. Nearly every community he built in the last ten years has had a suit or mechanic's lien against it. Not earth-shattering. But, five of the seven suits were by the same subcontractor, Builder's Alliance. Builder's Alliance is a front for Santo Infante's gang. They are big in sweetheart contracts and shakedowns. Now, my question is, why would a subcontractor continue to do business with a General Contractor who the sub sues on a regular basis? My guess is that Builder's Alliance sues Ross's Concept Living as a normal revenue stream. The suit is settled. Concept Living or the insurance company pays. Then Infante sends a special thank you to Marshall Ross.

"A brown paper bag loaded with cash would be Marshall Ross's cut for fleecing his own company and the insurance company. The last suit was the most recent court case. I'll bet Ross told Infante that their business relationship was over unless Ross got a bigger slice of the payout pie. Infante was pissed off and decided to end the business relationship on his terms before anybody got wise to the scam. Why the insurance company didn't bring this cozy partnership to light is interesting. I suspect someone at the insurance company is complicit in the illegal activities. I need to dig into the insurance company records. Maybe someone at that end was also getting money. Then, I'm going to dig into the tax records of Marshall Ross and his company. Follow the money. I think I've uncovered the real motive for Ross's murder."

Have they uncovered another possible suspect for Marshall's murder? But why the violent act that would end a sweetheart deal?

XIII

The elevator ride to the twelfth floor is non-stop. Most of the people in the building have already left for the weekend or are jamming the down elevators. Friday is a half-day of work for most of the denizens of floors ten and above. Two of the perks of seniority are upper floors with views and half-days on Friday. Some exploit the work policy by leaving their offices before noon. They have early tee or court times.

There is no receptionist. There is no noise of human activity. Liz has no idea where Marion Morrison's office is. She'll have to find it by walking the halls. Halfway down the long central corridor, a door opens and there he is.

"Hello, Detective."

"Hello, Mr. Morrison."

"Marion, please."

"Then Liz, if you please."

"Come in. Mr. Sly is already here."

She follows him through a reception area toward his office. They turn to the left and enter a conference room. Leonard is sipping water from his ever-present plastic bottle.

"We were waiting for you so we could discuss the information on the white boards. And hopefully, you could add some of what you have recently learned. Now we can get started."

"I know it sounds crazy and paranoid, but were you followed, Liz?"

"No. I left my car in the police lot and walked. As you had suggested, I walked through two department stores before circling back to this building. I'm sure no one was able to follow me. So let's begin."

"OK. The situation is this; we have three dead men. Killers unknown. Reasons unknown. Hector and Rosario were former members of Los Hermanos and Eduardo was a Muy Loco. What is their connection?"

"Gentlemen, I think I can shed some light on these points. We have been interviewing members of the two gangs and I've come to the conclusion that neither gang had anything to do with the murders. For all their posturing, they are more confused than we are. I also got a glimmer of something that is disconcerting. Both gangs appear to be connected to a source of muscle outside their little street worlds. I probed the possibility of a gang outside of Tampa making a move on the territory of either Los Hermanos or Muy Loco. The leaders dismissed this as crap, but they are looking outside their membership for help in dealing with the other gang. The phrase "told to wait" was used. If this is an accurate assessment of their situation, they are beholden to someone to protect them. There is no other force able to protect them other than the police force. But why would the force protect the gangs."

"Liz, that's great. If this outside force is stirring the pot for their own benefit, we may be looking at Street Cleaners' activities. I'll add that to the board. But what is the benefit they derive?"

"The power and money of control."

"Leonard, explain."

"They pit the gangs against each other to maintain the balance of power on the streets and thus in the city. The reason the gangs exist is because they are allowed to exist. Street Cleaners need the gangs to exist, because the gangs are a source of revenue for the Street Cleaners. Street Cleaners don't want either gang to become too powerful, so they kill a member or two and blame the other gang. Then they'll tell the gangs to wait for help. Help comes in the form of a reprisal…a member of the other gang is killed. Neither gang is guilty of murder. Each is beholden to the Street Cleaners. The brutality of the murders indicates to me that each was meant to send a message to both gangs. The message is that the gangs are not in charge. Street Cleaners are in charge."

"That goes on the board. But, Leonard, Hector Lopez was out of the life. Why kill him now?"

"Not sure. Liz?"

"We do know that Lopez had been receiving cash payments from an unknown source or sources after he left Los Hermanos. Could he have been a snitch taking payoffs? Were the payers Street Cleaners?"

"Liz, that's likely. But what did he tell the cops to be an earner? And why was he killed now?"

"Not so much *tell* the Street Cleaners but more like *do* for them. Maybe the payers were afraid Lopez was vulnerable to the legit police. Their fear may be based on whatever Lopez did or was doing for them. The payers wanted to tie-up a loose end."

"Another board entry. What about Rosario?"

"I'm afraid he was killed because he was seen talking to me. Street Cleaners could fear that he was going to identify them, so he was eliminated. Someone was keeping tabs on Rosario. Leonard, what about Montenegro?"

"And keeping tabs on you, Liz."

"That's closer than you may think. More on that aspect of our digging shortly."

"We know Montenegro was killed on police property. Killed at a place unknown outside the force. So, it's safe to assume, he was killed by police. What did he do to warrant such a heinous beating? His murderers were very angry. All three of our dead men had their tongues cut out. Normally, this is a not-too-subtle message that these guys were rats. But, in these cases, each tongue removal may be a false clue. A clue that we normally attribute to a gang killing. This may be a way for the Street Cleaners to direct the minds of the regular force investigating the murders away from one gang onto the other."

"Good point, Leonard."

"Marion, let me throw in another murder: Marshall Ross."

"Liz, didn't he die in an auto accident?"

"Auto, yes. Accident, no. Leonard was the first to spot the brake line tampering and that the tampering required knowledge of a BMW. Hector Lopez was a mechanic. He very well could have had that knowledge. Suppose Hector was paid by the Street Cleaners to crimp the line so that fluid leaked and thus rendered the brakes unavailable when needed. Ross dies in a fiery crash. Then the Street Cleaners kill Lopez to keep him quiet. His death was not gang related. It's crime related."

"OK, Liz, but why kill Ross?"

"Many think he got away with the murders of the two toddlers. In the eyes of Street Cleaners, the scales of justice were out of balance and had to be rebalanced. That's the vigilante way. We have chased down numerous leads from the non-grieving wife to hired guns to family and friends of the little boys. We have come up empty. But, here's an interesting twist. Detective Archie Leach thinks he has spotted a connection in previous insurance claims involving Ross Concept Living; the subcontractor, Builder's Alliance; and the insurance adjuster. Builder's Alliance is a front for Santo Infante's gang. They are big in sweetheart contracts and shakedowns.

Given the connection, this is what I think. An insurance claim is filed and found worthy of payment, even though the claim is not contested or negotiated because the adjuster OKs payment. The claim is paid, and all three guilty parties in white collar crime split the proceeds. What if the subcontractor got greedy? Ross would get mad and threaten some form of retaliatory action like exposure. Builder's Alliance wants to nip this action in the bud. They want Ross killed. But they don't want any visible connection between them and Ross. So on the recommendation of the Street Cleaners, Lopez is hired to kill Ross. He tampers with the brake line. Ross dies. Then, to eliminate any path back to the Street Cleaners or Santo Infante, Lopez has to die. The same scenario would also follow if the subcontractor got greedy and wanted to eliminate Ross."

"But what or who is the connection between Builder's Alliance and the Street Cleaners?"

"My guess is a relative. I don't know who."

"So if I understand you, all four murders should be hung on the Street Cleaners. That's almost too much to process."

"Here is something else to throw into the mix. Two years ago, the police raided the hang out of Los Hermanos. Three cops were killed in the shootout. They were killed by a shooter stationed across the street. They were shot in the back by Enrique Flores. I went to see Mr. Flores in the Lake Worth State Mental Institution. He revealed that Hector Lopez had warned him of the raid. Enrique was told to get his gun, go across the street, and fire when the police showed up. The only way Hector could have known about the raid is if he had been told by someone in the police department…a Street Cleaner.

"The only group that wanted maximum damage from a firefight between the police and Los Hermanos would be Street Cleaners. An attack from the rear of the surrounding police force would intensify the shooting to ensure maximum destruction and death. They wanted Los Hermanos dead, and they didn't care if a cop or two died in the process. My guess is that Los Hermanos was becoming too big and powerful to control in the usual ways, so they decided to cut off the head, or in this case, the heads of the snake. The only Los Hermanos not sent to prison to await execution was Flores. He was deemed to be suffering from a diminished capacity. So he sits in Lake Worth. Los Hermanos did not go away as a result of the raid and shootout. It simply was reborn with younger, more controllable leaders. The gang is a neighborhood force offering protection and dealing some drugs. Fairly harmless. Mission accomplished."

"Liz, I read the file about the shootout. I am sorry for your loss. But why would they want to kill your husband?"

"Thank you. He was just in the wrong place at the wrong time. I doubt an ulterior motive. There is one last item. And, this is unnerving. I am sure I've recently been followed. The car was a gray four-door with cracks in windshield and rust spots on the hood. One day a car followed me from home to work. I saw the same car when I was talking to the young punks of Los Hermanos. Then later, in the parking lot of my grocery store when I did some last minute Thanksgiving shopping, I saw a gray four-door with cracks in windshield and rust spots on the hood near my car in the parking lot. Then, my son told me a man came to the house asking for the boy's father, my husband. When Alex told him Sandy died years ago, the man said how dangerous police work was. Alex said the car was a gray four-door with cracks in windshield and rust spots on the hood. Coincidences? I think not.

"My son described the man as big with a big belly, baggy pants, a handlebar moustache, and a mullet. This is a similar description of one of the men who made payoffs to Hector. Maybe that's just a coincidence, but I think not. My son said that Max, our German shepherd mix, did not like the man. When he was talking to Alex, Max's fur was on end and he was growling deep and low. I trust Max's instincts. The only thing I can deduce from all these factors is that some member of the Street Cleaners is aware my digging, and wants me to know I am being watched. So, gentlemen, we are not alone."

"Marion, what can you do to protect Liz?"

"I can't put a policewoman under protective custody because we are investigating the local police force. But, the District Attorney's office has access to a small group of

Florida State Troopers who assist us in certain situations… situations we want to keep out of the newspapers, off the TV channels, out of the newspaper, and away from any local police. There is a woman on the squad. She could shadow Liz."

"No thanks. I refuse protection. Not out of false bravado but because I don't want the thugs to see that they have gotten to me, and therefore, us. If we show them that everything is status quo, they may just back off or will relax so much that they screw up."

"Very risky attitude."

"Marion, thanks for your offer but no thanks. Let's change the subject. What have you learned about the twelve men whose names we gave you?"

"My preliminary investigation has revealed nothing truly out of the ordinary. There are no black marks in anyone's personnel jacket. Twelve spotless records, of officers that have been on the force as long as each of these men is not unheard of. But, it's very, very rare. One oddity is that the name of one of three senior officers appears on the jacket of each of the men. Let me explain. Oachoa, Fernandez, Mettle, and Qito have the same Rabbi, Commander Kelly. Hernandez, Winters, Brawley, and Schliemann are safe beneath the wings of Commander Betancourt. Gracia, Antes, Montoya, and Salvatore owe their stellar careers to Commander Weber.

"I'm not sure what all that really means. But it appears to me that the Street Cleaners operates like a Sicilian mob. The Commanders are the members of a council that runs the show. They are the heads of three mob families. They are capos. We don't know if there is one individual above the three…a capo di tutti capi or boss of all bosses. The twelve men who are beholden to the three capos are captains or senior lieutenants. Just like in the mob. That's what it looks like to me. So I believe this avenue must be pursued. I have much more exploring.

"If we assume this organization functions like a mob, there is another avenue that we must consider – that of the wannabes. Their names are not on this list because they have no familial lock on Street Cleaner membership. But they are trying to become part of the gang. These are the foot soldiers. The true workers. They have to work their way to membership by performing tasks. If my assumption is accurate, these wannabes want a seat at the table, because of the monetary value of that seat. Money drives most enterprise…good and evil. These men see the amount of money Street Cleaners earn, and they want a piece of the money pie. They know a seat at the table is open to those who are the big earners or perform the most onerous tasks. Tasks that are beneath the Street Cleaner membership. Tasks like murder. Expanding on this, being a Street Cleaner means never having to worry about money. This is a far cry from the original premise of the organization…to make the streets safe. Now it is a business of making money for its members like any corporation or organized-crime family."

"Marion, I must get going. I promised my wife a nice dinner out tonight, and I don't want to screw up date night."

"Sure, Leonard. I was done with my report. Yes, indeed, I see it's time for dinner…six-thirty."

"Let me know when you want to meet again."

"How about next week at the same time in my office?"

"Great. See you then."

Leonard leaves Liz staring at the white boards with the names and events listed and thin lines connecting groups of names to three new names. There's so much evil written in black, red, and green markers. So much unsettling and unconnected information.

"Liz, do you have dinner plans?"

"My kids, why?"

"I'd like to continue this conversation, I can't do that by myself, and I'm hungry."

"I guess I can call them. Sure, why not?"

A phone call frees her for the evening. Her children seemed happy that she would not be home for dinner. Were they happy for her or for themselves?

Café LaMond is a trendy eatery for the lawyers and bankers who inhabit downtown during the day. At 7 PM on a Friday, the place is crowded and the bar is two deep. The customers are waiting to sample the latest creation of Pierre LaMond, the chef and owner. Pierre came to Tampa from Boston where he had a large following. The pressure of competition and the constant drive to stretch the envelope of dish creation, coupled with the ever-increasing, crippling cost of doing business, convinced him to leave. And he found an unfettered opportunity to work and live the good life here in Tampa. Now, he takes a weekly occasional day off from his duties.

"Two for dinner."

"Sir, there will be a one-hour wait. May I have your name?"

"Here is my card."

The hostess opens the reservation book to the last page and checks the names on a special list.

"Mr. Morrison, I'm sorry I didn't recognize you. It's nice of you to return. We will find you a table immediately. Would the kitchen be acceptable?"

"That would be great."

The hostess leads Liz and Marion through the bustling dining room; some diners are whispering, while some have voice levels augmented by alcohol. The three walk through the double swinging doors into the frenetic kitchen. As they enter, a middle-aged man who is in command of the chaos looks up from his duties, smiles, and waves. The couple is seated.

"Marion, this is almost too much. They obviously know you. How?"

"When I got divorced, I set several goals. One of them was to eat very well-prepared and delightfully delicious meals whenever I could. Dinner from a deli does not fall within that description. And, I don't aspire to be a chef at home. So regularly I give myself a real treat. I quickly came to know this place and made sure Chef Pierre came to know me. Thus, the immediate seating on Friday night. Would you like a cocktail?"

"I wish I could, but I'm technically on duty and I have to drive home after dinner. But, please feel free to have a cocktail."

"I'm lucky. I live and can dine within walking distance of my office. I have no family, so there is no reason to live in a community of lawns and pools outside the city. And yes, I'll have glass of wine."

"Marion, it's nice to see you again. Who have you brought to my humble eatery?"

"Pierre, permit me to introduce Liz Kimble."

"Well, Liz Kimble, you are a brave soul to be with this man in my kitchen. Would you like a glass of wine?"

"Yes, but no thank you."

"Marion, Pinot or Cabernet?"

"Pinot please, Pierre. And, as usual, we will put you in charge of our meals."

"Bon. I have a very nice grouper. Fresh from the Gulf. Excuse me, I must go to work."

"Marion, this is a strange place to continue our business discussion."

"A very safe and secure place. No prying eyes or eavesdropping. We can speak freely. I want to know why you won't accept my offer of protection."

"First, the protector would be in the way of my family life. My children would become involved in my work. I try very hard to keep my work and my family separate and distant. Alex and Cary have enough on their plates being teens. Protection to keep their mother safe from an unknown would be too much for them to process. Second, I am not a shrinking violet. Since I'm sure you've reviewed my personnel jacket, you are aware that I am an excellent shot and I am proficient in hand-to-hand combat. I can protect myself. So, there is no need for anyone to protect me."

"You win."

Having made her point, Liz smiles at Marion. A coy look between female and male. His wine arrives. The server also places on the table a plate of marinated mussels, a plate of jumbo shrimp, and two small plates. The freshly baked bread and lightly salted butter also arrive. Then individual salads. Cucumber slices, watercress, pitted Italian olives, diced sun-dried tomatoes splashed with a light lemon and tarragon vinaigrette dressing. The server is good. She just appears, takes care of her duties, and disappears. The grouper has been prepared en papillote. When the envelope is opened, the rich aroma of herbs and spices wafts over the diners. The server serves Liz first.

They eat in near silence.

"Excuse my exuberance, but this is marvelous."

"Liz, seafood preparation is only part of Pierre's reputation. His veal and lamb are exquisite."

The dinner then progresses with conversations about her children and how she got to Tampa. Liz steers clear of asking about his divorce.

"OK, what is the real reason you asked me out to dinner?"

"I was hungry and I wanted companionship that was not interested in my wallet. Plus, I wanted to get to know you better."

"Fair enough. Now you know as much as anyone on the force with the possible exception of Leonard."

"What do you really know about Leonard?"

"My children and I are good friends with Leonard and his wife, Helen. When Sandy was alive, my family had dinner with the Slys a few times a year. I know he was shot in the line of duty. He walks with a limp as a result. He was the first to spot the cause of Marshall Ross's accident and showed me the evidence at the Impound Lot. He walked me through the murder scene and explained the history of the Street Cleaners without going through channels. I believe he did so because he knew he could trust no one but me. He is a good man. Honest and trustworthy. Why do you ask?"

"No hidden agenda. I just wanted to know your feelings about him."

"Pardon my language, but bullshit. You were fishing."

"Yes, and I got the answer I was hoping for."

"I'll bet you asked him about me."

"I did, and he feels toward you as you do toward him."

"Spying on both your partners is nervy, don't you think?"

"We are in the initial stages of an investigation that could turn out to be very ugly and dangerous. I wanted to be positive I was working with stand-up cops."

"You are. By the way, I checked you out. You passed muster."

"And you called me nervy."

Liz's coyness shows in her smile and eyes. The server clears and returns with two small dishes of sorbet to cleanse the diners' palates. No coffee is ordered. The check arrives and Marion's Gold Card appears. After the receipt is completed and signed, the couple stands. Pierre approaches.

"No need to ask, the meal was fantastic."

"Thank you, Marion. Ms. Kimble, did you enjoy it as well."

"Very much. I wish I could cook that well. But, I'm afraid that my teens would not appreciate creations like we had. They're more meat and potatoes, mac and cheese, and barbecued chicken types."

"All it requires is imagination, years of training, time, and excellent, fresh elements."

"You lost me at imagination. The meal and the service were superb."

"Thank you. Please excuse me. I must get back to work. Have a pleasant evening."

The couple walks through the dining room and out the front door.

"I'll walk you to your car."

"There's no need."

"I insist. Besides, I want to walk off the meal."

"If you insist."

Five blocks later, they are at the police parking lot.

"Marion, thanks for the lovely evening. I truly enjoyed it."

"Next time...no shoptalk."

"If you insist."

"I do."

A lingering handshake is warm and almost affectionate. They go their separate ways. On the drive home, Liz smiles. A meal with a handsome, well-educated adult male. Did she just put herself out there? Can she consider this her first date in more than two years? It was nice. She thinks about the next time.

XIV

Before she gets two blocks from the parking lot, her phone rings.

"Liz, Liz Kimble. This is Helen, Helen Sly. Is Leonard with you?"

"No, he's not."

"Do you know where he might be?"

"No. He left after our meeting. Said he didn't want to be late for date night. That was well over an hour and a half ago."

"So he's not with you. I'm worried. Worried sick. He never came home and he never called me. I'm frightened something bad has happened to him."

"Let's not jump to conclusions. I'm sure there is a reasonable explanation. Let me do some digging and call you right back."

"Thanks. Please hurry."

Liz calls the squad room. No incident reports. She calls the 911 Dispatch Director. No calls involving Leonard. She is beginning to worry.

"Helen, nothing has been reported that pertains to Leonard. I'm downtown now. I'll drive to you. Can you tell me the route he would normally take from police headquarters to your house? I'll retrace it."

"He most likely would have driven north on I-275 to Bearss. Then east to Adamo. Then north to 147th Terrace. Hurry, please."

Liz begins to trace Leonard's path. She heads to I-275. Along the entire route, she finds nothing to indicate foul play. Route retraced, she finds Helen waiting by the front door.

"Did you see anything?"

"Sorry, no. You should call this in. Let the on-duty unies take the lead. They have more resources than I do. I'll be available by phone if you need anything, and I mean anything."

"Thanks for checking. I just don't know what could have happened or where he is. I'll let you know what the unies say and find. Again, thanks."

They hug. Liz is confused and concerned. Her mind is awhirl with half-random, disconnected thoughts. Dread begins to creep into her consciousness. Accident or murder? If murder, why? Do they know that Leonard is working with Liz and Marion?

"Hey, kids, Mom's home."

Four teenage feet come cascading down the stairs to confront Mom.

"You're late, young lady. Explain yourself."

"Yes, missy. Where have you been at this ungodly hour?"

"I don't think ten-thirty is an ungodly hour for an adult to be arriving home. I told you both I was having a working dinner with Marion Morrison, the new ADA. That's where I've been."

"Sure a business dinner. Until now? It must have been a great meal. Is this Marion a he or a she?"

"Marion Morrison is a gentleman."

"So, you were on a date with a man. Does his wife know he dates police lieutenants?"

"Marion is divorced."

"Ooooh, Mom is seeing a divorced man."

"I'm not seeing Marion…"

"Now it's Marion and not Mr. Morrison. How cozy."

"Dinner started at six-thirty. What took so long? Romantic dinners last longer than regular dinners or dinner with your children."

"Well, first of all, it was not a romantic dinner. It was a working dinner. We finished about eight. Then I had an errand to run."

"Don't try to change the subject. Let's get back to Marion. Is he cute? Is he handsome? Is he a true gentleman? Does he dress well? What does he look like? What are his intentions? What are yours?"

"Holy crap, Cary. You're worse than Torquemada."

"Who's Torki…whatever?"

"When you know, we can continue this interrogation. In the meantime, how was your evening?"

"Always trying to change the subject, aren't you, young lady?"

"Alex, I had a working dinner with an ADA, and then I ran an errand. That is the sum of my evening's activities. We're done talking about it. Is that clear?"

"Mom, Alex and I are excited for you. You need a life outside the department and beyond your adorable children who tonight waited patiently and anxiously by the front door for your return home. It's been two years. We're working hard to move on. Dad would have wanted us to have our own lives and not wallow in the sadness of his death. And by us, I mean all of us. I think you should put yourself out there. Don't hide at home or behind your badge. You're a good-looking, intelligent older woman. I'm sure there are lots of guys who would want to take you to dinner. We say… go for it."

Liz is stunned by the grown-up attitude of her daughter. She is also proud. Sandy would be proud, too. She has a great deal to think about.

"Older, eh? OK, you guys. It's bedtime. Yours and mine. Tomorrow you must attack the shrubs and the lawn. While I plant some flowers in the front beds. It looks like the ones I planted a while ago have decided to perish. Just so you know…I love you both very much and I deeply appreciate your interest in my life."

"That's love life, Mom. Good night."

The thundering herd of two scampers upstairs, while Liz gets a Rolling Rock from the fridge. It will work like a sleeping pill. She wonders what happened to Leonard, but there is nothing more she can do.

Liz retrieves the paper from the bed of dead flowers. Saturday morning is time for a relaxed look at the newspaper. There is the story above the fold on the front page. It hits her.

Bay Times Police Blotter

The body of Leonard Sly, Tampa Police Sergeant, was found in an empty lot at the corner of 22nd Street and Freedom Boulevard. At approximately one-thirty Saturday morning, patrons of Fuzzy's Fun Time Bar discovered Sergeant Sly's body slumped over the steering wheel of what was later determined to be his car. Police were called to the scene and identified the body. The incident report indicates Sergeant Sly died as a result of a gunshot wound to the head. As of this reporting, police are calling the death a suicide. The Sergeant's service revolver was found in his lap. It had been fired once. Sergeant Sly was a thirty-year veteran of the force. He worked at the police department's Impound Lot. He is survived by his wife, Helen, and two adult children.

Tears begin to roll down her cheeks. She can't re-read the article. Liz finds her phone and calls Helen.

"I'm so sorry, Helen. Is there anything I can do?"

Helen's sobbing is contagious. Liz starts.

"Oh, Liz, I don't know. I'm still processing the facts. I have to identify his body and retrieve his personal effects. I'd appreciate it if you went with me to the morgue. I'm not sure I can go there alone. The whole situation is overwhelming. I've called the children. They are on their way to Tampa today. We agreed the service must be held next week. Pfister will handle all the details. I have to meet with our attorney and our banker to understand what happens next for me.

But I can't do that until Monday. I know I need help, I just don't know what or who to ask."

"The department has someone on staff who knows all of that. They can be a big help. Let me do some digging. I'll get you their home phone number."

"Thank you, Liz."

"We can go to the morgue today, if want."

"Yes, I need to get that formality out of the way. Can we go there at two?"

"Two, it is. I'll see you then. Hang tough, Helen."

"Bless you, Liz."

Liz makes two more calls. She gets the name and number of the grief counselor from the lieutenant on duty in the squad room and calls Helen back. Then she calls the ME, Dr. Kovalewsky.

"Sorry to call you at home, but I need a huge favor."

"Name it."

"Sergeant Leonard Sly was found dead in his car early this morning. I am a good friend of Leonard and his wife, Helen. She wants to identify the body so Pfister can do the embalming for the funeral next week."

"So you want me to perform an autopsy today."

"By two this afternoon."

"It will be tight, but I can do that for one of ours."

"When you are doing what you do, please look for needle marks and keep any tox screen information out of your preliminary report. Indicate it will be included in the final report but call me with the results before the information is made available. OK?"

"OK and I won't ask why. I'll see you at two in my office."

"Thanks, Doctor."

Liz's must compose herself for the next call.

"Marion, did you read the paper today?"

"Yes, I saw the article about Leonard. I thought he was heading home for date night. He seemed excited about it. Why would he go to Ybor City?"

"I'm not convinced Leonard took his own life."

"What?"

"I think the subjects of our recent conversations are responsible for Leonard's death."

"Go on."

"Leonard was not depressed. Hell, he wasn't even sad. He was as emotionally strong as any of us. I think he was killed because he was working with us…me. Somehow, someway, the bad guys knew of our connection and they learned where he was going. They probably figured out why he was meeting with us. They knew Leonard was a treasure trove of historical information about who is who and what is what. They were afraid he would share this information with someone like you and me. So the cat is now out of the bag. The bad guys are becoming dangerously desperate. They have graduated from killing criminals to killing cops. And they appear to be everywhere. They must be stopped before this mess goes any farther."

"I'm already on it."

"How?"

"Look outside. Look across the street. Three houses down from yours."

"OK. Now what?"

"Do you see a green sedan parked in the driveway? Is the car facing the street or the garage?"

"The street."

"Can you see anyone in the car?"

"No. The windshield is heavily tinted.

"Good. The person you can't see is Sergeant Rose Widdix of the Florida Department of Law Enforcement. She's your bodyguard."

"I told you I didn't want a bodyguard because of my kids."

"I heard you. But that was before the events of last night. This is now. Sergeant Widdix will stay in your neighborhood to ensure nothing befalls you while you are at home. She will not follow you to work or when you have household errands to run on the weekend. She will not follow your children."

"Small consolation. I have to go. I'm meeting Helen at the ME's office so she can identify Leonard. I'll call you after that."

"Kids, I'm going to buy the flowering plants this morning. I'll bring them home. Then I have to go downtown this afternoon. I won't be long. You guys have all day for chores. Dinner tonight at Rigatony's."

During the drive to the morgue, Liz looks for the green sedan. It is not there. Rose is just protection when she is at home. She begins to feel maybe she would like protection when she is not at home.

Helen is strong. She calmly identifies Leonard's body, signs the form, gives Liz a serious hug, and heads home to await her children.

"Doctor, did you find anything worthy of note?"

"Yes, I did. I found a needle mark on the right side of Leonard's neck. The preliminary tox screen revealed a high level of opiates. What does this mean to you?"

"It means that Leonard was murdered. He was abducted, drugged, and then shot. Did you find gunshot residue on his hands?"

"Very little GSR. It's as if someone other than Leonard was holding Leonard's hand on the gun when it was fired. Who would kill Leonard?"

"Better you not ask or know for now. It's safer that way. I need you to violate procedure. I need you to create a second autopsy report. A bogus one indicating self-inflicted death and no drugs or telltale marks. This report will be the official one temporarily. But only for a short time. Then, I want you to give me the true report with all the true findings. Make no copies of the true report. I will take charge of it. And, no questions."

"Falsifying my report will get me fired and you suspended. If you're OK with that, then I guess I'm OK. I only hope you know what you're...we're doing."

"Our secret is safe with me. You are in no danger. If something arises, you will be protected. Your involvement will be praised by the District Attorney's office. You could be a hero."

"What does all this mean?"

"It means Leonard's death is the result of an ongoing investigation that requires deception on the part of the investigators: me and the ADA. Your hands will be clean. OK?"

"OK. The few times I met Leonard, he seemed like a stand-up guy. I hope you get his murderer."

"We will."

Father Renaldi of St. Regis refused to perform a funeral Mass for Leonard because he had committed suicide…a sin. Therefore, the 9 AM service would be held in the chapel of Pfister Mortuary. The chapel normally holds up to seventy-five people. Today, there is a standing-room- only crowd of well over one hundred and twenty five. On the surface, an observer would say that Leonard was well liked by everyone. Liz is examining faces to see if any of the twelve Street Cleaners and their rabbis are there to pay their last respects. Those who feared Leonard might tell others what he knew would have to continue the charade. She spots Gracia, Winters, Antes, and the three Commanders who she feels rule the roost. The service lasts forty-five minutes. The automobile processional to the public cemetery is eight cars and one hearse long. Helen chose a plot near Sandy's.

"Liz, thanks for being by my side during this ordeal. Leonard often said how much he valued his friendship with you and Sandy."

"Helen, I'm so sorry. Leonard was a dear friend and mentor. Will you be all right?"

"No life insurance from the department, because of the way Leonard died. We had small policies to cover our funerals. He was a real saver. I complained about his severe saving efforts. Now I'm grateful for them. I will receive his pension, modified by years of service. I have enough for a while. It will give me time to figure out what I'm going to do. Jennifer has asked me to come and live with her and her family. It's comforting to have a daughter who wants to take care of you when you need it. Leonard Jr. made the same offer. He lives alone in New York. So, that's out. But, I love the thought."

"While you sort things out, please consider me and my children your temporary family. That said, you are invited to dinner after your children leave. And, I won't take no for an answer. Agreed?'

"Agreed. Your timing is perfect, Leonard Jr. and Jennifer are returning to their homes early Friday. And for the first time in a week, I will be alone. I'm not sure I will be strong enough to be alone next week. I would love to see your two. Now, if you'll excuse me, I have to accept the formal condolences from people I'm not sure I know. See you soon."

"Marion, it was depressing. We need to talk in private. Let's meet in the park by the river. Twelve-thirty? I'll meet you by the fountain. I'll bring the sandwiches and drinks. My treat. Hope you like hot-pressed Cubans."

The downtown oasis is dedicated to Jose Marti. The park sits next to the river that empties into the bay, so there is normally a breeze. Trees, fountains, benches, and tables offer office workers and shoppers alike an enjoyable space for temporary rejuvenation. The park is populated by couples sharing food from refrigerated storage containers, people reading while they eat, and even a few people dozing before returning to their daily grind. Liz sits on the ground staring at the blades of grass. A thousand thoughts are bouncing around her brain like the ping-pong balls used in the lottery drawings.

"Excuse me, miss. Is this piece of terra firma taken?"

"Oh, my god. You startled me. It's you."

"You can dispense with the god reference. Call me Marion."

She smiles for the first time in two days. As they open the brown bags, she relates what she knows and has done. Marion takes it all in.

"I think I know how the bad guys figured out that Leonard was involved in the investigation. He gave me a blood sample from the outbuilding at the Impound Lot. I gave it to the ME hoping to corroborate that it was where Montenegro was killed. The ME never got back to me directly. He simply put the information into the file. A file anyone can access. This was Detective Dannello's case. He must have seen the entry and reported the new evidence to Gracia. Gracia put two and two together and came up with the conclusion that someone other than Dannello was nosing around the Montenegro killing. So the source of the information had to be silenced before more got out. Gracia got someone to follow Leonard downtown last Friday. This someone saw Leonard enter your office building. Gracia's conclusion was confirmed. Leonard is a rat and must die. My guess is he was killed by the same guy or guys that followed him. Murder of a cop by a cop is not only abhorrent, it's frightening."

"Your thinking is disconcertingly logical. You and I have got to maintain a low profile for the next few days. Whoever is behind this is becoming justifiably paranoid. They will be looking at everyone they don't know or trust."

"One more thing. At my request, the ME placed a sanitized death certificate in Leonard's file. I had the Doctor complete two death certificates. A true one for me that shows a needle mark on Leonard's neck, a high level of opiates in his blood, and very little GSR on his hand. Not enough to corroborate that he alone fired the gun into his head. Someone must have helped the unconscious sergeant fire the piece. And a sanitized, official one for prying eyes. Whoever reads the official report will feel that he or they are safe from any further investigation. This may buy us some time. It's not much, but it's something."

"Our meeting on Friday will be in a secure location...at my condo at 333 Riverview Terrace. Right after your tour, drive from the police headquarter's parking lot and leave your car in my building's garage. Meeting away from my office will be safer. I have to leave this respite and culinary delight. Gotta chase different bad guys. See you at four-thirty on Friday."

XV

Liz leaves police headquarters and drives as if she were going home. After five minutes, she makes a series of quick turns to lose any unwanted guests. Twenty minutes later, she pulls her minivan into the garage at 333 Riverview Terrace. Announcing herself at the concierge desk gets her to the locked elevator. The doors are opened from the desk. Her chariot awaits. The PH button is already glowing. Doors close and she starts the uninterrupted ride. Destination reached. Doors open to reveal a foyer warmly lit, with large paintings on the other three walls. The small rug looks to be Chinese.

"Welcome. Would you like something to drink?"

"Thank you. Water would be nice."

The living room has floor-to-ceiling, wall-to-wall windows on two sides and more large paintings on the other two walls. The views are spectacular. Streetlights are already on, while office lights are being turned off. The sun is gripping the horizon and holding on for dear life before it falls into the Gulf. Marion's furniture is modern with clean, functional lines. Its simplicity is an interesting visual counterbalance to the intricacies of the Impressionist and Constructivism paintings hung on the walls. She has no way of determining if the furniture and paintings are originals or very good copies. But if they are copies, they must be almost as expensive as originals. The space and furnishings speak of a man with good taste and the money to enjoy it. She will keep all of her questions to herself.

"I have some appetizers we can nibble on while we work. They're on the dining table. Help yourself. And to answer your question before you ask it, yes, I bought them from LaMond."

"Just to let you know, I did not see the green sedan of Ms. Widdix on my trip here."

"That's good. She is not to leave her post at your house. There are two keys to good protection: invisibility until it is necessary to become visible, and consistency. Shall we begin?"

For the next ninety minutes, Liz and Marion pour over the facts and assumptions of this ever-expanding and confusing situation. They question everything, and even question the questions. There is no white board, so Marion notes any conclusions and unanswered questions on his legal pad.

"Time for a break. I'm going to have a glass of wine. May I pour one for you?"

"I'll have what you're having."

Standing before one of the large windows, she waits for her drink. Liz is focused on the view, yet sees Marion's reflection as he approaches.

"Cusamano Merlot, vino d'notte, madam."

"Thank you."

"I need to tell you something that I found intriguing when I dug through the archives."

He already knew the truth of his discovery and hoped it would not hurt her too much.

"OK. History can be intriguing because it tells us why we are where we are."

They both take big sips of wine.

"Three years ago, my predecessor, Marvin Lembetick, created a file whose title was simply SC. He had uncovered some preliminary facts about this SC and was working with someone identified only as 3523. Nowhere in the file is SC shown to be a specific individual. Rather it appears to be an amorphous group. The file is light on facts, but contains hints, innuendos, and several names. Lembetick's file contained the names of eight of the fifteen names on our list. All eight were observed by 3523 during a work week. I believe that 3523 was code for a cop.

"Two of these names, Salvatore and Qito, appear numerous times in the file. This 3523 indicated he felt those two were vulnerable to approach. He dug up information to use as leverage against the two. Both cops were selling protection to downtown merchants. If convicted, they would go to jail and lose everything. All for about five hundred a week. Too much to lose for so little. A notation in Lembetick's handwriting reveals he briefly and unofficially spoke to these two men, and they both seemed nervous. He thought both men might have consciences, and that they could be persuaded to talk freely in the DA's office.

"Qito is a nephew of your Lieutenant Gracia and Salvatore's mother's maiden name is Infante. Lembetick planned to have a serious second sit-down with these men "within the next two weeks." Then, two years ago last month there were no further entries in the file and it lay unattended during the remainder of Lembetick's service. I found it buried behind another file that dealt with possible corruption in two precincts. The corruption cases were investigated and taken to trial. But this file never came to light."

While Marion is explaining what he found, Liz feels has she slipped into a parallel universe somewhere outside the room. She can hear Marion as if he were fifty feet away. His voice, although faint, echoes in her brain. She stands still in stunned silence. Liz has to focus on the here and now. To come back to reality, she squeezes her hands into fists of rage. Fingernails dig into the palms of her hands. Tears well in her eyes, but she refuses to cry. Her hand holding the wine glass is shaking. In fact, her entire body is trembling. Suddenly, she explodes into a non-stop, high volume verbal stream while gesturing emphatically.

"My husband's badge number was 3523 Lembetick was working with Sandy before Lembetick could sit down with Qito and Salvatore and explain the information dug up by Sandy my husband was killed murdered on the orders of the Tampa PD just like Leonard those bastards they kill their own to protect their enterprise of corruption Marion what the fuck do we do now?"

"Breathe, Liz, breathe. Stop talking and breathe."

Marion is standing before her gently holding her shoulders and looking into her eyes. She feels his strong calm and stops her rant. Ever so slightly, she steps into his space. They are nose to nose. They are breathing each other's breath. Seeking protection from the evil, ugly truth, she leans her tear dampened cheek against his chest and finds comfort. Her normal breathing returns. She lifts her head and thanks him with her eyes. They separate.

"You're still shaking. Perhaps you should sit and collect your thoughts. Your glass is empty. Would you like a refill? Or water? Our next step is to connect all the dots to be sure we have all the players and incidents clearly defined. We'll go from point A to point B, the whole way to point Z if need be to get all the answers. We can take this next step when you are ready."

"Water, not wine. I'm ready for our connect-the-dots time. Let's nail the bastards."

Liz has calmed down. Her rage has been re-focused to drive her forward. She has a strange feeling about Marion. Something she hasn't felt for years: trust. During the next ninety minutes, everything is reviewed and written on Marion's legal pad. The Street Cleaners are a far-reaching criminal conspiracy enterprise, while the names of those known to be involved in the recent spate of crimes are simply components. Hector Lopez, Umberto Rosario, Enrique Flores, Eduardo Montenegro, Leonard Sly, Alexander Kimble, Los Hermanos, and Muy Loco are all somehow connected to the Street Cleaners' fifteen names. Liz feels the surge of power as the entire picture emerges from the fog. Her thinking is deliberate, driven by her emotion to right terrible wrongs.

"Well, that about does it. All the players are in the picture, and their activities duly noted."

"What about Marshall Ross, Marion? Why was he killed? What if what I put forth previously is true? The Street Cleaners were asked to have him killed for reasons beyond the deaths of the two children. What if he had been involved with Santo Infante in a series of insurance scams and he was reneging on his part of the deal? Infante would be viciously angry. Would he go to his nephew, a Street Cleaner, to seek revenge? I think so, to keep his hands clean. Salvatore could contact Lopez, a mechanic, to rig the car. Lopez is then killed because he has too much information on the Street Cleaners and the murders of Sandy and Ross. Lopez had become a real liability, so they made him dead. He was murdered to cover up two other murders. Nice and neat, while the police chase their tails trying to link his murder to anyone else."

"That's a plausible scenario. So his name belongs in our schematic. Now, how about a celebratory glass of wine? I'll open a second bottle."

"I'd like another glass. No, I need another glass."

Marion refills both glasses.

"Liz, we know the truth, but we don't have the proof."

"We'll have to talk with Qito and Salvatore. Hint at what we know and how their involvement could earn them many years in jail, if not a visit to Ol' Sparky. If threatened with execution, one or both will reveal the inner workings of the organization."

"I'll call them on Monday. They may want to bring their PBA lawyer. I have to be clear that this is just a friendly chat about an investigation that the DA's office is conducting, and thus doesn't need to involve lawyers. I'll be sure that they think I need their help in pursuing someone else. You can sit in a room adjoining my conference room so you can hear what they say. But you'll have to remain invisible."

"Invisible, my ass! My husband was murdered on the orders of these cops. And now they have someone following me and threatening my children. I want to crush these bugs. I won't be a shrinking violet."

"I didn't mean to exclude you. Or that you should fade away. It's just that when I question the two cops, I don't want them to associate my actions with you...at least for now. They must think they are talking to me and me alone about some other investigation. For now, I have an obligation to keep you safe."

"For now. Very soon, I want them to know that I caused their downfall...that I hold them responsible for Sandy's death and that they must pay for their crimes."

After the emotional turmoil and multiple glasses of wine, Liz is spent and not sure she's able to drive home. She sits on the couch trying to absorb the significance and enormity of what she has just learned. Then she stands and paces expressionless. She is so engrossed in processing everything, that without knowing it, she is standing at the table finishing off the large of plate of appetizers. Marion remains quiet for twenty minutes.

"Liz, did you tell your children when you would be home?"

"Oh. Sorry, Marion, I zoned out for a spell. Yes, I told them that I would be home by eleven. So, it's about two hours until my curfew."

"Would you like something substantial to eat?"

"Thanks, no. I just Hoovered the tray of goodies. I am full. I think I want to get home to my children. I'll beat curfew. An early arrival to loved ones and a good night's sleep will be proper tonic for me tonight.

"OK."

As they walk to the foyer, Liz turns to Marion and gently kisses him on the cheek. He turns and reciprocates. At the elevator, he delicately kisses her lips. She responds with long-suppressed fervor and they become locked in a head-to-head, hip-to-hip embrace. Slowly they peel away, stare into each other's eyes, and smile. The elevator door opens, and she enters. Marion looks longingly into the closing elevator doors, turns and retrieves his cell phone.

"She's on her way to the garage. Tuck her in."

Cary is in the kitchen.

"Mom, you're home early. Is everything OK?"

"Yes, everything is OK."

"How was your second date?"

"Very nice, and it was *not* a date."

"Ooooooooooh! Defensive."

"It was a very nice evening in which two adults shared grown-up conversation, a little wine, and some food. Nothing more."

"OK, Mom, if you say so. Wink. Wink."

Alex is watching TV on the patio.

"Hey, Mom, Billy Kelly invited me to his house for a sleepover tomorrow. Are you good with that?"

"Sure. That leaves Cary and me alone for a girls' night."

"Sorry, my crew made plans for dinner and a movie."

"Well, I guess I'm all alone on Saturday night. I'm a grown-up. I can handle that. It will be a struggle, but somehow I'll manage. Wink. Wink."

Liz heads upstairs to wash and change into comfortable clothes. Halfway up, she realizes that bravado is not her style; her heart is racing and she is sweating. As she enters her bedroom, she begins to tremble. Quickly the door to her sanctuary is closed. Liz sits on the edge of the bed staring at the wall. Still raw from learning the truth about Sandy's death and her encounter with Marion, her emotions are in free fall. Her head spins. Images race: Marion's face, Sandy's form, big black dogs snarling, shadowy rooms, and standing on a ledge overlooking a canyon with no bottom in sight, all race in her mind's eye simultaneously.

Preaching self-reliance and independence to her children has unintended consequences. Suddenly her mind jumps to different subjects and images. Little birds are leaving their nest her Saturday will be filled with chores so she can concentrate on keeping her mind off being alone or being lonely will not be as easy as she hopes getting through the weekend without disquieting dreams is the real issue dreams like the ones she has when she is reminded of her loss of Sandy the arguments they had and the times she screwed up on the job always leave her upset the dogs are barking and growling at her the canyon wall is shifting beneath her she has to steel herself in the knowledge that she is on the right path to solving her biggest mystery Sandy is there his form and his smell comfort her she her head echoes with the lyrics he used to sing to her, "You're everything I hoped for you're everything I need…"

Slowly she opens her eyes. She is sitting on the floor, naked, beneath one of Sandy's shirts. Her knees are folded up against her chest. Liz feels cold and clammy. She rests her head against the mattress. Emotional fatigue has given way to physical exhaustion. She just wants to rest for five minutes. She covers her face with her husband's shirt. She wants to acquire his strength through her olfactory system. After the brief respite, Liz heads to the bathroom. The water is turned on, and she steps into the shower still wearing his shirt. Drying herself, she realizes she is hungry. Liz heads downstairs to be with her children.

XVI

"Lieutenant Qito, thank you for coming to my office today."

"I brought my PBA attorney."

"Although unnecessary to these discussions, I always welcome the help of other legal counsel. And your name, sir?"

"G. Wendell Haass. Let me ask, what charges are being brought today?"

"No charges. The lieutenant and I will just have a friendly conversation about several situations unrelated to him, but ones on which he might give us some insight. Is that acceptable to you?"

"Yes."

"Fine. Lieutenant Qito, are you familiar with the murder of Marshall Ross?"

"I read he had died. I was unaware that anybody had classified his death as murder."

"That's it?"

"That's it for that."

"What do you know about the history of Hector Lopez and his murder?"

"Lopez had been a member of Los Hermanos until a few years back. He left the gang and, I heard, he was living the civilian life. I have no idea why he was murdered."

"What do you know about the history of Umberto Rosario and his murder?"

"Rosario had been a member of Los Hermanos until recently. He left the gang and, I heard, he was living the civilian life. I have no idea why he was murdered."

"What do you know about the history of Eduardo Montenegro and his murder?"

"Montenegro was a member of Muy Loco. I heard he was beaten to death by Los Hermanos in retaliation for the murders of Lopez and Rosario."

A single painfully well rehearsed response to two different questions.

"What do you know about Los Hermanos?"

"A street gang that the department put out of business two years ago."

"Are they a factor in crime today?"

"No. I guess there may be a few young punk wannabe thugs. But the gang is gone."

"What do you know about Muy Loco?"

"I hear they are as crazy as their name says. The guys in the Gang Unit claim to have their eyes on the gang 24/7."

"What do you know about the murder of Detective Sandy Kimble?"

"He was shot in the back during a raid on the Los Hermanos hangout two years ago. A guy named Enrique Flores was the shooter. He is a guest of the state at a mental rehabilitation center over in Lake Worth."

"What do you know about the death of Sergeant Leonard Sly?"

"I heard he ate his gun in some abandoned lot downtown."

"What if I told you he did not commit suicide? What if you learned he was murdered? What would you say then?

"I wouldn't believe you. The ME's report confirmed suicide."

"OK."

"What do you know about an organization referred to as the Street Cleaners?"

"Who?"

"Street Cleaners."

Silence falls over the room. The PBA lawyer doesn't even whisper in his client's ear. Qito is fidgeting. He taps his fingers and his eyes dart left, right, up, and down. His "tells." He is trying to hide something, but his conscience is aware of knowledge he doesn't want to reveal.

"Let me repeat; what do you know about an organization euphemistically referred to as Street Cleaners?"

"I've never heard of any organization like that."

"Are you sure?"

"Mr. Morrison, my client has answered that question. He has no knowledge of an organization known as Street Cleaners."

The use of the word "known" as opposed to "referred to as" is Mr. Haass's "tell." He now knows the purpose of this sit-down. Is he worried that Morrison may be connecting his client to the Street Cleaners?

"Let me tell you about the Street Cleaners."

Marion launches into a history lesson. Mostly factual with some fictional embellishment, from the Bolito Wars to the present.

"Now that you know that the Street Cleaners started as a subset of the police force, and that they now operate as vigilantes, what can you tell me about their membership?"

"I don't know no fucking vigilantes. I know cops. Hardworking guys doing the dangerous job of protecting the citizens of Tampa."

Perspiration has appeared on Qito's upper lip and Haass is tapping the fingers of his right hand.

"Well, that's about it. Thanks for your time. I may need to get in touch with you again so stay close. And by the way, please sign this confidentiality agreement that states you will keep our conversation to yourself. As if it never happened. Thanks again."

Qito and Haass leave the conference room through the main door. Two minutes later, Liz enters through the side door.

"It's obvious he knows more than he is saying. Did you see him twitch?"

"Liz, this is not my first rodeo. We have planted the seeds of worry. Qito's memory is long enough to remember his conversations with Lembetick. He is probably fearfully aware that the District Attorney's office has reopened the investigation due to the recent rash of murders. Later today and despite the confidentiality agreement, Qito will pass this information and the vague details of our discussion along to his commander who will pass it throughout the group. Tomorrow, when we talk to Salvatore, he will be so guarded that he will be easy to trip up. The Street Cleaners will get the message that the DA's office is digging with the goal to expose them and bring them down. But they don't want to come out of the shadows. They'll just try to stonewall every inquiry. We'll know tomorrow how many nerves we hit today."

On her way home, Liz thinks she sees the gray, rust-pocked car following her. When she pulls onto her street, the car drives on. She quickly and emphatically hugs both her babies.

"Captain Salvatore, thank you for coming to my office today."

"I brought my PBA attorney."

"Although unnecessary to these discussions, I always welcome the help of other legal counsel. And your name, sir?"

"Branson Reynolds. What charges are being brought today?"

"No charges. The captain and I will just have a friendly conversation about several situations unrelated to him, but ones on which he might give us some insight. Is that acceptable to you?"

"Yes."

"Fine. Captain Salvatore, are you familiar with the murder of Marshall Ross?"

"I read he died in a car accident. I was unaware that anyone had classified his death as murder."

"That's it?"

"That's it for that."

"OK."

"What do you know about the history of Hector Lopez and his murder?"

"Lopez had been a member of L-L-Los Hermanos until a few years back. He left the gang and, I heard, he was living the civilian life. I have no idea why he was murdered."

"What do you know about the history of Umberto Rosario and his murder?"

"Rosario had been a member of Los Hermanos until recently. He left the g-g-gang. I have no idea why he was m-m-murdered."

The same rehearsed response as from Qito.

"What do you know about the history of Eduardo Montenegro and his murder?"

"Montenegro was a member of M-M-Muy Loco. I heard he was beaten to death by Los Hermanos in retaliation for the murders of Lopez and Rosario."

"What do you know about Los Hermanos?"

"A street gang that the department put out of business two years ago."

"Are they a factor in crime today?"

"No. I guess there may be a few young punk wannabes. But the gang is gone."

"What do you know about Muy Loco?"

"I hear they are as crazy as their name says. The guys in the Gang Unit claim to have their eyes on the gang 24/7."

"What do you know about the murder of Detective Sandy Kimble?"

"He was shot in the back during a raid on the Los Hermanos hangout. A g-g-guy named Enrique Flores was the shooter. Flores is in a state m-m-m-mental institution over in Lake Worth."

"What do you know about the death of Sergeant Leonard Sly?"

"I heard he ate his gun in some abandoned lot downtown."

"What if I told you he did not commit suicide? What if I told you he was murdered? What would you say then?"

"I wouldn't believe you. The ME's report confirmed suicide."

"OK."

"What do you know about an organization euphemistically referred to as the Street Cleaners?"

"Who?"

"Street Cleaners."

Silence falls over the room. The PBA lawyer doesn't even whisper in his client's ear. He's either a very good poker player or he's clueless. Salvatore shifts twice on his ass cheeks, and coughs nervously. He folds and unfolds his hands while his eyes dart to each wall in the room. These are his "tells." His lips say no-no, but his soul is telling his body yes-yes.

"Let me repeat; what do you know about an organization euphemistically referred to as Street Cleaners?"

"I've never heard of the organization."

"Are you sure?"

"Mr. Morrison, my client has answered that question. He has no knowledge of an organization you call – Street Cleaners."

"Let me tell you about Street Cleaners."

Marion repeats his history lesson. Mostly factual with some fictional embellishment from the Bolito Wars to the present.

"Now that you know that the Street Cleaners were a subset of the police force and that they now operate as vigilantes, what can you tell me about their membership?"

"I don't know no f-f-f-fucking vigilantes. I know cops. Hard-working guys doing the dangerous job of protecting the citizens of Tampa."

Another canned answer.

"Captain, what do you know about Santo Infante?"

"He is my uncle."

"Are you aware that your uncle is the boss of a crime family?"

"I don't know anything about that."

"In all your time on the police force, you mean to tell me that you've never heard or read anything that implies that Santo Infante is the boss of an organized crime enterprise? A crime family?"

"Never. He is my mother's brother. That's all I know about him. I see him mostly at family holiday gatherings."

"Which family?"

"My client resents the implication of that question. He obviously meant his natural family and not the alleged crime family to which you alluded."

"When was the last time you spoke to your uncle?"

"Thanksgiving dinner at my mother's house."

Sweat is glistening on Salvatore's forehead. A result of two factors: the questions about his relationship with Uncle Santo and a thermostat set at eighty-five. Liz noted Salvatore stammering during the Q and A session. He knows he's in a seat that is very hot in more ways than thermal.

"Well, that's about it. Thanks for your time. I may need to get in touch with you again so stay close. And by the way, please sign this confidentiality agreement that states you will keep our conversation to yourself. As if it never happened. Thanks again."

Salvatore and Reynolds leave the conference room through the main door. Two minutes later, Liz enters through the side door.

"It's obvious he knows more than he is saying. I think we have enough to expand the inquiry into the Street Cleaners. I will invite several other lieutenants and captains to have pleasant sit-downs with me over the next few days. I'll randomly select names from the list you gave me. If I kick the bee's nest hard enough and often enough, we'll get the honey we want. For the time being, I want you to keep your head down…buried in paperwork…hide in plain sight, as it were. For your safety, you must not be associated with this investigation."

"How will you get what you want without confronting them directly? They will all have plausible deniability. They will look like honest, hard-working members of the force being persecuted by the new ADA, who's trying to make his bones. With their years of service and tons of commendations, the public would side with them. If you fail to get information leading to an indictment, you'll be in your job less than a year before you're ridden out of town on a rail."

"Liz, I have resources. Before you leave, I want to share some interesting facts. Let's go into another conference room down the hall."

Marion unlocks the windowless door to reveal a long table holding stacks of paper at various heights.

"We started gathering the financial data of the fifteen men on our list. We have acquired complete bank, credit card, and investment records of Qito and Salvatore, as well as their wives. So far, we've turned up a few intriguing facts. The information set off a few alarm bells. Take a look at the stack for Lieutenant Qito and tell me what you see highlighted."

"Bank records show regular deposits of his wages and the normal plethora of checks written and electronic debits issued to pay the mortgage, utilities, telephone, and two credit card accounts. The mortgage payment seems high based on his income, but there is nothing out of the ordinary that jumps out at me."

"Now take a look at the financial records of Maria Alphonso, aka Mrs. Armando Qito. What do see?"

"She makes regular deposits. Income from her job, I assume. I see debit notations for groceries, gasoline, or incidentals. So, she must run her household on her salary."

"Yet, she invests six thousand dollars each month with Morgan Stanley. See information about investment accounts. OK, where does the cash come from? Maria is a Customer Service Manager at Hillsborough Gas and Electric. Her salary is forty-five thousand dollars before taxes. Her pay stubs indicate her take-home pay is twenty-six fifty-four per month. Yet, she is able to invest an average of six thousand dollars each month. All of which is not invested electronically. It is invested via cashier's checks. Where does the six thousand per month come from?"

"Cash from a side business…or her husband."

"She has no side business but she does have a husband. I'll bet that the additional money is Lieutenant Qito's income from various Street Cleaner enterprises, such as payoffs and kickbacks from street gangs. Street Cleaners get the cash for looking the other way as bad stuff happens. Bad stuff like robbery, extortion, and auto theft. These are crimes in which neither bodily harm nor murder is a component so they never make the front page or get mentioned on the evening news. Really under the radar.

"The finances of the overall operation are a classic pyramid. The foot soldiers are the real earners. They do the deeds and collect the money. They get to keep a portion of the cash each month. The bulk of the money is then sent up the ladder. Ultimately to the three commanders. Everybody wins, except the guys at the top win bigger. Crime is protected and the cops get rich.

"This is why Qito can afford a house in Avalon valued at over five hundred thousand. He and his wife pay for normal, traceable expenses out of their salaries while the couple invests the cash he acquires from his illegal activities. Cash he earns for being a Street Cleaner.

"When we looked at the couple's investment accounts, all of which are in his wife's name, we learned that she has a nice little nest egg–slightly north of seven hundred and fifty thousand dollars. Maria and Armando are living up to their visible means yet have amassed a boatload of money for retirement. The only way this is possible is through the infusion of regular cash payments from Street Cleaners."

"What about Salvatore?"

"A similar pattern of more cash than income."

"OK, we have two. What about the others?"

"We have proof about the questionable finances of Qito and Salvatore, but we can't prove the source of the extra income. When we determine the source of the extra income, we will be able to go forward with the case. That's why we need to examine the records of the other alleged members of the alleged gang. Once we can see a pattern, we have true enterprise corruption. Right now two does not make a pattern sufficient for a RICO indictment."

"If Qito and Salvatore are the tips of the iceberg, the criminal corruption must be huge over the lifetime of the Street Cleaners. Millions and millions during the past sixty years, stolen from the citizens in small chunks. Protection has its price. What can I do to help?"

"As we dig deeper, your existence will be perceived as a real and present danger to their existence. They will put all the pieces together and come to the conclusion that you are a danger that must be eliminated."

"You are not very comforting."

"I didn't mean to frighten you, but you need to know the truth. I have arranged to have someone watch you."

"I know, Rose Widdix."

"She watches your house. I've arranged for someone else to watch you when you drive to and from work, and when you go out on calls."

"Who? Can they be trusted? What about my children?"

"My resources are from the Florida Department of Law Enforcement. Commander Ishmael is a dear, longtime friend. We share the same cultural and legal values. He and the people under his command can be trusted. Your children are also being observed...on their way to and from school. But, I advise you to curtail their evenings away from home. At least for the next few days. Then they will be safe to roam like normal teens."

"How long have you had the FDLE watching me?"

"For a few days. I believed in what you and Leonard told me."

"Were you also watching Leonard?"

"Yes, but we lost him. We screwed up."

"Please, don't screw up watching me."

"I won't. I promise. One more item. I'll need the names of the Los Hermanos and Muy Loco gang members you spoke to. I want to have a friendly chat with them. I want to learn more about their relationship with the police. Plus, after the FDLE picks them up and brings them here for our sit downs, they will tell their handler. Then everyone in Street Cleaners will feel the noose tightening around their collective necks."

"What do I do now?"

"Go back to work. Work as usual. Bury yourself in the computer files and the details of your other open cases. We are very close to asking for expansive indictments from the grand jury.

In the next few days, I'll gather more financial information and talk to a few more bad guys.

XVII

Liz never made reservations to go to Key West. She had to hold off given the large case and its complications hanging over her head. So, she wants to get a special item for Cary's Christmas. That means no shopping at the mall: Cary's hangout. She saw what she wanted at Friedman Family Fine Jewelry and she has the money originally intended for the trip. Liz leaves police headquarters for the pleasant ten-block walk to the store. Along the way, she stops at a food truck for lunch, a burrito and water. The day is unseasonably warm, the air is clear, and the sun is bright. The sidewalks are crowded with shoppers hoping to finish last-minute shopping – before the last minute. The occasional jostle is met with a smile and a courteous "excuse me."

The crowd thins as she approaches a three-block, cobblestone street that is home to two-story jewelry stores, three beauty salons, numerous female and male clothing and accessories boutiques, a very trendy coffee and tea shop, and a chocolatier. All high-end outlets, selling expensive, exclusive items supported by superior, fawning service. Each door is distinctively colored to catch the eye of every shopper. Small patches of well-tended grass that separate the often-swept sidewalk and the curb of the street for forty-eight weeks of the year are now covered with spray-on snow. Poinsettias on pedestals are sentries at several store doors.

Old-fashioned gas lit street lamps will bathe the three blocks in a warm orange glow commencing an hour before sunset. For the season, the street lamps and doorways are festooned with garlands and wreathes. Some have small lights entwined within. Because it is the midday shopping hour, carolers are strolling the three blocks. They will be on the sidewalk until two with an encore at five.

The entire environment is an old-fashioned oasis among the impersonal canyons created by massive marble and steel facades. These edifices of progress and greatness, built within the past fifteen years, manifest a modern metropolis, while this short one-way street tells the story of seasons past. Liz is swept back to a Dickensian image of Christmas when everyone was cordial, and loving excitement filled the air. She remembers going downtown as a little girl with her mother and father to see the sights. This time of year it was much colder up north and the snow was real. Bundled against the cold, she and her sister would sip hot cider and snack on roasted chestnuts. As now, there were carolers.

"O, come all ye faithful…"

Liz is snapped out of her reverie by the screech of tires as a vehicle turns onto the street. The thump-thump-thump of the tires on cobblestone increases in volume. An admonition. She turns to see the source of the warning. A massive black SUV is racing down the street. As it nears Liz, the rear window on the passenger side is lowered and she notices the muzzle and barrel of a gun just inside the open window. It's not a handgun. The barrel is too long. Instinctively, Liz begins to drop to the side walk as bullets commence their lethal spray. She hears noises of metal striking metal and the cracking of plate glass. Screams arise from other shoppers. The flame-hot pain in her left arm tells her she's been hit. The second shot grazes her forehead as she twists during the fall to the sidewalk. The drive-by happens so fast that she is unable to reach her gun beneath her jacket and fire off retaliatory rounds. She tries to get up, but becomes woozy and slowly settles back onto the sidewalk. Despite the fact that the letters and digits were partially hidden by a translucent plastic shield, she is able take notice of the last three digits of the license plate, 8V1, before her eyes close.

"Hey, Mom, you're on the front page of the paper. Look."

The teens come bounding into Liz's bedroom. She vaguely recollects how and when she got to her own bed. The past twenty-four hours are a blur due to the shooting and the heavy dose of pain medication. Alex is holding the newspaper in front of his face so she can't miss the article. She was already awake recounting the events by tracing her fingers over the bandages on her upper left arm and forehead. The pain is real but not severe. Modern chemistry taken in moderation will ease her transition back to normal. Alex hands her the paper.

"The man who brought you home told us you received two superficial wounds, and that bed rest would be the best medicine. You shouldn't drive or try to do housework for a couple of days. Just rest. Did you get some neat stitches? The man that brought you home last night said his name was Marion Morrison. He is an Assistant District Attorney working with you on some case. Is he the man you've been meeting with over dinner? He seems nice."

"Alex, Mr. Morrison is more than just nice."

"Cary, the man helped Mom."

"Alex, you are so dense."

"Enough, you two. Your discussion is not helping my throbbing head. Cary, would you get me a glass of water so I can take a pain pill?"

"Mom, read the paper."

Shooting Downtown
by Harold Shade

At approximately twelve-thirty Tuesday afternoon, last-minute holiday shoppers strolled the three-block stretch of downtown known as Elegant Lane. Suddenly, a vehicle raced through the street and a gunman fired a hail of bullets striking several shops and a shopper, Police Detective Elizabeth Kimble. Witnesses report the vehicle was a late-model black SUV. No license plate information was available.

The shops have been a source of unrest and accused of discrimination among the downtown Hispanic and African-American communities. Alleged price gouging, a restrictive in-store dress code, and biased customer service are the chief complaints. Police are pursuing a possible motive for the shooting by talking to community leaders.

Detective Kimble, the only shopper struck by bullets, was struck twice; her left arm was hit, while a second bullet grazed her forehead. Neither wound is life-threatening. A police spokesman stated that Detective Kimble has taken medical leave. He went on to state "This type of crime, the terrorist attack on law-abiding merchants and coupled with the shooting of an innocent bystander, is most heinous, and the Tampa Police will not rest until the perpetrators are arrested and convicted. We are talking to store owners and managers to learn if they may have had any issues with members of the urban communities. Detective Kimble has served this city admirably over the past ten years. Her late husband, Alexander 'Sandy Kimble,' was a much-decorated officer. He was murdered two years ago in a gang-related incident. The Kimble family has served above and beyond and suffered more than the citizens of Tampa can imagine. We wish Detective Elizabeth Kimble a speedy recovery and look forward to having her back on duty soon. We have a description of the SUV and its driver, and are pursuing multiple leads at this time. If anyone has any information about the vehicle or the people inside the vehicle, please call 800-500-5555. All calls will be held in strict confidence. The EL Merchant's Association is offering a $10,000 reward for information leading to the arrest and conviction of the gunman and driver."

"Look at the pictures. There's your official police department photo, Dad's police photo, a picture of the three blocks of Elegant Lane, bullet holes in the storefront window, and a diagram of the SUV's path. Is this last photo of your blood on the sidewalk?"

"Yes, Alex, that's my blood. Gawd, I hate that photo of me."

"Some guy named Harold Shade stopped by since you got home. He gave me this card. He is the same guy who wrote the article in the newspaper. He said he wants to interview you for a follow-up article."

Alex perks up with the sound of the doorbell.

"I'll get it."

He races down the stairs. Liz can hear muffled conversation. Alex races up the stairs.

"Mr. Morrison is here. He is waiting by the front door. Should I let him in? Do you want to talk to him?"

"Yes, let him in. Ask him to be patient. I'll be down shortly. I need to look presentable."

"Getting all pretty for Mr. Morrison. He *is* the guy you've been seeing for those late night working dinners?"

"Yes, Cary, we are working together. That's all."

"If you say so, Detective. Wink. Wink."

Cary goes to the top of the stairs and peers at the man waiting in the doorway. She walks back to Liz with a Cheshire cat grin.

"He's kinda cute…for an older guy."

"That's enough. Now scoot. I have to clean up."

Liz wonders when Marion brought her home what did he say to her children? Did he put her into bed? Into her pajamas? Liz struggles to find a sweatshirt to cover her left arm and hide the bandage. She can't hide the bandage on her forehead. She delicately washes her face, brushes her teeth, runs a brush through her hair, and applies some lipstick. She is as ready as she can be.

"Marion, it's nice to see you, regardless of the circumstances. Or should I say it's nice to see you again. Let's go to the outside porch. I've been cooped up for too long and could use some fresh air. Alex and Cary, please give us complete privacy. Gottit?"

"Liz, how are you feeling?"

"Fine. Just sore in two places. My entire left arm is stiff."

"I'm sorry this happened."

"I thought you had someone following me."

"We did, but only when you were in your car: to and from work and when you went out on a call. Not when you go for a shopping stroll at noon."

"Well, young man, it's fine protection you've been providing me."

"I'm truly sorry and will make it up to you. You won't be alone anymore."

"It's OK. You're forgiven. But I have a few questions for you. What did you tell Alex and Cary? How did I get into my pajamas?"

"I told Alex and Cary that you were shot but would recuperate fully in a few days. They understood and were fascinated by your wounds. I have no idea how you were able to undress yourself and put on your pajamas. I suspect Cary helped. Now I have a question for you. Who knew where you were going?"

"Gracia. I told him I was going to Friedman's to pick up a gift for Cary. Why?"

"Just curious."

"Just curious, my ass. He's the connection to my shooting and Leonard's death."

"I think that's spot on."

"Now I have some information for you. I saw the last three digits of the SUV's license… 8V1. That should help the police nail the bastards."

"Given that we're only a few days from the indictments, I don't want to give any member of the TPD a heads-up. The FDLE will track down the SUV and its driver."

"Where does that leave me?"

"At home recuperating."

"Pardon my language again, but home, my ass. I am so deep into this pile of crap that all I see is brown and it stinks. I'll be back at my desk on Monday."

"I can't stop you. I doubt if anyone could. You have the right to be angry at the people responsible for Sandy's murder, Leonard's murder, and your injuries. It's just that you are safer here than on the street. That said, I want you to look at some photos. We have been watching about twenty TPD detectives above and beyond the original twelve and the three commanders, who we think might be involved with the Street Cleaners. I'd like to show you a series of photos. If you can identify anybody, tell me where, when, and why."

After two six-packs of photos.

"Bingo! That heavyset bastard with the handlebar moustache and a mullet is the guy who was following me and who came to my door and spoke to Alex. But, just to be absolutely positive, please show the six-pack to Alex for confirmation."

"Not yet. A few more."

On the next six-pack, Liz's eyes widen.

"Bingo again! I never met him, but I think he is the partner of the first guy I recognized. Umberto Rosario told me two guys came to give Hector Lopez money. One was the first guy with all the hair and the other had no face hair and was bald. Who are they?"

"Officers Raymond Wovent and Bruno Weingarten. They work the Gang Unit and report to Captain Schliemann, who we suspect of being a Street Cleaner. He reports to Commander Betancourt. These guys are Street Cleaners in training, or wannabes."

"So, Gracia knows where I am going. He calls Schliemann, who tells Wovent and Weingarten. These guys then reach out to a gang, my guess is Muy Loco, to do the deed. Muy Loco is pissed at me for the way I disrespected them when we met the first time. So they happily accept the job. Plus, I'll bet they got paid."

"Again, you're spot on. I had a nice chat with Geraldo Jimenez and Alberto Cosmarti, the guys you met with Dannello. They were startled when the FDLE not TPD scooped them off the street. The FDLE did not offer the comfort the two of them expect from TPD. Given their native criminal intelligence, I am sure they will help us connect lots of dots. They know who you are and that you represent a curtailment of their lifestyle. So, they were, no doubt, all too eager to kill you. I am thankful they failed. I'll have concrete proof of their involvement once we find the SUV and have state techies go over it with a fine-tooth comb and fact-finding chemicals."

"Marion, I know your scenario is correct. It all started with Gracia."

"I have to go. I need to pursue these matters. I need to collect financial information on Wovent and Weingarten. This undercover part of our case will be over very soon. I will be strengthening the protection of your house this weekend. Please keep your children at home. They should not go out once they are home from school on Friday."

"Jaysus, we're all in jail at home."

"Liz, don't consider it jail. Consider that you will be safe in a fortress. I'm officially inviting myself for dinner on all three nights of the weekend to ensure the safety of Alex,

Cary, and you. To make your life easy, I'll shop, cook, serve, and clean up those nights."

"The man who came for dinner."

"What won't your children eat?"

"Dirty carpet and wooden furniture. Everything else that can be chewed and swallowed will be devoured. They're teenagers with commensurate non-discriminatory appetites."

"I know a few recipes. Nothing too exotic. I think Alex and Cary will like the meals. Then it's set. I'll be here on Friday around five. I do have to advise you that I'll have two cell phones and a laptop with me in case something critical happens before Monday. So consider these three nights working evenings. By the way, how many guns do you have in the house?"

"Now you're frightening me. One, my Sig Sauer."

"As of today, the Street Cleaners can feel the ever-increasing discomfort of the tightening noose. I believe they tried to kill you once. I just want to be sure, that if they try again, we're ready."

"Do you carry a gun?"

"Under normal circumstances, no. But, I am licensed to carry a concealed weapon. It's part of the job specs. I selected a Desert Eagle 50 caliber."

"Jaysus. A cannon. Wait a minute. I see what you're doing. I am not in jail or in a fortress. You want to use me and my children as bait. You're tying the nanny goat and her two kids to stakes in an open field and you're waiting for the wolves to attack. And when they start to attack to devour the tethered bait, the wolves are killed by the noble herder. That's crap. I can deal with your risky game, but I will not put my children in harm's way. No parent in their right mind would use their children as bait for killers."

"You and your children are not being used as bait. These guys already know where you live. It would not be difficult for them to visit you. I just want to be absolutely sure that the three of you are safe until the bad guys are put in jail and are no longer a danger to you."

"And when will that be?"

"Monday or Tuesday at the latest. Consider their arrests a Christmas gift from you and me to the people of Tampa. If all goes as I have planned, the bad guys will be arrested within the next ninety-six hours. Who they are and how many of them are out there is yet to be determined. That's my job before I arrive here on Friday. You've got to trust me for a few more days."

"I trust you. But here is my part of the deal; I will tell my children that they are housebound this weekend, and that they are not going to Key West between Christmas and New Year's. But you will tell them why."

"That's a deal. See you Friday around five. By the by, I'm very glad you're all right. I'm glad both professionally and personally."

As Marion leaves, Liz realizes her relationship with him is more than cop/ADA. It's becoming woman/man. She wants to tell him she is glad she is all right both professionally and personally. She wants to tell him she is glad he will be in her home for three evenings.

"Alex. Cary. Come in here. We need to talk."

She outlines the teens' clean-up duty for Friday immediately after school lets out for the Christmas break. Her excuse is that, like homework, if the chores are done early there is more time to play. She tells them they will not be going to Key West because of her injuries. They understand it's because she was shot. She does not explain that she wants her home to be presentable for a special guest. Should she buy flowers?

Liz peels back the tape and gauze on her forehead to examine the wound. It has stopped seeping. A scab is beginning to form. No stitches, just two small butterflies. She tosses the piece of gauze and the holding tape into the bathroom trash. Delicately she washes the wound, pats it dry, and applies the ointment the ER doctor gave her. She knows a smaller bandage resides somewhere in the large plastic box that's on the bottom shelf of the bathroom closet. The box contains all manner of miscellaneous items; a bottle of aspirin, laxatives, decongestants, antihistamines, hotel-sized shampoo bottles and bars of scented neatly wrapped soap liberated from beach hotels during long-ago get-away weekends with Sandy, two unopened toothbrushes, gauze, medical tape, a bottle of wart remover, nail clippers, a pair of scissors, shoelaces, a tube of very old cortisone cream, expired birth control pills, and several condoms. Ah, hah! A box of various-sized bandages. Her target: one just large enough to cover her forehead wound. The covering is gently applied.

Now to the left arm. The stiffness and soreness is gradually abating. Given the choice between drugs or natural healing, she prefers nature's way. It's still very tender around the entry and exit sites…beneath the bicep, on the under part of the arm, in what the kids call the waitress wattle. The three little butterflies applied at the ER to each of the wounds must stay in place for three more days. The bulky covering on her arm can be removed now. Tape is delicately pulled and bloody gauze is unwrapped. They join the forehead bandage in the trash. She examines the two arm wounds. The caked-on blood is washed away, the spots are dried, ointment is applied, and two large bandages cover the dark red areas on her arm. Her cell phone. Restricted call.

"Hello, Liz Kimble."

"Lizzie, this is Shannon. Are you all right? I read you had been shot while shopping. Jaysus, Christmas shoppers must be a lot meaner and more aggressive than those here in Jax."

"I'm fine. The wounds are superficial."

"Sorry, I didn't call sooner. But, I've been on the street roundin' up bad guys. I just came in to the station house this morning. Is the newspaper report accurate? You were a collateral victim of a drive-by. The guys were aiming for the stores. You just happened to be in the wrong place at the wrong time."

"Not really. Answer me this. On a sidewalk filled with real and window shoppers, how is it possible that only one person was hit by someone firing an automatic weapon from a moving car and that one person is a cop?"

"Holy crap, you *were* the target. Why?"

"We have been digging into a very sordid aspect of the city's law enforcement. That's all I can say."

"Beyond you, who are the we?"

"An ADA."

"Male or female?"

"Male."

"Is he cute? Is he single?"

"Yes and yes."

"Lizzie, you dog."

"It's strictly professional."

"OK. Wink. Wink. If you say so."

"How serious are your wounds?"

"A through and through in the upper left arm and a scratch on my forehead."

"You have acquired the cop's badge of courage. Congrats. Do not have the forehead scar surgically concealed. Guys find a chick with a scar to be very sexy. At least that's been my experience."

"The guys you meet on the job might feel that way, but I can't imagine Marion lusting after me because I have a scar on my forehead."

"Interesting choice of words…Marion and lusting. Marion, eh. If he is not gay, apparently, he's more to you than you're telling me or even yourself. I hope he feels the same way."

"I seriously doubt he's gay. But the subject of how he feels about me has never come up, and I doubt it ever will."

"Sure. Sure. Lizzie, this is me, Shannon, the person who knows you better than anyone else does. I wish only the best for you. There's my pager. I gotta scoot. I'll call next week. Love ya."

"Love ya, too."

Who is Marion to Liz? Who is Liz to Marion? The kids will be home from school shortly. They have not yet been told that they are housebound for the weekend. There will be wailing, gnashing of teeth, and beating of breasts.

XVIII

"What!? That's not fair. Why are we being punished?"

"Cary, this is not a punishment. Remember Mr. Morrison, the ADA who came to see me yesterday? He's coming for dinner tonight. He'll prepare our dinners, and we will enjoy his company. That's all I can say for now. He will give you all the details. All the whys and wherefores. You have to trust me that this arrangement is only for the weekend. It's job related."

"But I made plans with my crew for Friday and Saturday nights. What do I tell them?"

"Tell them that you have to stay home to take care of your wounded mother, and that you will be free to hang out after Christmas for the balance of the break."

"What about during the day on Saturday and Sunday? May I go to the mall?"

"No. Sorry. You and Alex are to stay home with me until I say it's all right to leave."

"It's just not fair."

"Alex, do you understand?"

"I think so. I thought we were going to the Keys. But with your wounds, I quickly realized that's off the table."

"It has been temporarily delayed. I promise we will go. I just don't know when."

"This guy has upset our Christmas plans. A man we don't know is coming to our house to cook us dinner, and we can't leave the house for the entire weekend. Very strange. What's the real skinny?"

"Mr. Morrison will give you all the details when he arrives…in two hours. That's all I can tell you for now. You guys have got to trust me on this. All will become clear tonight. I'll make it up to you, I promise. It's now chore time for you guys. Start downstairs. Do the upstairs later, if there is time. Mr. Morrison will only see the first floor. Alex, make sure the patio and the porch are clean."

Two hours drags for the laboring teens and for Liz, who is emotionally confused. Getting ready takes so much time and energy that she needs coffee just to get back to even. Standing in the kitchen waiting for the drips of coffee to stop, she wonders about Marion. Who is he really? Leonard put his trust in him and was murdered. She put her trust in him and was shot. Why does she trust him now? Marion is a politician, and all politicians have hidden agendas. Is he trying to make his bones on the bodies of dead and wounded cops? What does he want to do or be? State office? He's covered all the needed job bases. His resume is solid gold, just as his references must be. What about his divorce? From whom and why? Does he have children? Could he possibly be gay? Not based on their kiss. Maybe he's bi. Is he seeing other women? How will Cary and Alex react to him? He to them? Why is she agonizing? Does he mean more to her than she wants to admit? She must trust her instincts. But what are they saying amid all the mental chatter? Is her mental chatter expressing her instincts? The doorbell interrupts her anxious introspection. She walks with anticipation to the door.

"Marion, it's nice to see you."

"Liz, it's always nice to see you. Could Alex help me with the food? It's on trays and in pots gently resting on the back seat of my car and in the trunk."

Max comes to the front door to check out this human and the food smells emanating from the car. His reaction to Marion is neutral; he does not growl, nor does he wag his tail and jump up. He stands guard in the front hall and watches Marion's every move.

"Liz, how friendly is the dog?"

"Very friendly, if he feels you are no threats to the three humans that share his realm. Don't try to pet him. He will come to you if he feels you are trustworthy."

"Your Christmas decorations are very homey. The wreaths and garlands give off a woodsy aroma. And, the tree is spot on. Not so big as to overpower the living room, yet well decorated to make a pleasant statement. And no blinking lights, plastic reindeer, or plaster crèche. Plus, I hear the sound of orchestral versions of Christmas hymns and songs. I see that Santa has shipped some of the gifts ahead of his arrival."

"A Christmas traditionalist in my house. Or are you a home décor critic from the *Times*? On the day before Christmas, I start with the *Messiah* four-disc set. I put them into the changer, crank up the volume, and relish in one of the world's greatest, most inspired musical tributes… albeit mostly an Easter opus. What you smell came from an aerosol can. I cannot tell a lie."

"Not an aficionado or a published critic. Just someone who likes the statement of personal caring that abides in this season. The smells, sights, and sounds of Christmas years ago, as opposed to the gaudy excesses of noise, bright colors, and guilt encouraged by manufacturers and retailers."

"Childhood memories?"

"Very much so. You are fortunate to have children with whom you share the true spirit of the season. And, they are fortunate to have a mother who wants to share that spirit. But, that's as far down memory lane as I care to travel."

"Alex, Mr. Morrison needs your help, and if you want to eat dinner tonight, you will stop what you're doing and carry the food into the house."

She watches as two men work a simple task. They chat and smile. Max follows the containers.

"The tray and salad bowl can go on the counter, and both pots on the stove. Thanks for your help, Alex."

"Glad to help when there is food involved. Can't wait to dig in. The smell is terrific."

"Hope you're hungry. I brought enough for eight."

"I am. Mom, the taskmaster, has had me on housecleaning duty all afternoon. She really wanted the cave to look special for you. I even picked some flowers from beds in front of the house and placed them in the dining room, living room, and patio. Her orders."

"Nice touch, Liz. Alex, please corral your sister so the four of us can talk about this weekend."

With all four on the patio, Marion begins to explain the reason for his weekend visit.

"Your mother and I are investigating crime and corruption in the Tampa Police Department. She came to my office with Sergeant Sly a few weeks ago with some frightening information and reasonable assumptions. The recent rash of violence caused her to suspect there is an evil element where she works. And, we have since learned that the evil is pervasive throughout the department. So our investigation covered ancient files to the present activities. Because we are getting close to arresting the criminals, your mother and I have a ton of details to confirm before next week. So, this is a working weekend for us…"

In thirty minutes, he tells the children enough to satisfy their curiosity and justify his presence, but none of the frightening details: the murders of their father, Leonard Sly, Marshall Ross, Hector Lopez, Umberto Rosario, and Eduardo Montenegro. He never mentions the car across the street watching their house, the fact that their mother has had a protection detail for a few days, and that they have had their own observation detail.

"I have a question. No offense meant, but why are you here now? I mean, if this is a big working weekend, wouldn't you do better in your office?"

"Good question, Alex. The District Attorney's office plans to spring the trap of arrest on the bad guys this very weekend. Given some recent events, I believe these bad guys have already determined that your mother is involved in the investigation. They may think she could be the cause of their downfall. Thus, my concern is that they may try something stupid to influence her actions. And, since she is home recuperating from a shooting incident, that's where I want to be to ensure nothing goes wrong. Plus, I am connected to those that need to talk to me by means of two cell phones and a computer. So it's not important where I am physically. And I choose to be here with you guys."

"You mean they would try to hurt or kill Mom?"

"Cary, that's not a real possibility. But, representing the District Attorney's office, my duty is to guarantee her safety. I want nothing to befall her. I simply want to be absolutely positively sure your mother and you two are safe and sound. By Christmas day, this will all be over. I am here for a couple of evenings just as a precaution. Besides, I have no family with whom I could celebrate, so I chose yours."

"Sir, do you carry a gun like Mom?"

"Carry? No. But I'm licensed to, Alex."

"What do we do if the bad guys come to the house?"

"Again, an almost non-existent scenario. But, if it were to happen, I will deal with them."

"What does Mom do?"

"As a police detective, she will help me. As your mother, she will make sure you're safe. Now, if there are no more questions, I have to get to the kitchen and prep dinner."

Liz sees concern on the faces of her children. They are good soldiers and will do what they are told. She sees they are frightened by the threat of the unknown. The unknown can be terrifying when the unknown includes is the possibility of violence.

"OK? Now who's hungry?"

"What's for dinner?"

"Spare ribs, scalloped potatoes, green beans, and salad, Cary. Plus, good fresh French bread to sop up the sauce. All compliments of a restaurant downtown, LaMond. I just ordered, picked up, and delivered here. Consider me the delivery man not the chef. Dinner will be ready in less than thirty minutes. Now I take on the Herculean task of reheating."

Liz and the children disappear upstairs to wash up. Max follows Marion into the kitchen. He smells food...and not from a bag or can.

"OK, everybody, dinner is on the table."

Marion's phone rings.

"Sorry, I have to take this. Please help yourself and start."

He steps onto the outside porch and slides closed the glass door that separates the patio and porch. While he talks, he writes notes in his folder. The conversation lasts fifteen minutes.

"Sorry about the disturbance. That's a problem with working weekends. Everybody wants you to work for them. How is everything?"

"Delicious."

"Fantastic. Mom, we have to have spare ribs again...real soon."

The four, like a traditional family, eat and converse between bites. Alex and Cary tell Marion all about their school: academics, the theater, and athletics. Marion touches on the high points of his job. He relates his career and his accomplishments. He never mentions his divorce. The children clean their plates and devour seconds of everything except salad.

"I see neither of you guys liked the meal."

"We call it Hoovering. We inhale everything on our plates and look for more."

"I have clean-up. The three of you just relax."

"Marion, I'll give you a hand. Alex. Cary. You can watch TV or, heaven forbid, start the reports and papers which are due after the Christmas break."

The faces of the two children lengthen. But they know that if they start their school assignments now they won't be a panicky burden at the end of break. Off they go to their rooms. They leave Marion and Liz to KP. The little food that remained after dinner is stored in the fridge. Max gets nothing. He mopes upstairs to be with Cary. The kitchen workers steal glances at each other but immediately look away when caught. Staring lovingly without being noticed by the object of your affection is quite difficult. Each smiles when caught.

"Done is done. Food brought, served, and kitchen cleaned as advertised. Now we need to talk in private."

"You look concerned? Let's step onto the patio."

"The call I got was from the FDLE. They found the black SUV thanks to your license plate information. There was GSR on the inside of the passenger-side rear door. The shooter's door. There was a single shell casing on the rear floor that was dusted for prints. Up popped Geraldo Jimenez. The steering wheel and door handles had been wiped down, but not entirely. Alberto Cosmarti had driven the SUV, but it's owned by Jimenez. When the FDLE arrived at their doors for the second time in less than twenty-four hours, the two immediately lawyered up. So, both upstanding young men are being held as material witnesses somewhere near Tampa. It is the same with the

Los Hermanos: Roberto Ricardo, Jose Hernandez, and Benito de Vila. Scooped up as material witnesses and deposited somewhere close by. For their own protection, of course.

"Once they call lawyers, it will take hours for their lawyers to find their clients due to bad directions and miscommunications. But the perps will be on the street by late afternoon or early evening tomorrow. We will have them under surveillance; watching them like an osprey watches the bay water for food. My guess is that, upon hearing from these bad guys, their lawyers will notify someone in the police department. That person will spread the news that we are getting dangerously closer to ending their enterprise. The end of the Street Cleaners is at hand."

"What does that mean for me…us?"

"It means we are almost there, but we can't let down our guard for a few more days. Now you and I have to get to work."

After an hour and a-half of going over all the details twice, Marion makes a call.

"It's time to bring down the hammer."

A simple directive. He hangs up.

"And what does that mean?"

"Around two AM tomorrow, in the dark of very early morning, the FDLE will commence arresting the fifteen Street Cleaners that we know of. The Grand Jury gave me indictments against all of them. The round-up will be simultaneous so that there can be no tip-offs. After the swoop and scoop, they will sit in a holding tank until their lawyers, personal or PBA rep, can get to them.

"Then it's over by sunrise tomorrow. Thank gawd, Marion."

"Not exactly. We can make cases of enterprise corruption, attempted murder, murder, extortion, and bribery of an official against the fifteen whom we know. Unfortunately, we don't know whom we don't know. I am hoping that someone within the group will give up the names of anybody above commanders at the top as well as any and all wannabes at the bottom. I leave the truth extraction up to the FDLE. Until such time that we get all their names and arrest them, these unknowns are disconcerting unknowns. How they will react in the face of being trapped is the issue. At best, the wannabes will disappear. That's my hope."

"Or, at worst, they could attempt retaliation against those who caught the bosses. That's me and you, Marion."

"Retaliation is not likely. But, that is why you and your children must be watched and protected for the next few days."

His response is small comfort.

"Were you able to get wine in your provisional acquisition?"

"How unthinking of me. I have a nice bottle of Merlot for the adults. Interesting how we use the phrase "nice bottle" as if we had a choice of buying swill, vinegar, or drinkable wine. Regardless, the wine is in the kitchen. I'll get it."

Liz has moved outside to the porch to enjoy the cool clean winter air and to stare at the myriad stars. Marion returns with the uncorked bottle and two glasses. He pours. They sit on a chaise. The air is brisk. The sky is pitch-black, a perfect background for the twinkling stars. They truly look like they are twinkling. There is no moon.

"To a successful end to this case."

"I'll drink to that."

"One more toast. I toast to you. I'm glad Liz Kimble came into my life."

"I'm glad I met you, too."

They sit quietly. Marion reaches out his hand to take hers. She gives it willingly. His phone rings. They both frown.

"Yes. That's great. Let me know when you have them in the tank. Thanks for all your help. Me, too."

He turns to Liz.

"More members will be stashed away shortly."

Marion and Liz settle into a second glass of wine. They have reviewed all the facts for the umpteenth time and now want to relax. She slides over to sit next to him. When she arrives at his side, he leans in to her and kisses her deeply. She kisses back just as deep. One kiss leads to a second. Arousal is rearing his head. Suddenly, the footsteps of two teens as they clamber down the stairs. The amorous foray comes to a screeching halt before it really begins. A plaintive cry from the kitchen.

"What's for dessert?"

"There are four small tarts inside the box on the bottom shelf of the fridge. Help yourself."

"Wait, why don't you each have two?"

"Thanks for dinner, Mr. Morrison. And the tarts."

"You're welcome, Cary."

Their culinary expedition a success, the two teens race upstairs. Liz looks into Marion's eyes.

"Where were we?"

"Here."

He pulls her close. Their lips lock. Their bodies are at an angle awkwardly pressed together. The temporary interruption has heightened their desire. Tongues explore mouths. Hands grip tightly. Breathing that started deep is becoming shallow and rapid. Hands are sliding over upper torsos and necks. In a flash, Liz pulls away.

"Wait."

"For what, Liz?"

"It's neither the time nor the place for this. I want to take this to the next level. But I can't with my kids upstairs. I don't want them coming upon us rutting on the chaise."

"Agreed. But how do we keep our desires in check? And for how long?"

"I don't know and I don't know. Let's think about this conundrum for a few days."

"Fair enough. Uh-oh, the wine bottle is empty. I must have bought a bottle with a hole in the bottom. It's eleven. I think it's time for me to leave. I'll return tomorrow around five, if that's OK."

A part of Liz wants Marion to stay. But the maternal part of her wants time to sort through her feelings and how to explain the situation to Cary and Alex.

"Alex. Cary. Mr. Morrison is leaving."

The two children come down the stairs.

"Thanks for dinner, Mr. Morrison. It was terrific."

"Yeah, thanks for dinner. I hope I'm not being rude, but what's for dinner tomorrow?"

"It's not rude to be curious, Alex. Tomorrow's meal will consist of a special recipe of mac and cheese, a vegetable medley, and salad."

"The dinner was great. Mom could learn a lot from the chef at LaMond."

"I could, too. I hate to cook, but I love good food. So I purchase great meals from a great chef whenever I can. Tomorrow I can."

"Don't lose his telephone number."

"I won't Alex. See you both tomorrow."

"I'll help you carry the pots to your car."

"Thanks, Liz. Good night, you guys."

Max stands in the doorway watching every move of the two adults. He is acting parental. The items are loaded into the trunk. As Marion approaches the driver's side door, Liz intercepts him. She wraps her arms around his neck and presses her body against his from toes to lips. She can no longer feel the pain in her arm. The kiss she initiates originated in her loins. Slowly, she rubs her hips against his until both arousals start. She can feel his. She likes it but pulls away.

"Drive safely. See you tomorrow."

"One last item; do not walk the dog in the neighborhood tonight or tomorrow. Let him roam and relieve himself in the backyard until this is over and everyone we want has been arrested. OK?"

"OK."

Marion looks over at Rose Widdix's car. He hopes she has not witnessed anything, and if she saw anything, he hopes she will forget what she saw. All the way home, he plays out various scenarios involving Liz. Because these are his scenarios, they all end to his liking. Tomorrow is the big day: a day of fireworks. Yet, he fears possible retaliation. His job tomorrow will be to stand between good and evil.

XIX

Saturday morning arrives. Nothing special for the majority of Tampa's population. Very special for fifteen members of the Tampa Police Department. Arrested and held in a FDLE secure location, the men wait for their one telephone call. They no longer have possession of their cell phones, and the closest payphone is eight blocks away. Or so they are told. They are blindfolded and driven there one at a time. Reaching all of their lawyers takes more than four hours. Since they have no idea where they are being held, the lawyers must call the FDLE to ascertain the location. Unfortunately, the FDLE telephone lines seem to be busy all the time.

The sun pokes its fingers through the horizontal blinds in three bedrooms. Nature's alarm clock makes staying in bed an effort. Liz is the first to rise. Teens will sleep until noon if it weren't for their bladders and olfactory senses that tell them breakfast is being prepared…bacon, eggs, and biscuits. They stagger down the stairs and plop into chairs. They are like little birds looking to their mother to feed them. The pre-holiday world is frenetically alive beyond the Kimble home.

Commerce and charity go hand in hand this time of year. And the most vivid display of this strange couple is found at the mall. Because this is the last Saturday before Christmas, there are lines of cars waiting to get into the parking lot of the International Mall. At 6 AM, there are lines of people waiting for the stores to open at 7. The emotional, guilt-driven stress of the season is evident in the faces of the shoppers. Some are dressed in winter garb as if they were living in Boston. Floridians will accept any excuse to wear heavy, yet quite fashionable winter clothing in fifty-degree weather. There is a boy with costume reindeer antlers on his head. Another is dressed like an elf. Standing at the mall entrances, are Santas ringing bells seeking donations for the needy.

Because it is real winter up north, Tampa and the surrounding area are hit with the usual influx of homeless seeking warmth and the kindness of the South. Several of them are working the lines of shoppers requesting money from those that have it. A veritable gold mine for those with their hands outstretched.

The lines have attracted coffee carts selling a roll and small cup of coffee for five dollars. Several people buy this meager breakfast for those less fortunate. The coffee cart business is brisk but will end when the stores open. The homeless will not depart when the carts do. They will wait outside the main entrance for shoppers to leave the store and hit them up one more time for cash. No one knows where this money goes. Some say to pay for a flophouse bed. Some say for the next meal. Many say the money goes to buy a large bottle of cheap wine to ease their pain, keep them warm, and help them sleep.

Marion Morrison slept fitfully. Between one-hour naps, he was on the phone with various members of his task force. He has reviewed the minutia of the vast case so often he can recite them. The brilliant sunrise flooding through the large windows of his aerie is his cue to prepare for the next steps. He punches in a new number on his phone.

"Is this Harold Shade?"

"Yes. Who is this?"

"This is ADA Marion Morrison. Sorry to awaken you, but I have important information for you. If you would be so kind as to come and see me, I will give you the story of your life. Can you be here in an hour?"

"I rarely get calls from the District Attorney's office so you have piqued my interest. I can be at your building in twenty minutes."

"I am not in my office. I am at home. The address is..."

Public exposure of evil is like shining a light on a floor covered with cockroaches. They scurry looking for a place to hide, because they don't want to be noticed then crushed. In this situation, there is no place for these human vermin to hide. A front-page story will bring them into the light of public scrutiny and drive them out of their nest into a much larger house with small eight-by-twelve rooms. Marion showers and shaves before his guest arrives. He is only partially refreshed.

"Yes, please send him up."

"Welcome, Mr. Shade, would you like some fresh coffee?"

"Yes, indeed."

"What I am about to tell you can't be published until Christmas Day."

"Why the delay?"

"We have not completed our work because it is quite extensive in scope. Plus, you'll need a day to digest what I tell you, and there will be more information for you tomorrow. Thus, my request for you to develop your story and sit on it for forty-eight hours. During my presentation of the facts, please hold your questions. When I am finished telling you what we know and what we are doing about it, you may ask me anything you wish. You may record what I am about to tell you or you can rely solely on your notes. Let me begin by explaining an organization chart…"

Forty-five minutes later, the presentation of the facts is complete just as it was with the Grand Jury. The reporter's scribbling in his notepad takes up six pages. He takes a picture of the organization chart with his phone. The recorder is turned off, his pen laid to rest on the pad, and Harold Shade leans back in his chair smiling.

"That's almost unbelievable. I'm sure you're aware of the ramifications of your investigation. If the men you mentioned are convicted, there will be a total upheaval in the police department. Many men in blue will be jailed creating extensive voids in police leadership. There will be a citizen's uproar. And, if this corruption is found in city government, the citizens will want blood. A new administration with aggressive oversight riding herd on a new police department. I'm not sure the city can handle such extensive turmoil without resorting to some form of vigilantism. If the people can't trust those hired to protect them, they may take protection into their own hands. That's the dangerous, yet logical, extension of your efforts. How do you plan to avoid that eventuality?"

"First, I don't think the city will fall into a paroxysm of riotous anarchy. So far, the corruption can be found in a small but influential number of police department middle management: much less than one-tenth of one percent of the total force. Second, the city has checks and balances plus bench strength to maintain a well-functioning department. So, I don't think your overarching concern is a real possibility. Just what about the specific aspects of what you just heard raises questions?"

"Let me get this straight. This is a widespread investigation that started with the murder of a retired OG of Los Hermanos."

"It actually goes back to the assassination of Detective Alexander Kimble two years ago. But the events that opened our investigation were the murders of Marshall Ross and Hector Lopez."

"And you did all this by yourself?"

"No, the investigation was driven by Detective Elizabeth Kimble. She did the legwork, unearthed the facts, and put herself in harm's way. I just put her work into perspective. She deserves most of the credit."

"Why is she not here with you now?"

"She is at home with her children getting ready for Christmas."

"Do you think she is safe from reprisal?"

"Yes."

"May I talk to her?"

"On Monday you will be invited to her home. She is still recuperating from two gunshot wounds."

"Why has no one ever mentioned these Street Cleaners before?"

"They worked hard to stay off the radar. Plus, they are led by police commanders who are just below the Deputy Chiefs and Chief. People in these high places know how to hide things they feel would put them in a bad light or that would be disruptive to their enterprise."

"How can you explain the role of the two street gangs?"

"They worked for the Street Cleaners. Muy Loco and Los Hermanos were allowed to thrive only if they kicked a portion of their ill-gotten gains back to the cops. The Street Cleaners are, therefore, ultimately accountable for the vast majority of the extortion, burglaries, smash and grabs, robberies, and car thefts in the city. We are confident the street gangs will roll on their police handlers and, thus, prove our working theory. And we will inexorably move up the food chain getting cooperation at every step. Working up the food chain is a time-honored process in major investigations."

"Do you suspect any Deputy Chiefs or the Chief herself?"

"Not so far."

"What about the Mayor or anyone on the City Council?"

"Not so far."

"When will you know?"

"When those we have arrested begin to talk openly and honestly to us about their organization and its activities. Particularly the commanders. They may be willing and able to point their fingers at those above them who turned a blind eye to this long-standing enterprise."

"When will I be able to interview the fifteen men you arrested?"

"Wednesday, after they are arraigned, they will be available for interviews. Whether any of them grant interviews is a separate question."

"When will we have a follow-up conversation?"

"As I said, Monday if things go as planned. That way the entire story can be read by the good citizens of Tampa on Tuesday. A special Christmas gift."

"What things? What do you hope will happen?"

"I can't tell you what things now. I will tell you more when we meet again."

"One last question. What is your relationship with Detective Kimble?"

"We are professionals seeking justice. That's all."

"Nothing more?"

"Nothing more."

"I want to go home, digest my notes, format an outline of my story, and await your call. Thanks for the exclusive. But, why me?"

"I revealed all of this to you for two reasons. First, the public has a right to know the truth about those entrusted with their safekeeping. Print is the best way to get the entire story out in detail. And second, my sources tell me you are a man of discretion who would not leak any information about our investigation until he knew he would not put anyone in danger."

"Thank you for your trust. Now I must get to work creating a story outline."

Marion contacts his FDLE team. Everything is going according to plan. Once the lawyers arrive and the detainees are released, the state cops will withdraw and head back to their base. But the lawyers have not yet arrived. The detainees are very cranky. It seems the concrete floors and metal-framed beds are not to their liking. And they are hungry. No food. The escorted bathroom visits make it seem like jail. Marion thinks...tough shit! Their time in detention is just a taste of their next fifteen-to-twenty-five years.

He calls LaMond. They are prepping his meal. It will be ready by four. It is now nap time.

❧　❧

"Hey, kids, Mr. Morrison and dinner are here. Alex, help carry the pots, pans, and whatever into the kitchen. Cary, double-check the patio. I think we'll eat out there tonight. Welcome back, Marion. I see you have brought enough food to feed us well for some time."

Max unfolds his body from its sleep position and wanders into the kitchen. He smells food. Slowly, he approaches Marion and sniffs him. The dog's tail begins to wag. A friend who brings food is here.

"Hi, guys. Alex, thanks for the help. Liz, I brought wine for us and sweet tea for your children. Hey, Cary, how was your day?"

"Since we couldn't leave the house, I spent nearly all day finishing the assignments for after break. I guess I should be thankful for that. But I really don't like being cooped up all day. Too much like school. Somehow I'll survive."

"All of these precautions won't be necessary much longer. Hang in there."

"Alex, how was your day?"

"Homework. Gave Max exercise in the backyard. Worked on my two papers. How long will this faux-incarceration last?"

"Not much longer. Now you guys leave your mother and me alone so we can talk…if you don't mind. Dinner will be ready in about forty-five minutes."

"What's in the special mac and cheese?"

"Seafood; lump crab meat, shrimp, and lobster."

"Sounds incredible. Cary, let's leave the adults to talk. Wink. Wink."

They leave the first floor to Liz and Marion. Immediately, he sweeps her into his arms and kisses her deeply. She is not prepared for the attack but responds in kind after two seconds.

"OK, Marion what has transpired since last night?"

"Boy, talk about ice water."

"Time and place are critical components for the culmination of…"

"I know. I just wanted you to know that I feel the same today as I did last evening…only more so."

"Me, too. But, not here. Not now."

They walk to the screened-in porch holding hands.

"The arrests have been made. The criminals have lawyers or been assigned a lawyer from the Public Defender's office. The massive arraignment is set for Wednesday, the day after Christmas. I spoke to Harold Shade and gave him enough information for him to start a story that will appear Christmas day. We should talk to him Monday and help him fill in the blanks. Tonight we wait to see if there is any blowback."

"Now I am frightened. What do you mean by blowback?"

"Undoubtedly, the Street Cleaners have gotten word to wannabes not arrested to stay out of sight. Depending on the strength of their resolve, I guess some wannabes, those without families, will flee. Get out of Dodge now that the sheriff knows who they are."

"Will any of them seek revenge upon me and my family?"

"Not a chance. I have men watching as many of the wannabes as we know. My guys will keep close tabs on them so no harm can befall us. Besides, we have Rose across the street. She's our warning system."

"I am not as blindly optimistic as you are. I am a mother of two children. My instincts are flight not fight."

"That's why I have taken every precaution to avoid any harm coming to you and your family."

"I hear you. But, I'm still wary. I think I'll keep my service piece within arm's reach tonight. Wherever I go, it goes. What about you? Where is your cannon?"

"In my briefcase that will not leave my side tonight. Now, if we don't want a rebellion on our hands, I'd better prep dinner. The tray of mac and cheese in the oven at 300 for thirty minutes. The mixture of vegetables will take fifteen minutes. And, for the adults, a pre-dinner glass of wine."

"I could use a drink."

The winter sun is setting. The sky is orange and deep blue, and the sun's wide fingers spread across the sky.

Shadows are short-lived. Drinks in hand, the two celebrate the close of a peaceful and successful day.

"I never asked, and I am hesitant now. But, what happened to your marriage? If I am treading on sacred ground, tell me."

"Not sacred ground. I was working too hard climbing up the ladder and I did not pay enough attention to my wife. She found someone who would lavish her massive ego with praise. After a year of the mess, we agreed to seek a divorce. Marriage counseling was considered but it was not viable. I gave her the property she wanted and a lump-sum payment to go away so that she would not be a hindrance to my drive for success. She took everything I offered and settled into a life with the other man, who, it turns out, had a big cocaine habit. He hooked her. She pissed through the money I gave her and sold some of my former possessions to pay for their drugs. About a year and a half after our divorce was settled, she petitioned the court for more money. The court said no. I left Fort Myers and began work in the Appellate Division in Lakeland. I am happy and don't care if she is or not. That's the abridged version. Does it answer your question?"

"I didn't mean to pick at old scabs."

"No apology necessary. I am happy doing what I'm doing. And I thought I was happy being a loner until I met you. You changed those feelings. I'm glad about the change. Let's eat. You call your children. I'll get the food onto plates."

"What's the crust on the mac and cheese? It's fantastic."

"A combination of Romano, Asiago, and Parmesan cheeses mixed with bread crumbs."

"The seafood is a great idea."

"Not mine, Alex. Remember, I simply order and pick up. Your compliments should go to the kitchen staff at LaMond. It's the chef's recipe."

"Tell him thanks for me, will you?"

"Yes, I will."

"Mom, you've got to get this recipe."

Another evening meal with conversation about the season.

"Mr. Morrison. How many more days will we be housebound?"

"One or two more at most, Cary. Then you will be sprung from this jail."

"It's just that I am missing the biggest weekend at the mall with my crew."

"Sorry to cause you any inconvenience, but your safety is my highest concern. Now who wants seconds?"

Marion and Liz carry four plates into the kitchen. Mac and cheese and the vegetable medley are spooned onto the teens' plates, while the adult plates receive more salad. Dinner continues.

"Sir, are you married?"

"No, Cary. Divorced. My ex lives in Fort Myers."

"Do you have children?"

"Not that fortunate."

"So if you weren't here babysitting us, you would be spending Christmas alone. Right?"

"Well, technically not alone. Just not with family. I have several long-time friends who invite me to their homes for Thanksgiving and Christmas. I think they feel sorry for me during the holidays. So I am rarely alone on those special days."

"But this is better. Right?"

"As your generation says…waaaaay better."

"We're glad you're here regardless of the reason."

"Thank you."

"OK, you two, as a pre-Christmas gift to Marion, you will be responsible for bussing and clean-up."

"I'll do my part. Not sure about Mr. Wisenheimer."

"Don't speak for me, little sister, I'm already on it."

Alex stands and circles the table collecting plates and silverware. The adults sit and stare at each other.

XX

"I think it's wise for me to stay a little later tonight than I did last night."

"Why?"

"If any blowback is going to happen, it might happen tonight."

"So, I was right when I said you expected trouble."

"Not necessarily right. I just don't want to take any unnecessary risks."

"If you're more concerned than you let on, you can sleep on the couch."

"That would be awkward when Alex and Cary get up in the morning. To save us the embarrassment of explaining my presence, I'll stay until twelve. By then they'll be asleep. I'm sure everything will be fine."

"If that's what you want, OK."

"That's what is right. Thanks."

"Now tell me, what's the latest?"

"The fab fifteen have been arrested and are out of their retention cells. They are undoubtedly meeting with their lawyers who are aware of the detailed charges. They'll be drafting motions of dismissal today and tomorrow. At the arraignments on Wednesday, I'll have to be sharp. One of the FDLE officers thinks he has spotted two weak links in the chain of evil. He thinks we can learn the names of those above and below the captains and lieutenants busted. He'll give me a call sometime with a status update. Can I get you another glass of wine?"

"The man not only brings great food, he waits on me. What will he think of next?"

"You know what I'm thinking. But I've been admonished…not here. Not now."

"Throwing my words back in my face."

They laugh.

"Where's Max?"

"He's upstairs with Cary. It's where he goes when she goes to her room. Max is devoted to her."

"I can see why. She is kind, considerate, and she obviously loves him."

"Where is my glass of wine? Snap to it, knave."

"Right away, your haughty highness."

He returns holding the second bottle. They settle into an evening of flirtatious conversation. Softly touching as they speak. Not in the traditional, socially acceptable Southern hand-on-hand, but fingers tracing lines and circles on each other's arms and cheeks. This prelude to petting consumes the next fleeting hours as they reveal their plans and hopes. Occasionally, one or the other will impart a small buss on a forehead, cheek, or lips.

"Well, lovely maiden, it is time for me to depart."

"So soon."

"I will return on the morrow. Do you have a grill?"

"Yes, why?"

"Steak, corn, and baked potato."

"LaMond?"

"No, I confess. From the over-priced superior quality food mart downtown and my fridge. I'll be here about five. By then I'll have all the information I need to move forward and release you from home jail. With your help, I can load the tray into the car. No need to call Alex."

Marion carries the cleaned tray to his car. He hands the tray to Liz so he can open the trunk. Job completed, he turns to say good night and is greeted by an attacking mouth and hands that touch his buns and cup is man parts. Liz's hands are all over his body in a fever pitch. She feels his arousal, while he struggles to control himself.

"What was that all about?"

"I wanted you to know what awaits you when we both can say...here and now."

"I don't know if you dream, but I do. And tonight's dream will be all about you and us. See you tomorrow."

Marion backs his car out of the driveway and heads toward downtown. Liz watches the tail lights disappear around a corner. Before she enters the house, she glances over to Rose Widdix's car. Liz makes sure all the doors are locked, and turns on the exterior security flood lights, front and rear. Excited about her prospects with Marion, she is nonetheless concerned about a real and present danger.

In restless slumber, Liz hears the ticking of a clock. Her eyes see nothing in the dark of her dream world, but the feeling in her soul is concern. She is frozen in her place. Is she standing or prone? Is she in bed? What is the source of the ticking sound? It doesn't get louder. She hears another sound. Rolling thunder. Far away. It does not become louder. Still the ticking. Its cadence is faster. Why would her clock do that? Louder now, the thunder rolls but does not crack as during a storm. There are no flashes of lightning to brighten the air outside. Where is the storm? The thunder pauses, as if to catch its breath.

Her eyes pop open as if on command. The ticking and thunder are still in her ears. She sits up and leaves her bed. Opening the door to her bedroom, Liz sees Max pacing on the tile floor in the hall. Why would he leave Cary's bedroom? His growl is deeper and more threatening than she can recall. Something sinister is bringing Max's protective instincts to the fore. She quickly returns to her room, opens the lock box, and removes her Sig Sauer. Making sure there is a cartridge in the chamber, she puts on a pair of shorts and a sweatshirt. Gun in hand and an extra clip in her waistband, Liz heads downstairs with Max close behind. Whatever spooked Max is still within his sensory range. She checks the front door, the sliding door to the patio, and the door to the garage. All three are locked. She notes that the security flood lights in the backyard are off. She fears someone somehow got to them. Liz does not turn on any lights inside the house. Remaining in the darkness gives her a small advantage in dealing with whatever is outside. The kitchen is not pitch- black as she would like. She can see the major details of the kitchen in the muted green, blue and red of the LED lights on the fridge, stove and microwave. She realizes that in these lights she casts a shadow. The shadow can be traced back to a target by whoever is outside, so she stays crouched. Max's rolling thunder has become a threatening growl.

"Mom, what's going on with you and Max? Why are you in the dark?"

"I'm not sure what's going on, Cary. I just know that Max has been spooked by something outside."

Cary turns on the lights in the kitchen. Both mother and child are awash in fluorescent glow. Immediately a bullet crashes through the porch screen and patio sliding door. It smacks into the kitchen wall. Cary yelps.

"Turn off the lights, now!"

Liz closes her eyes momentarily to adjust them back to the darkness. She peers into the backyard to find the source of the shot. All is eerily quiet. She notes that the muzzle flash was to her left. She thinks she sees a shadow move across the yard, hunched over as it runs. Then six more slugs find their way into the kitchen wall. These from a different source. Liz now knows there are at least two shooters. The porch screen is shredded and shards of glass from the sliding glass door sprinkle the patio and the kitchen floors. Max fires off five big barks. Loud enough to awaken Alex and the neighbors. The intruders are too close for his liking.

"Cary, go upstairs immediately. Call 9-1-1. Tell them you are reporting a home invasion. Tell them I am Detective Kimble. Tell them shots have been fired. Tell them the scene requires at least two patrol cars. Go now, damn it. Now. And stay upstairs."

"Mom, what's all the ruckus?"

"Alex, don't come downstairs. Stay with your sister upstairs while she calls 9-1-1. Both of you remain upstairs until I tell you that you can come down. I need Max down here with me. Stay with me, Max. Good boy."

Liz kneels on the kitchen floor and peers into the darkness, hoping to see the forms of the shooters. Can she wait for whomever to come to her? That would be to her advantage but a significant risk to her children. She must lure them into exposure outside. Get them to fire again so she can note their locations.

"WHO THE HELL ARE YOU AND WHAT DO YOU WANT?"

Silence.

"I KNOW THERE ARE TWO OF YOU AND THAT YOU'RE AFRAID TO COME INTO MY HOUSE AND CONFRONT ME FACE-TO-FACE. FUCKING COWARDS!"

Eight more slugs hit the wall. Four, each from the two far corners of the yard. Liz fires at the locations. She hears no cry of pain, but is sure she got their attention. All is quiet. Cary whispers down the stairs.

"I called 9-1-1. They said they're sending help."

"Stay upstairs until they arrive."

She turns and focuses on the yard. Is one shadow moving toward the house? She fires. She peers into the darkness. The reports from her gun do not seem to arouse curiosity among the neighbors. Liz does not see that any lights in the surrounding homes have been turned on. Fireworks, of course. Fireworks are set off at every major holiday. It is a Southern tradition. The neighbors must think someone is celebrating early. Where the hell are the patrol cars? Everything is quiet. Too quiet. Everything except Max, who is pacing. His warning growl has become a whimper as if he senses mortal danger. He can't do anything but be afraid.

"Cary, I need you to call Max upstairs to be with you. He is frightened and he needs your strength. Call him now."

At the disappearance of the dog and the fading of her words, a barrage of slugs rakes the patio and kitchen. Glass and china are shattered and wood is splintered all over the floors. The intruders have replaced handguns with automatic weapons. Liz checks the clip in her gun, as well as the extra clip in her waistband. Then a new noise: the report of a heavy caliber weapon surprises her. Six shots from the rear outside wall of the house. This shooting generates return fire from automatic weapons directed at the outer wall of the garage. The muzzle flashes from the far corners of the yard silhouette the two shooters. One is standing. One is crouched. She returns fire. The standing shooter crumples like wet paper and falls in a heap. Four more large caliber slugs hit the crouching shooter and the fence behind him. He takes his final dirt nap.

"Liz, have you been hit? Are you all right?"

Marion's voice, though strained and faint, is comfort after the cacophony of gunfire.

"I'm fine, but the house is a mess. Are you OK?"

"I've been hit. I think twice. I'm woozy. I'll have to go to a hospital. Can you come out here? Do you have a flashlight? I want to see who these shooters are."

"Kids, it's safe to come downstairs."

Max and the children race down the stairs. The big dog rushes to Liz and sniffs her. Satisfied she is not hurt, he trots outside to inspect the carnage. His tail is wagging at this new game of seek and sniff.

"Mommy! Mommy, are you all right?"

Cary rushes to her mother and hugs her emphatically. The girl is trembling, and her skin is cold and clammy. She is shedding no tears. Liz recognizes the signs of shock.

"I'm fine. Can't say the same for the porch screen, the patio, and kitchen. They shot the fridge and the stove. Watch your step down here. There are glass and porcelain shards all over the floor. Cary, go back upstairs and put on a sweater, you're shivering. Alex, bring me the big flashlight from the garage. I need to inspect outside."

He hands Liz the flashlight after he hugs her. He is standing tall and brave like his father.

"Mom, this was like a shootout at the OK Corral. The Clantons against the Earps. Were you hit?"

"No, I'm fine. Not sure about Marion."

"He's still here?"

She can hear multiple police sirens coming closer from different directions. Gingerly, she exits through what once was a sliding door, onto the patio, then through what is left of the porch screen to the backyard.

"Marion? There you are. Where were you hit? How badly are you hurt?"

Marion is propped up against the outside rear wall of the garage. Two blood pools have formed on his shirt: one on his right shoulder and one on the right side below his rib cage. This one appears to be getting larger.

"I'm hangin' on. Breathing is difficult. Did you call for an ambulance?"

"Alex, bring the police back here and tell them that Mr. Morrison has been shot. He needs medical attention. Tell the officers that we will need two EMT vans. One for a trip to the ER and one for a trip to the morgue."

Aroused by the sirens and flashing lights, the neighbors have come from all surrounding homes to observe the results of the chaos. Liz can hear milling around in front of her home. With the patrolmen tending to Marion, she goes back to the kitchen and peers through a front window. Some members of the small crowd are clothed and some have wrapped their pajama-clad bodies with bathrobes. Clusters have formed. They do not speak to the police. They just observe. Liz steps through the front door.

"Liz, are you and your kids all right? Tom, I told you it wasn't fireworks. I know fireworks."

"Martha, thanks for asking. We're fine. The house is a mess. Sorry to disturb you."

"Nothing like a little excitement before Christmas."

"Tom, glad to see you."

"Hey, Liz, Jeanie and I are here. Is there anything we can do to help?"

"Not sure. Give me a minute to sort through the events."

She turns and returns to the backyard and the garage wall where Marion is seated on the ground resting against the cinder block wall.

"Marion, you are a dear friend. You came back to protect my family and me."

"Never left. Watching your house from the backyard of property beside yours. Feared attack might occur so I decided to hang ar…"

Marion slips into unconsciousness and slumps to his left onto the ground. Max is standing by his side. When the EMTs arrive, Max stares at them and growls a low warning to not hurt this good human. A patrolman tells Liz that he requested a senior officer and a Crime Analysis Team.

"Max. It's OK. These men have to take Mr. Morrison to the hospital. Cary, call Max, please. Will Marion be all right?"

"Mr. Morrison was hit twice. He is losing blood. The bullet that hit his side must have nicked something important before exiting. That will be determined by the doctors at County General. From the trauma of being shot, he is drifting in and out. His vitals are weak but stable. We have to hurry."

Liz walks to two police officers, and recounts the details of the evening's mayhem. Not all the details, just the ones pertinent to the shooting. Halfway through her explanation, a sector SUV with a senior officer arrives followed by a Crime Analysis Team van. Liz approaches Lieutenant Minter and walks with him and the patrolmen to the two bodies she identifies as Raymond Wovent and Bruno Weingarten. Both are dead. Wovent has two large entry holes in his chest and there are also several large holes in the stockade fence thanks to Marion. Weingarten was hit twice, once in the chest and once in the head. Her kill.

The cacophonous confusion of the gunfight has morphed into the controlled chaos of police fact finding and gathering...statements, nearly fifty shell casing identification cones, most of them outside the house, multiple vehicles, gurneys, klieg lights, and numerous police officials walking gingerly around the expansive crime scene. She stands amidst the thorough investigators...each with a singular purpose. Protocol requires that all police weapons used during a shooting must be retrieved for review and analysis by forensics. Four handguns and two department-issued AR-15s are loaded into the CAT van. Protocol also requires that the police officer involved in the shooting must visit a Department shrink to ensure that the shooter's mind is clear and clean. That will have to wait until after Christmas.

The patrolmen take the remainder of her statement about the evening and the would-be assassins. She tells them why she thinks the two bad guys were at her house on the Saturday night before Christmas. The patrolmen act surprised that two detectives would try to assassinate a fellow detective and an ADA. Lieutenant Minter does not act surprised.

In the front of her house is muted activity: uniformed police, flashing lights, and the ubiquitous yellow tape to warn those not involved to stay away. The neighbors are standing on their side of the tape. Their conversations and questions are not audible to Liz.

"Kids, after the police leave and give us the OK, we'll have to get this mess cleaned up. Alex, get the two large tarps we use for camping. Plus, a box of large staple nails and the big hammer from the tool bench. You'll need to hang the tarps over the recently created entrance to the patio. Cary, get the push broom, the regular broom, work gloves, and both large trash containers from the garage. You and I will be in charge of trash collection and removal. While you're gathering the tools of our new trades, I want to walk across the street. I'll be right back. When we're done here, we'll all go out for breakfast."

Then she spots Cary standing stock-still staring into the backyard. Holding her sweater in her hand, she is trembling. In the bright light of a crime scene, Liz can see Cary's skin is pale. Mother rushes to child. Liz looks into Cary's eyes.

They are vacant. She approaches one EMT and whispers in his ear. He immediately retrieves a blanket from the van and drapes it over Cary. He returns to Liz. He whispers.

"Your daughter is in shock. I want to take her to County General and have her examined there. She seems to have been substantially impacted by the events.

"Cary, sweetie, I want you to go with these men to the hospital. Just a precaution. On the ride, would you hold Mr. Morrison's hand? He needs your strength. Alex and I will be right behind the van. We'll meet you at the hospital."

The girl appears to be in another universe. Max, her protector, is by her side.

Liz puts her arm around Cary for support and guidance. The girl goes limp and falls into her mother's arms. The EMT helps Liz place Cary on a gurney and into the van. Max growls at the EMT.

"Max, come to me. Cary is OK. Good boy. Good boy. Alex, make sure Max is back in Cary's room."

"Martha. Tom. Jeanie. Bob. Would you do me a huge favor? I need to go to the hospital to be with Cary. They want to examine her. But I'm concerned about leaving the house unattended. Would you watch the place until I return? I won't be gone more than two hours. If it's any longer than that, I'll call. I would really appreciate it."

"Go and be with your daughter."

"We'll watch your house."

"Give her our best."

"Our thoughts are with you and your family."

One van with the wounded departs for County General. The other van with the corpses heads for the ME's domain. Shortly thereafter, the patrol cars and sector SUV pull out of the driveway. Lieutenant Minter has agreed to keep this event under wraps for seventy-two hours. No newspaper. No TV. Ninety minutes after the last shot was fired, the inside of Liz's house is empty of people. She walks across the street and approaches the guardian car.

"Are you Rose Widdix?"

"Yes, I am Special Agent Widdix."

"I'm here to tell you, your duty is over. You can go home."

"Only ADA Morrison has the authority to tell me to leave my post. I'll call him to confirm."

"He won't answer, because I am holding his phone. See. Let me tell you why I have his phone."

In five minutes, Liz gives Rose the very abridged version of what transpired across the street.

"Special Agent, let me ask why didn't you come my house when you heard the gunfire? Did you not think it was worth investigating the commotion? Or were you asleep at your post? No need to answer me. You'll have a chance to explain your actions or lack thereof to ADA Morrison and Commander Ishmael.

Liz does not wait for an answer. There are many more important issues at hand. She heads back to her shattered home. Special Agent Widdix hurriedly drives off as if running away.

"Alex, honey, get in the car. We are going to the hospital."

"What about the house? What's wrong with Cary?"

"The house will be watched by our neighbors. Cary is being taken to the ER for an examination strictly as a precaution. Her body's reaction to the shooting indicates shock. But I want to be sure it's nothing too serious. How about you? How do you feel?"

"Really angry that those guys came to our house and very relieved that you and Mr. Morrison were not killed. I am really, really pumped. Wait until the guys hear what went down at my house. It's like the O.K. Corral. You and Mr. Morrison were like the Earps who took care of the Clantons. Wait until the guys at school hear about our Christmas."

Liz thinks…testosterone. The adult male is channeling through the child. He is truly becoming his father.

"I put the tarps on the patio. I'll start trash detail after I hang the tarps. There is so much damage all over. But, we may not need Cary for clean-up. The two of us ought to be able to handle it."

"Sweetie, you're great. Later today, I'll call an emergency clean-up company and they'll finish what we start. Plus, we'll go to Home Depot and buy sheets of plywood to replace the tarps. That will be our new backyard view until we can get replacement screens for the porch and a sliding glass door for the patio. Maybe we can paint a beach scene on the plywood panels. We'll need to take inventory of all the broken vases and china. The insurance claim will be substantial. We can sweep after the big chunks are in the trash containers. Whatever we miss the first time, the clean-up company can get. The mess isn't going anywhere until we make it go."

"Mom, what about Mr. Morrison? Will he be all right?"

"Good question, Alex. The EMTs said Marion was very weak but stable. We'll check in on him after we check on Cary. Plus, I want the doctor to take a look at you."

"Aw, Mom, I'm fine."

"I'm sure you feel that way now. I just want to be medically sure. Now let's get moving. Get in the car."

"Why don't we take both of them breakfast? I'll bet they'll be hungry, and everybody knows how lousy hospital food is."

"Good thinking, Alex, except let's see how they are doing before we bring food into the hospital.

Male teenagers very often think with their stomachs.

XXI

Liz wonders if ERs all over the country have a look and smell similar to County General. Subtle colors, the hint of antiseptic in the air, bright lights, the calm almost seductive female voice over the intercom, and the scurrying of caregivers...each with a singular purpose. Are the ERs and those who work in them engineered that way?

"I'd like to see Caroline Kimble."

"And you are?"

Liz flashes her badge in the face of the nurse at admissions as if she were talking to a perp. Her aggression is driven by the desire for her child's safety.

"Her mother, Police Detective First Grade Elizabeth Kimble. Now, where is Cary?"

"Your daughter is in the examining room."

"Where is that?"

"Down this hall. First door on the left. And who is the young man with you."

"My son, her brother. I will vouch for him. Thanks for the information."

Mother and son take a thirty-step rapid walk, turn the corner and come face-to-face with a male nurse, the ER sentry.

"How can I help you?"

"I want to see Caroline Kimble. I'm her mother, Police Detective First Grade Elizabeth Kimble. This is my son, her brother."

"She's being examined presently in room three. You can see her shortly. Please wait here."

After five minutes that seem like five hours, a young female doctor comes from behind a curtain.

"Mrs. Kimble, your daughter is OK. She recently suffered a trauma. I did not ask her what happened. Do you know exactly what happened?"

Within two minutes, the doctor has a grasp of the cause.

"The gunfire and the threat of harm caused her to suffer a mild psychological trauma. She'll bounce back. Young people generally do. You can take her home shortly. Make sure she gets a lot of rest. Keep her in bed or resting on a couch for the next twenty-four to forty-eight hours. Water and some light food will help. Nothing that could upset her stomach. No medications are required. I suggest you have her looked at by her regular doctor within a week or so. You can take her to the discharge desk as soon as she is dressed."

"I would like to see her now. Cary, it's Mom and Alex. Are you decent?"

"Mommy, I'm in here."

Mother and son quickly rush to Cary's side.

"What happened, Mommy?"

"I'll explain on the way home. First, I want the doctor to take a look at Alex."

"Doctor, he was with his sister during the gunfight. I know he is not showing any signs of shock. I just want to be sure he is fine."

Ten minutes pass as Alex's vitals are taken and the doctor performs a few tests to confirm the boy's well-being.

"Mrs. Kimble, your son is healthy. As a precaution, keep an eye on him over the next week to ten days to be sure nothing adverse boomerangs. The chances are very slim, but we want to be sure. You should have him checked out by his regular doctor in two weeks."

"Thank you. Alex, stay with your sister. When she is ready to leave, both of you wait for me in the lobby. I'll swing by and get you both after I see Marion. Then we can leave."

Another long hall. Another nurse's desk.

"Good morning, I want to see Marion Morrison."

"Are you his wife?"

Liz blushes.

"Sorry, only relatives are allowed to see patients in this part of the hospital."

"I am Tampa Police Department Detective First Grade Elizabeth Kimble, here is my badge. Assistant District Attorney Morrison was wounded defending my family and me. I want to see him now, please."

"Yes, ma'am. Room 432, bed A."

"Thank you."

Liz gingerly enters the room. There is Marion on the bed. A nurse is attending him, reading the beeping monitor and checking the tube from the IV stand beside the bed.

"How is he?"

"His body suffered shock caused by the two bullet injuries. The one on his side was a through-and-through.

278

But when passing through it nicked his liver. The scratch was leaking when he was brought in. Surgery was performed to close the leak. We put a patch on the nick. We stitched the entry and exit wounds. We also had to remove the bile and blood from around the liver to prevent complications. The other bullet lodged in his pectoral muscle. It appears to have ricocheted off something very hard before it hit him, because it had flattened and didn't penetrate too deeply. We removed it easily. No major damage other than the minor scrape on his liver. The liver is a self-regenerating organ so with proper care, rest and diet, he will be fine in ten days to two weeks. His bruised ribs will heal if they're stabilized. That means he has to be taped and he must rest. We'll need to keep him here for forty-eight hours to monitor the impact of the surgery and his recuperative process. After release, like most men, he will complain about his mortal injury, but your husband will be fine."

"He's not…"

"Lots of TLC, ma'am."

Liz decides not to correct the misconception. She approaches the body on the bed and grasps his hand. His eyelids open halfway. Marion sees Liz and grins. His face reflects weak, yet heartfelt appreciation. She leans into him, kisses his forehead and whispers.

"Hey there, soldier. You were protected by an ugly garden gnome. I'll explain that later. The nurse tells me you'll be fine. Cranky, but fine. After you're released, you'll need bed rest and a healthy dose of mothering. I'm great at mothering. I've a lot of practice. So, when I spring you from this joint, you're coming home with Alex, Cary, Max, and me. You'll enjoy our Christmas. That's an order."

"I…"

"Shush. Rest."

She turns to the nurse.

"When will he be discharged?"

"My guess is in two days. Monday mid-morning. By then his liver will be on the mend and on the way back to normal. The new blood we gave him will have started to heal him. He is receiving antibiotics and a prescription for them will be given to him at discharge. Monday he'll be strong enough to leave. But no physical activity for at least a week."

She knows he heard the nurse. Marion is living proof that no good deed goes unpunished. She leans into his ear.

"Listen closely…I want you now…here."

His eyes open wide as he offers a pained whispered response.

"Not fair."

She smiles and kisses him. This time on the lips. Her hips bounce and sway a little more than usual as she leaves his space. She is glad that she didn't correct the nurse's incorrect presumption about their relationship.

Forms are signed and the family of three walks slowly to the minivan.

"Mom, the sun is coming up and I'm hungry. Can we stop to get something from the drive-thru?"

Breakfast is acquired…to go. Liz thinks this new day will be a good, but busy day: making sure Cary rests, cleaning the mess, grocery shopping, and creating a space for Marion. A massive amount of work, but it's what the mother in her looks forward to because it's her home, her family, and her man. She wonders if she will have FDLE protection on her trip to the store. Or even at home now that Special Agent Widdix is no longer parked across the street.

As she turns the car onto her street, Liz notices four large trash containers at the curb in front of her house. They are filled with debris and the yellow crime scene tape from the house. Entering, the three Kimbles are greeted by neighbors standing in the war zone.

"Welcome home, Kimbles. We tried to return this area to some semblance of normal, but all we could do was clean the residue of the firefight. Aside from the obvious holes and missing pieces of wood, the porch, patio, and kitchen seem to be functional."

The tarps have been hung, the large splinters of wood and shards of glass picked up, and the countertops and floor obviously swept and wiped clean.

"What is this? What did you guys do?"

"Acted neighborly."

Tears begin to well.

"This goes above and beyond. How can I thank you?"

"We thank you. We did nothing compared to what you do and did. Every day you go to work to protect us. Last night, the bad guys came to our neighborhood, and you protected us in our homes. What we did is a small tip of the hat. We got you some ready-to-reheat-and-eat dishes from the grocery store. Thought you would not be in the mood to cook. Now we have to scoot. Leave you and your children alone."

"Mrs. Benn, thanks a ton. I was not looking forward to the clean-up."

"Alex, your family has been through too much as it is. It's the least we could do. Tom, we're leaving."

"Bob and I got your back, as they say. Liz, if there is anything else you need, just let us know."

Neighbors gone, Liz helps Cary upstairs to her bed. Max is waiting for the love of his life. His tail thumps dramatically on her bed as he raises his head and perks his ears. Cary gets into bed trying not to disturb her dear friend. He moves to make space for her.

"After you've rested, I'll get you something to eat. It is important for you to rest for the next few days. Alex and I will be downstairs if you need anything."

Liz leans over her daughter and kisses her cheek.

"Love you, sweetie."

"Backatchya, Mom."

The girl's eyes are no longer vacant and a small smile is visible. Downstairs, Alex has already finished his Woodsman Breakfast consisting of three eggs, two sausage patties, three strips of bacon, hash browns, a stack of pancakes, and a biscuit. Liz nibbles on her Sun-Lite Special consisting of fruit, yogurt, and oatmeal. Over her coffee, she stares at Marion's phone. Did he open it sometime last night during the gunfight? It fell at his side when he was hit, and she retrieved it before the EMTs carted him off to the hospital. No password is required to access his contact list. She quickly finds the name.

"Commander Ishmael, this is Elizabeth Kimble. I'm calling on ADA Morrison's cell phone because he can't.

He was shot earlier today. He is out of the woods and is temporarily recuperating at County General."

"Can you give me some proof of your identity?"

"My TPD badge number is 8739. I have two children, Alex and Cary. Anything else?"

"Your badge number will be sufficient. I can access the TPD database. Got it, Detective Kimble. That explains it."

"What?"

"Very early this morning, I received a call from Marion. He whispered something that I could not make out. I heard several explosions. Then nothing. He must have dialed then rolled over on the phone. I called back, but the call went directly to voice mail.

"Under what circumstances was ADA Morrison shot?"

"Defending my children and me against the attack of Detectives Wovent and Weingarten."

"How badly was he hit?"

"He took two in the upper right half of his body...one just below the rib cage and one in his shoulder. His liver was slightly nicked and he lost a lot of blood but nothing life threatening. He's resting comfortably. He will be released in two days."

"Were you hit, Detective?"

"No. Thanks for asking. I am now speaking for Marion. I need to know a status report of your activities since you scooped up the fifteen men on our list."

"Several of the lower-level Street Cleaners gave us the names of others in the department who are wannabes."

"Who?"

"Dannello. Leach. Rasko. Brennan. That's all we have so far, but I estimate we'll have others before the end of the day. If that's all you need, I have to cut this short. We're approaching Rasko's house. I want to surprise him in his pajamas."

"Thanks for the information. Please keep me in the loop."

"Gladly. Marion is a good friend. Give him my best and tell him when recovers he owes me dinner at LaMond. Time to use my legal pooper scooper on more bad cops."

"The more poop the better."

She surveys her recently remodeled kitchen. Not quite what she had in mind. Rather than be depressed, she views it as a canvas upon which she will paint a masterpiece of modernity and comfort. Maybe eliminate the partial wall between the kitchen and dining room to create an expansive looking space from kitchen through to the porch outside. A multi-functional great room. Something she has wanted to do for a while. The coffee has had precious little energizing effect. Her eyelids are beginning to droop. Her muscles are relaxed. An early morning nap is in order. Why should she be the only one in the house who is awake?

"Mommy, I'm hungry."

The plea of her daughter standing at the foot of her bed is a joyous alarm clock to Liz. Like a little bird in the nest chirping for the sustenance of love. It's time for her to rise and be the nurturing parent; a job she enjoys.

"Before we go downstairs, Mom needs a hug."

The clasp is as strong as the bond. Two women and a happy dog go to the kitchen.

"Alex selected a breakfast he said you would like, scrambled eggs, bacon, strawberries, and pancakes with lots of syrup. Huzzah! The microwave is working despite the hole in its outer shell."

Alex comes bounding down the stairs.

"Cary, how ya feeling?"

"Better."

"Alex, please feed Max. I'm sure he is hungry after staying up all night."

The family is on the mend. Now to mend the house. Liz goes to the filing cabinet in the garage and digs through the contracts, warrantees, tax returns, and various miscellaneous papers until she finds the homeowners insurance policy with the name and number to call. She calls, explains what happened, and what is needed. She is told an adjuster will be summoned to arrive before five today. She will visit Marion after the required walk through.

"Hey there, Mr. Morrison."

"Alex. Cary. It's great to see you. Are you guys all right?"

"I'm great. Not sure about Mr. Wisenheimer."

"I'm greater. When are you getting released?"

"Not sure, Alex. I am at the mercy of the hospital staff. Where's your Mom?"

"She stopped to talk to someone at the nurses' desk. She'll be here in a few minutes."

"What does the house look like? How's Max, Cary?"

"My Max is fine. He acts as if nothing happened. But he seems confused because he can't go outside the usual way. The house looks like a Middle East war zone shown on TV news programs. The insurance adjuster said he'll have workmen out to start the repairs the day after Christmas. Mom wants to make some changes in the layout and color. So we have to think about what we would like before they arrive. We're getting new appliances."

"Well, I see you three have gotten reacquainted. Marion, how do you feel?"

"I hurt a lot, and I feel like I want to get out of here very soon."

"The doctor says we can retrieve you tomorrow before noon…assuming you successfully continue on your road to recovery. I have made a bed in the living room. You will be our guest for a few days. We want to be sure you're properly healing. After three days, I'll bring you back here for a check-up by professionals. If they're OK with it, you can return to your own home."

"I'll need clothes and toilet articles. Plus, I will want my work files. They are on the floor next to my desk in the living room."

"Your home is our first stop after we leave here."

"You'll need my keys."

"I already have them."

"You think of everything."

"I'm a cop. I'm trained to think of everything."

Liz winks at Marion and blows him a kiss, hoping the children don't see.

They see and smile.

XXII

"I am a responsible adult so I am responsible for you. You will be recovering in our living room for a few days before I take you to your home. The bed linens are beside the couch. Alex has cleaned the small bathroom off the garage, and your toiletries are there. I didn't know what you wore when you weren't working so I brought several changes of comfortable casual clothes. Hope you find the accommodations satisfactory. If there is anything missing or anything you need to be more comfortable, tell me."

"There is something that would make me feel better."

"Not here. Not now."

With that, Marion Morrison became a recuperating houseguest.

"Hey, Mr. Morrison, how you feeling?"

"Sore and very appreciative, Alex. You guys have gone out of your way to take care of me."

"You should see the kitchen. You can see where the bullets hit the walls, stove and fridge."

"I'll look later, thanks."

"Mr. Morrison, Max wants to say hello."

"Bring him on, Cary."

The four-legged warning system and protector rushes up to Marion. His tail nearly knocks a lamp off the end table by the couch. Sniffing becomes nuzzling. Max bounces with joy.

"Since your spot is near the Christmas tree, it's almost like you're a special present."

"I accept that role. Unfortunately, I have no gifts for my caregivers. I've been busy at the hospital. So, I will treat for dinner at LaMond tonight."

"Well, I don't know…"

"You have no say, Liz. I already made reservations for us at five-thirty. In the kitchen. But before that, you and I have a date with someone important."

"Who is more important than we are?"

"Harold Shade."

"The reporter?"

"I asked him to come here around two. We're going to have a tell-all sit-down with the media."

"Is that wise?"

"The sooner we get the public behind us, the safer we'll be. The arrests have been made and the massive court appearance for all the crooked cops is scheduled for Wednesday. But I want the story to break on Christmas day, so everyone can read it and be joyful they are protected by decent members of law enforcement like you and Leonard."

"Leonard. In all of the commotion, I had almost forgotten about him."

"Did you bring the files I asked for?"

"I'm a cop. I know how to follow orders."

"Yeah, sure. That's why your house was shot up. Someone was pleased you were following orders."

Liz displays a sheepish grin.

Marion is beginning to feel comfortable in his temporary home.

"I would like to clean up before Mr. Shade arrives."

"The small bathroom is through the door in the kitchen and at the rear of the garage."

👁 👁

"Mom, there's a Mr. Harold Shade here to see Mr. Morrison."

"I'll be right down. Let him in and ask him to wait in the kitchen or what's left of it. Make sure Mr. Morrison knows Mr. Shade is here."

Coffee poured. Introductions all around. Marion begins to relate the case details. Harold takes notes, records everything, and periodically interrupts with a question for either Marion or Liz. The process takes nearly two hours.

"Do you mind if I take some shots? To make the story very real to my readers, they need to see the people involved and the scene of the crime. I need one each of you two, and several of the house and backyard."

While he is taking the photos, Harold asks a few more questions, including a summary one.

"What do you hope to accomplish with this case? First, Detective Kimble."

"Make the police department something the citizens of Tampa can trust in all situations."

"ADA Morrison?"

"Detective Kimble and I are of one voice. The group known as Street Cleaners is like a cancer that must be excised before it metastasizes and kills the department and the city. The people expect and deserve to be served and protected by honest cops."

"Now here is the tricky question. Do you fear retaliation?"

"The attempted retaliation occurred a few nights ago and it failed miserably. I believe that we have exposed the evil to the sunlight of public scrutiny. Your article will be the final spotlight on the evil and provide the citizens with real transparency. I hope that doesn't come across as arrogant. But, if we missed anyone, they will be addressed when we hear more from the men already arrested. Facing long jail terms, most criminals express a desire to cooperate with law enforcement to minimize their punishment. These dirty cops are slightly different, because they fear being in jail with people they put there. That could be a life-shortening situation."

"That's it. Now I have to file the story. Deadline is in two hours. This will make good holiday reading. Thanks for the exclusive. I owe you."

Liz closes the door and leans into Marion. Their embrace lasts about a minute. She pulls away and calls out to her children.

"Alex and Cary, get cleaned up. We're leaving for dinner in thirty minutes."

"We normally eat in our kitchen. I've never eaten in the kitchen of a restaurant. What can we order?"

"Cary, the meal has already been ordered. Duck a l'orange, wild rice, green beans, pearl onions, and an endive salad."

Chef LaMond leaves his post and comes to the table.

"Marion, these must be the charming young man and young lady you mentioned. Welcome, Alex and Cary to my humble eatery. I hope you enjoy your meal. If there's anything you desire, let me know. Now, I must get back to work if we hope to close by eight."

"Marion…"

"Shush, Liz, just enjoy the meal."

The feast commences and is completed with very little conversation from the hungry diners.

"I've never had duck before. It was great. Mom, we have to have this at home."

"I'll work on it."

The lime sorbet arrives.

"While you are cleansing your palate, allow me to present you each with a token of my appreciation."

Marion calls the server, who retrieves three small packages.

"Marion…"

"Shush, Liz, just enjoy the moment. Cary, you get to open your gift first."

"An ID bracelet. How cool is that?"

"Alex, now you."

"I got one, too."

"Sorry I did not have time to have them engraved. I was temporarily vacationing at County General. So, later this week I will take the bracelets to the jeweler for that. Each of you must write down exactly what you want on your bracelet. Now, Liz."

"A necklace with a locket. How very thoughtful."

"You can decide what pictures you want in the locket."

"My children."

Four well-fed and happy people leave the restaurant, get into Mom's minivan, and head for home. Marion is exhausted from the activity of the day. His head bobs as he fights sleep in the car.

Max is happy to see them. Marion walks to an SUV that has been following them to and from the restaurant. He speaks to the driver and the SUV departs. The teens rush to their rooms and log on to their computers. They will be occupied until they go to bed. Marion and Liz sit in the living room before the tree.

"I feel like a kid. Sitting here and wanting to do something that my parents, upstairs, don't want me to do. Faux-parental control from a distance."

"Me, too. But I have to throw you out of my bedroom. I need to rest."

"You need to know that although Max stays with Cary, he patrols the house occasionally during the night. Thank gawd he was on patrol the other night. So don't be shocked if he visits you. He likes you, so he'll probably sniff you while you sleep. Good night, Marion."

They kiss.

The morning sun announces Christmas. Liz rises and goes downstairs to check on Marion. A delicate kiss on his forehead causes his eyes to open. He pulls her onto him so they can feel each other's body while their kisses become deeper and deeper. Slowly, she pulls away and smiles lovingly at this new man in her life. This good man in her life.

"The children will be rarin' to go in a few minutes. I suggest you tend to your morning bathroom ritual before they come storming into the living room. What would you like for breakfast?"

"Coffee to start. I'm still a little disoriented from the events and being in a strange woman's house…alone on the couch. Plus, I can't make a decision as important as food with a foggy mind."

"I can hear them already stirring upstairs. When they were very young, they would sit at the top of the stairs and wait for their father and me to give them the OK to come to the Christmas tree and see what Santa brought. You'd better hurry."

"As soon as you allow me to rise, I will tend to my morning ritual."

"But what if I don't want to leave my superior position?"

"Then you can explain this couch situation to your children."

"OK. When you're done, please give me a hand in the kitchen. I'm nuking breakfast. Juice, sweet rolls, and link sausages; a breakfast every teen craves…sugar, fat, and sodium."

"A left hand is all I can give."

He enters the kitchen ready for the day…a day of family and joy.

"Would you go outside near the front door and get the paper? You may have to search for it. The delivery boy has a good arm, but he is not very accurate. Thanks."

He cannot find the paper anywhere on the lawn or in the flower beds so he looks in the mailbox. Bingo! Wrapped in the familiar plastic sleeve. He reaches in, grabs the paper, unfolds it, and begins to read the lead article on the front page while standing in front of the mailbox. The headline screams…

Cop Cabal Crushed
By Harold Shade

Sitting in the pleasant surroundings of a suburban family home the day before Christmas, two local heroes revealed the work and danger that went into exposing a criminal cabal among decorated senior officers of the Tampa Police Department.

Assistant District Attorney, Marion Morrison and Police Detective First Grade, Elizabeth Kimble gave this reporter the details of more than fifteen names and their crimes which include murder, attempted murder, extortion, and bribery of a public official. Real organized crime in Tampa: the Tampa Police Department. The organization, known as Street Cleaners is an exclusive, all-boys club that got its start during the Bolito Wars. However, within the past few weeks, this cabal of crime allegedly was responsible for the deaths of…

He will finish the article when he is inside. Before closing the mailbox door, Marion peers back inside. He notices a bulging medium-size manila envelope. As he removes the envelope from the mailbox, out falls a plastic sleeve. This one is tied with a pink ribbon and contains the remains of a big rat: gutted with blood and entrails in full display. Immediately, he lifts the sleeve, walks to one of the trash bins, and deposits the parcel. As he re-wraps the paper, Marion grabs his phone and dials. He whispers, explains what he just discovered, and listens. The conversation continues. His tone, anger, and volume increase with each sentence he utters.

"I don't care if it's their fucking wedding day. They're probably at home opening gifts with their families. I don't care if they're on the crapper. I want you to find the sonsabitches and arrest them. And don't be nice about it. I want them arrested in front of their wives and children. Rub their noses on the floor when you cuff them. Drag them out of their homes in cuffs bitching and moaning. I want them to experience a huge load humiliation in front of family for what they did. I want them taken to the holding cell in their goddamned pajamas or underwear. Do it now! Not an hour from now. Now! Thank you."

Marion re-enters the house.

"What was that all about?"

"I called Commander Ishmael. We are tying up any loose ends. It seems the FDLE could not find two miscreants. Wanders and Baker are the names given them by a wannabe. Ishmael is in the process of arresting them now. So let's enjoy Christmas. Go. Be with your children."

"Why weren't they arrested with the others?"

"He told me that Wanders and Baker were not at their usual haunts yesterday. But he assures me that the last two

Street Cleaners will be arrested at their homes before we have a second cup of coffee."

"Then it will be over except for the trial."

"Yes."

"Are you sure? I don't want to put my children through any more of this."

"Yes, I'm sure."

I hope so echoes in both their minds.

Printed in the United States
By Bookmasters